Rhodes' HOME

To my darling Amanda,
such a wise, loving, gentle soul
for one so young. Your gift
to see the promise in those around
you that others would miss — the
gift of a hope-filled spirit...

Carol Knuth

my treasure of a child. I met
you September 29, 1981 — & my
world changed... I found I had
so many reasons for my future.

Dream Swept Publishing

This book is a work of fiction, inspired by true events. Names of characters and places are fictional, created by the author's imagination.

Rhodes' Home. Copyright © 2013 by Carol Knuth

Dream Swept Publishing, LLC.
P.O. Box 18522
Erlanger, KY 41018

First paperback edition

ISBN: 0985924322

ISBN-13: 9780985924324

Printed in the United States of America

I dedicate this book to many special people…

To my husband, thank you for your support and encouragement during this laborious writing and publishing journey, for understanding my dream, and for believing in me.

To my children, as little girls you filled my life with purpose, love, and meaning, and now as women, you each represent the most enchanting miracles of love, and strength.

To my grandchildren, may you always know how much you are loved, the joy you are to me, and to the world.

To my parents, who many years ago took on the challenge of healing and giving hope to the young, lost, teenage girl that I was. Thank you for continuing to be an example of unconditional love, and providing me with a place that I can always call home.

To my very special sisters and brother, thank you for sharing your home and your parents with me, and continuing to share your lives with me…and for your love, always.

To my siblings of origin, thank you for inspiring me to reach for more on my life journey. To my oldest sisters, you were my earliest inspirations to fight the bad guys. Thank you for being my little girl heroes that saved the day by making me laugh when I was afraid, for loving me, for never giving up and never letting me go.

May your dreams open a door to limitless possibilities...

Rhodes'
HOME

1

Over the past month, 16-year-old, Emma Snow had felt little pieces of her fall away, as one by one, the girls she had spent the last year with—walking to school, eating meals, pouring out hopes, dreams, and nightmares—had packed their bags and moved on, either to their old lives or somewhere new. With each goodbye, each tear shed, sobbing as the girls clutched each other, Emma had begun to withdraw. The pain was unbearable. A year had been spent teaching Emma to open her heart, to let others in to love her and to love back. Now as her cottage mates were being ripped away from her, not gradually, but in a mad rush to meet the states deadline for the closure of the children's home, Emma recoiled from the world, vowing never to allow anyone in again. Emma still had no home lined up, had no idea what lie in wait for her outside the grounds of the home.

"Emma," Mrs. Hays said, knocking on her bedroom door. The old rule which stated the girls couldn't be in their bedrooms during the day had been eliminated when more than half of the girls had been transferred out of the children's home.

Lying on her side on her bed, Emma stared blankly out her window. She had her own room now, almost able to have her pick of rooms since most of the girls had moved away.

"Emma, I need to talk to you. You know the foster mom that brought you to the home last year—Audrey?" Mrs. Hays asked.

"Yeah," Emma said in a muffled voice. Of course she knew Audrey, and she knew *all* the cottage mother's knew Audrey too. Emma had written Audrey almost every night while she had been living at the home. The cottage mothers all knew that because they read every incoming and outgoing letter the kids wrote.

"She's going to come pick you up tomorrow. You need to pack your things tonight," Mrs. Hays said.

Turning her head toward her cottage mother, Emma opened her mouth to protest but nothing came out. She had been dreading this day for months, and now it was here. She wouldn't leave, she thought. If they wanted her to leave, she wasn't going to make it easy on them. They would have to use force to remove her. They would have to *carry* her out, she thought, and turned back toward the window.

"I'm not packing!" she said angrily. "I'm not leaving. There are still kids here. I have nowhere to go!" Turning back toward Mrs. Hays, she hissed, "I have nowhere to go."

"Emma, you *have* to pack. You can't stay here. This place is going to be locked up in a few weeks," Mrs. Hays pleaded.

Crying now, Emma said, "What about the other kids that are still here that have nowhere to go? I don't see you kicking them out!"

"They can't stay here either. Oh, Emma. I know this really sucks. I am so sorry," Mrs. Hays said.

The cottage mother laid her hand on Emma's shoulder to comfort her, but knew there was nothing she could say that would make what was happening any better. What could she say to a child that had been beaten down so many times by life—and now it was happening again. How many times, Mrs. Hays wondered as she walked out of the bedroom, could a child get back up and try again.

Rough fabric from the orange and brown couch in the common room scratched Emma's cheek as she pressed her tear stained face into it. She clung to the couch as the few remaining girls at the cottage tried to rip her from it. Audrey had arrived over two hours ago to take Emma away from the home; from there she was to be taken to a temporary foster home until a permanent placement became available.

Emma lay sobbing on the couch as Audrey, kneeling beside her, begged her to please go pack her things. Mrs. Simpson, the cottage mother on duty, had given Audrey a black garbage bag and now Audrey was trying to coax Emma to pack her things into it so she could take her away. Mrs. Simpson was part of the skeleton crew of cottage parents, all that was left of the adults that had cared for the kids. Most of the other cottage parents had found other jobs, and had left Emma too.

"Emma, please," Audrey begged. "I'll help you pack your things if you want."

"No," Emma wailed. "I'm not leaving. You can't make me go back out there. You are *insane* if you think I'm going back out into that fucking world where people do horrible things. Leave me alone!" she screamed.

Emma cried, exhausted, and thought, *if they think I am going to walk, willingly, out of the glass door of this cottage, out into the fucked up world they call society, they are insane!*

Corey knelt down by Emma's face and wiped her cheek, and with tears of her own, said, "Emma you have to go. We all do."

"I can't," Emma, wept. "I can't go back out there, to whatever is out there. I just can't do it again."

Corey leaned over, wrapped her arms around Emma, and cried with her, as the two other remaining cottage mates came over and held Emma too, creating an emotional barrier from the world. They all cried together for a while as Audrey and Mrs. Simpson stood back with tears in their eyes, and watched the girls comfort one another.

In defeat, Emma rolled off the couch; her eyes almost swollen shut from hours of crying, and held out her hand for the garbage bag. Slowly, she walked to her bedroom, and not caring anymore, dumped everything that belonged to her into the mouth of the black garbage bag. She was numb—heard a buzzing in her ears—her motions automatic as she drug the bag behind her.

Audrey took the garbage bag from Emma, noticing the dark circles under her eyes and swollen face. The girl Audrey looked at was a ghost of the girl she had seen just months ago. Then, Emma had glowed—smiled—so excited about her future and all she had accomplished, but that had been before the announcement of the children's home closure.

Patiently, Audrey waited by the door as Emma sobbed her goodbyes.

As Audrey drove off grounds of the children's home, Emma looked back at her home, the place where she had been loved, accepted, and safe for the past year. Only after the grounds of the home had slipped out of her sight, did she turn around in her seat. Emma stared straight ahead through the windshield of the car—she didn't blink—she was numb—not caring anymore. Exhausted, she leaned her head against the passenger side window. Closing her eyes to the world, a tear trickled down her cheek, as she wondered, *what next...*

2

Audrey glanced across the car at the young girl huddled on the seat, her head pressed against the passenger side window—limp—worn out from weeks of not knowing what would happen to her, where she would go next. She could only imagine what it would be like to be a young girl with no place to call home, never having the security of knowing where she would sleep that night.

"Em," Audrey said, trying to sound cheerful. "I thought we'd go camping this weekend. Just get out of town for a few days. What do you say?"

Camping, Emma considered. She didn't want to go *camping*. She wanted to be left alone, not sit around some stupid campfire. That's what you did, you sat around a fire when you went camping; at least she assumed that's what people did on such trips. Crossing her arms across her chest, Emma stared out the window and watched a field whiz by under the blazing afternoon sun. Besides, it was too damn hot to sit around a fire, and where was she going to sleep, she wondered. How *big* was the camper, or was it a tent? That was all she needed right now, to be crammed into some tiny tent with other people. If she had to be cooped up with people all weekend she would peel her skin off, she thought hysterically.

"We have the camper all packed," Audrey said cheerfully. "We're going with another couple." Looking over at Emma slumped against the passenger car door, Audrey continued, "They have a daughter about your age."

Groaning inwardly, Emma stared across the car at Audrey. She was just trying to make her feel better, Emma knew that, but being with people was the last thing she wanted or needed right now. The foster kid on display thing was really just *not* what she needed right now, as she did not have the energy to play the nice little girl.

She hadn't eaten all day. Her head felt as if little men were inside with miniature ice picks chipping away at her skull, and she was exhausted. The comfort of her home, *her home,* was all she wanted. She didn't belong wherever it was Audrey was going to take her, to some campground to be around people who were obviously happy, had families...friends... very much not like her. She was sick of being different from everyone, and quite frankly, sitting in some little campsite was going to amplify how different and very much alone she was. What was Audrey thinking, she wondered, as she examined the woman she estimated to be in her forties. Had the woman taken leave of her senses, Emma wondered sarcastically?

Feeling dead inside, Emma sighed and stared out the window. Emma knew Audrey was delaying the inevitable, dropping her off at another temporary foster home. The camping trip was just a segue back into the real world, well at least her real world...the world of the never knowing what the day would bring or what home the day would bring. Audrey had served as one in a series of foster mothers for Emma. Over a year ago, Emma had lived with Audrey's family for a few months. Audrey's home had been one of the better foster homes Emma had stayed at, and Emma loved Audrey, but Audrey was no longer a foster mother, so Emma was being thrust out into the foster life game of chance again, where one just never knew what they would get. But for now, she knew she was safe...*for now.*

In a few days, Audrey was to deliver Emma to the Matthews' foster home. Emma had stayed at the Matthews' home over a year ago. It was the home where her caseworker had taken her after she had been beaten up by a different foster mother. It was a day that would forever be imprinted on Emma's mind. She had been living with a lady named Sheila, an unmarried foster mother. At first, Emma had loved living at the home. But one night Emma woke to find Sheila's twenty-year-old son lying next to her in her bed, groping her. In a panic, she had struggled to be free, and once she managed to pull herself away and get to her feet, shaking from shock, anger, and revulsion, she had insisted he leave the bedroom she shared with his sister, a few years older than her.

Sheila's home had even more disturbing issues than Sheila's son George. There had also been the matter of Sheila's boyfriend, Eric. He was creepily friendly, and at one point tried to convince Emma to strip at a club for money. In his sleazy, whiny voice, he had assured her that he should hold onto the money for her, and that they should keep it a secret. Emma had finally told her foster mother, Sheila, what her son and her boyfriend, Eric, had done to her. Sheila had been furious when she had learned what had happened to Emma...*furious at Emma*. It had become a tremendous argument, ending with Sheila shrieking at her son to hold Emma down so she could beat her.

While Emma did not take Eric up on his offer of a life as a stripper, and who knew what else, the event had affected her. It tore away a little more of her faith in men. To her, life had presented a parade of men from her earliest memories; first, her father's groping hands; her step-grandfather; foster brother; and even her foster mother's boyfriend. But it wasn't just the groping hands of all these men, it was the message from the adults in her life that she meant so little to them, and to the world, that they didn't care to keep her safe. *She didn't matter.*

When she had lived with her dad, many in her family, and even the community, knew about the bad things that were happening to her, but they hadn't saved her, instead they had left little girls to the mercy of a rapist. And then later, in foster homes—no one had saved her. At one abusive foster home, she'd had to run to the police to have them intervene, to save the children at the home, and then there had been the situation at Sheila's home. Emma was fairly certain that Sheila had not been charged with assault after beating her up, nor had her son been charged for sexual assault, and she had no idea what Eric should have been charged with, just knew it was wrong. Emma had reported it all to one of her caseworkers, what Sheila's son had done, what her boyfriend had done, and the beating from Sheila. Her caseworker had seen the bruises and the swelling on her face, but all he had cared about was a weekend get away with his friends. There was no foster home to move her to, he had told her, a clear indicator that he thought Sheila's home was better than no home at all. He hadn't listened to her. No one did. Why would they, she reflected. Who was she to be heard?

As a little girl, she had hoped for a different life—free from the bad things—but it seemed as if God just gave her more of the same. She wondered if it would always be that way, or could God, if He really existed, save her. So many whys. Why was this her life? Why did these things happen, and could, and would, her life ever be different?

It wasn't that Emma didn't like the Matthews family. She did. At one time, she had lived with them for a month or two. Mr. Matthews was a doctor at the local hospital and his wife was a homemaker. They were old for parents—in their fifties. When she had been placed at their home over a year ago, she had known their home was just a short-term foster home. She had known the potential for her stay could have been from a few days to almost a year. After the abuse from Sheila's home, and the home she had stayed at down south, Emma was skeptical at the state's ability to provide a safe home for her. Her intent while at the Matthews' home was to remain as emotionally distant as possible, however, it hadn't taken long for Emma to become comfortable, to feel safe, and to trust her newest parents. Against her will, she had fallen in love with the Matthews family and hoped it would be her last foster home stop. They had inspired within her, trust. She had met few men like Mr. Matthews and had certainly never lived with a father figure like him.

He had a quirky sense of humor, which she had loved. He had even created a new name for her of sorts, Emma-Emma. He would say her name twice, in quick succession. It was what he did with all the children in his home, and it made her feel as if she belonged. But of course, that had been many homes ago.

Hours later, Emma stood in the blazing sun staring at the small metal camper in an almost deserted campground. So, she thought as she squinted at the cream-colored camper with one lone ribbon of chocolate brown stripe running the length of its side. So here we are...camping. *Hurrah!* Sarcasm seeped from her, her mode of coping with the newest shit in her life. Placing her weight on her left leg, she placed her hand on her right hip, and considered her home for the weekend, and thought, well, now you *are* homeless.

Emma looked around the small campsite, at the small camper with logs lodged behind the wheels, picnic table positioned nearby for meals, and the few lawn chairs placed in a semi circle ready for occupants. Turning away from the small campsite, grass more brown than green under the hot Indian summer, she frowned as she thought, this is a place people escape to be in nature, noticing the gravel road, and absence of trees. It was a big open space, with no trees...no nature, so what was the point, she wondered.

Hearing the door to the camper open, Emma turned toward the camper.

"Emma, why don't you walk to the recreational building?" Audrey asked, as she stepped down the camper steps. Pointing, Audrey said, "It's over there. You can see the building from here."

Emma turned and looked in the direction of Audrey's finger, and noticed a small brown building with black roof a short distance down the dusty graveled road.

"There are a couple kids there now. Julie, my friend's daughter, walked over about half an hour ago," Audrey encouraged.

Fine, Emma thought. What else did she have to do? "Okay," she said quietly.

Shoving her hands into the pockets of her blue jean shorts, Emma walked with her head down, watching her shoes kick up gravel dust. She hadn't said more than a few words to Audrey since they had left the children's home. It was as if her vocal chords were paralyzed right along with her hope. She was numb. She couldn't feel, barely felt the scorching sun on her bare arms, and she wanted to remain that way...numb from caring, anger, and hoping. If she could remain numb, nothing could hurt her ever again. Never again, she thought, never again would she allow anyone or anything to hurt her.

Emma heard a boy's voice as she opened the door to the recreation building and felt a cool blast of air. She hadn't realized how hot she had been until she walked into the cool building. She walked toward the voices and saw two tall boys with brown hair and a girl that looked to be about her age, shorter than she was with sun streaked blonde hair. The young blonde girl was wearing a pair of shorts, similar to Emma's, a pair of flip-flops, and a navy blue t-shirt. The boys were both wearing blue jeans and t-shirts, comfortable in the air-conditioned building.

"Hey," the girl Emma knew must be Julie said, with a broad grin.

The two boys turned toward her, and checking her out, smiled.

"Hey," Emma mumbled. Emma felt the three teens' eyes on her as she walked over to the pool table to watch the game they were playing.

"Do you want something to drink?" Julie asked. "They have pop in the fridge in the other room."

"Sure," Emma said with a forced smile.

Several hours later, Emma plodded along beside Julie down the gravel road toward their campsite. It had been a quiet afternoon of watching Julie and the boys play pool. She had watched and listened to the teens laughing and joking around. They hadn't tried to exclude her. She knew she could jump in at any time and laugh, right along with them, but why bother, she wondered. What was the point? She just wasn't in the mood, so, bored out of her mind, she leaned against a wall and watched as pool cues struck the little white ball, smacking it into whatever colored ball was nearest.

Lulled by the warm breeze, Emma wished there was somewhere to take a nap. She was exhausted. In the distance, she saw Audrey sitting at the picnic table holding cards in her hands. Her husband and their camping neighbors were sitting at the table with her, cigarettes lit up and drinks in front of them. As she walked into the small campsite, Emma heard them laughing as they played their card game. It seemed to be what the old folks did, played cards.

Flopping down on one of the abandoned green and white striped fold up lawn chairs, Emma leaned back and watched the adults as they laughed and joked while playing their game. Closing her eyes, she could still hear the sounds of their voices as she drifted into a dreamless sleep.

3

"Here we are," Audrey said with feigned cheerfulness.

Emma looked out the car window at the familiar red brick house, once a place of comfort and belonging, but no more. A great deal had happened in the year and a half since she had lived with the Matthews family. Had it been that long, Emma reflected. Time seemed to have sped by since her time with Sheila's family, and the hands that groped in the night. Here she was again, and now Emma was older, stronger, and finally realized there would be no home for her—no one to call mom and dad—just a roof over her head. There would never be a close attachment with anyone, not as she had imagined it would be with a real family. After all, she was now 16, and a junior in high school. *How could it be possible to grow roots somewhere this late in her childhood?* She had to face it…having a home, something more than a place to put her garbage bag filled with her belongings, would not be.

Emma closed the passenger car door, then opened the rear passenger door and grabbed her heavy black garbage bag containing all of her belongings off the seat, closing the door with her hip. She followed Audrey up the narrow sidewalk to the stoop that led to the enclosed porch where they waited for Mrs. Matthews to answer the door.

"Come in," Mrs. Matthews invited.

Emma placed her bag just inside the door and followed the two older ladies to the kitchen, just as she remembered it. As she looked around the kitchen, Emma noticed little seemed to have changed in her absence, even the lock on the refrigerator was still in place guarding its contents. After a brief meeting revisiting the rules of the house, Audrey left Emma alone with Mrs. Matthews.

It was uncomfortably quiet in the house. The other girls that lived there wouldn't be home for another two hours. The ticking of the over-sized clock placed in the hallway near the entryway sounded loud to Emma as she walked passed. Grabbing her garbage bag, Emma followed Mrs. Matthews up the plush carpeted stairs to the bedroom she had occupied over a year ago.

"You can put your things over there," Mrs. Matthews said, as she pointed to a white dresser with fancy swirls carved into it.

Not saying anything, Emma heaved her black plastic garbage bag into the corner of the bedroom, knowing she would never place any of the items into the dresser. She knew there was no point. She wouldn't be staying long. Audrey had assured her that it was a priority to find her a permanent home.

Emma sat on the edge of the twin bed as Mrs. Matthews walked out of the pretty bedroom. Slumping her shoulders, Emma sighed, and looked around the room, at the bed covered with a fluffy white comforter, at the soft pink accents, and the pink floral pictures hung on the walls, not nauseatingly pink, but a pleasant soft color. She remembered arriving at the Matthews' home the first time—now it felt different, but the same. Then, she had tried to keep a wall up so she wouldn't grow close to the family, not wanting to have her heart broken when they didn't want her and made her leave. But she had fallen in love with the doctor and his wife, he with his funny antics, and she with her stern but loving rules. Then one day, she had come home from school to find her caseworker sitting at the kitchen table with Mrs. Matthews—waiting to tell her she was being moved to a new home. Emma had been devastated and embarrassed that she had allowed her heart to open to her temporary family, and she had promised herself never to let anyone into her heart again. Emma knew the Matthews were special people, but also knew not to get too close. To do so would hurt because she wasn't staying.

Being at the Matthews' home felt different this time, she reflected as she sat on the soft bed, staring at the familiar room. She wasn't a kid anymore. In two years, she'd be on her own. It was time to stop believing in fairy tales...in dreams. She knew the children services, where Audrey worked, were looking for a permanent place for her to live. And with Audrey involved, Emma was sure she wouldn't end up someplace like Sheila's home. Not that it mattered anymore, Emma thought. Just another strange place...a place she would never belong.

A few days later, Emma had the beige receiver of the telephone pressed against her ear listening as Audrey shared the news that they had found a foster home for her.

"It's a real nice family," Audrey said. "Their last name is Rhodes, and they live about twenty minutes from here...near a small town. When I say small, I mean small. The population is less than 400 people, and their house is outside of town, in the country. It will be so quaint, but of course, if you don't like them you don't have to stay," she said quickly. "It's just a visit to see what you think of the family," she explained.

Emma rolled her eyes absently as she wrapped the rubbery cord of the telephone around one of her fingers. A real nice family she thought. *Really.* Did it matter, she wondered, as she half listened to Audrey. She knew Audrey meant well, but the woman had no idea if indeed the Rhodes foster family was *"real nice."* For all she knew, they could turn out to be like Sheila. No one really knew for sure what a foster family was like. Most people didn't come right out and say they were sickos.

"Fine," Emma sighed into the receiver. "That's fine."

She didn't care where the state sent her. She was pretty sure it wouldn't work out anyway. They might as well just get this next home out of the way so she could move onto God only knew what.

"That's fine, Audrey," Emma mumbled.

"Just pack a few things," Audrey said. "It's just for the weekend," she reassured Emma in her deep and oddly comforting voice. But Emma was not to be taken in again by anyone. She had no intention of becoming soft and letting anyone back in her heart, not even Audrey.

After Emma placed the receiver back onto the cradle of the telephone, she slowly and quietly walked back to her bedroom on the second floor. She wasn't sharing a bedroom with anyone, just as she had not the last time she had stayed at the Matthews' home. The other girls that lived at the home had a bedroom near her own, and as she lay on her pretty, white bedspread, she could see the three girls laughing and talking across the room through their open door. The girls she had known, had laughed with, and hung out with before she had moved to the children's home, now watched her when they thought she didn't see. Their eyes darted toward her, questioning, and with fear, and Emma knew it was because she had lived at a children's home. She knew what everyone thought about those kinds of places, and not long ago, she had thought the same thing. They thought it was a place where they stuck kids no one wanted, a place kids had to be tough to make it. Before she had moved to the children's home, the year before, Emma had only one reference for such places, a movie she had watched about a young girl that had been raped by other girls at a children's home. Emma had been terrified when Audrey had announced that she was taking her to a children's home for a visit, and then the visit had confirmed her fears when a group of crazy looking girls had run screaming down a hall toward her. But once Emma had moved to the home, become one of the students, it hadn't taken her long to realize that her fears were baseless, and that the reality was that it was a place of safety and love for kids. No one could hurt her there, and they hadn't.

A visit at a foster home, Emma considered. She rolled onto her side, and her black garbage bag, still filled with all her worldly possessions, caught her eye. Tucking a hand under the frilly white pillow, Emma curled her legs toward her. It didn't matter where she went, she thought as she closed her eyes, soon falling into a fitful sleep—running from the man that chased her in her dreams.

4

Emma stared at the passing fields, not yet harvest time, lush with corn. Emma loved it during the summer when the fields—her favorite the cornfields—like a sea of green, swayed and sighed in the wind. Audrey had been driving for twenty-five minutes, first through the town of Largo, then through the country—the fields broken up by an occasional country house or red barn. Then they had driven through the tiny town of New Point. If she'd closed her eyes for a moment or two, Emma would have missed the town. Now they were driving through country again, almost to the Rhodes' house, where she would be spending the weekend.

She felt the car slow down, and looked out of the passenger window at a two-story green house—a covered porch stretching across the entire front of the house—set back from the road on a hill. The house had a peaked roofline, with a section to the right jutted out, disrupting the neat lines of the house. As Audrey turned right onto the gravel drive, Emma noticed the house was larger than it had appeared from the road. She looked back up at the roof, noticing a chimney, and then looked to the left, out of Audrey's window, at several large farm outbuildings and a huge red barn. Emma caught a glimpse of a brown colored horse held captive in a small fenced section in front of the barn. She heard the sound of dogs barking, and not the type of barks you'd expect from small dogs, then saw them, two large dogs running toward the car. They weren't bolting toward the car; it was more of a leisurely saunter.

The car pulled up in front of the house as Emma continued to look around, catching sight of what looked to be a two-story, slate gray wooden playhouse with white trim accents to the left of the house, near the fields lining the back of the house. It looked like a miniature Victorian house, she thought curiously, wondering what it looked like on the inside. She turned around and counted the various buildings on the property, besides the barn, there were three metal buildings—one the shape and size of the red barn, and the other two the shape and size of horse stables, one with a giant red tractor parked in the front. Emma wondered if the Rhodes family had other animals besides horses. They certainly had enough space for chickens, cows and an entire stable of horses, she considered. Turning back around on her seat, Emma examined the side of the green house, at the garage with a large door, providing access for vehicles, at a small window to the left, and at a door, she suspected led into the house.

They were now sitting in the middle of nowhere, a five minute-drive outside of New Point, Indiana. Not that it mattered, Emma thought. If she lived here, where would she go anyway? She didn't know anyone.

"Now remember," Audrey said, "this is just a visit. If you don't feel comfortable with the Rhodes family, you don't have to live here. We can keep looking."

It didn't really matter, Emma groaned inwardly. She climbed out of the car as the two large dogs, possibly rabid, continued barking, and brushed up against her.

The door on the side of the house opened and a woman with dark brown hair stepped outside. Smiling she asked, "Did you find the house alright?"

Emma examined the woman who she suspected was Mrs. Rhodes, her foster mother for the weekend. She looked normal enough, Emma considered, but then, one never really knew. It wasn't as if bad people made the announcement, *Hi, I'm so-and-so, and I plan to make your time here a living hell.* No, typically, they kept that part of a foster kids visit a secret, to be discovered later.

Emma sat quietly in the Rhodes' kitchen, perched on a white metal chair with cushioned seat, her arms resting on the round white table. She took in her surroundings as Mrs. Rhodes and Audrey chatted over several cups of coffee. Trying not to draw attention to herself, Emma glanced around the small kitchen at the white metal cabinets, and at pots and pans dangling from a black metal contraption that hung from the ceiling just above the stove. The stove was unlike any she had ever seen before, with a smooth top, no apparent place for pots or skillets to be heated. She wondered how it worked, noticing the four round circles on the surface, assuming they served as a source of heating food. Beyond the stove and black contraption, she saw a wallpapered room. She squinted her eyes and saw a large window, and through it, she saw the red barn, one of the outbuildings, and the driveway they had driven up half an hour ago. The large window, you would think would brighten the room, but instead made it difficult for Emma to see the pattern of the wallpaper—a white background with some type of brown and mostly soft blue, more teal in color than blue. Emma shifted on her seat to see more of the room just beyond the kitchen and noticed a red brick fireplace with a wooden mantle and paneling above with a small, pretty, wooden clock placed in the center. She assumed there must be a TV in the room somewhere beyond her view. Cozy, she thought. After the two ladies finished off the pot of coffee, Audrey left, leaving Emma alone in the two-story farmhouse with her temporary foster mother.

The weekend passed quietly and quickly with Emma observing the five children and parents of the home. Her contribution was at a minimum, having nothing to share, nothing to say, no memories binding her to the newest strangers in her life. Mr. and Mrs. Rhodes were in their thirties, and had five children, three teenage daughters, a pre-teen daughter, and a five-year-old son. Their oldest daughter, Carmen, had graduated high school the year before and would be attending college down south in a few weeks. Carmen, a pretty, young woman, of the same height as Emma, five foot three, with shoulder length corn silk blonde hair, a broad smile, and an easy laugh, had been adopted by the Rhodes family when she was eight years old, enough time, in Emma's estimation, to feel a part of the family. Emma, the oldest of the Rhodes' biological children, was one year younger than Emma, and Emma wondered how she felt now that her big sister was leaving and some new girl was moving in…someone older. Emma had always fit into the family order at either the bottom or middle of the hierarchy, and this was the first time she was at the top, as the oldest child. It was not a position she wanted. Emma reflected, Emma, the Rhodes' oldest biological daughter, looked like her mother, and the rest of the kids in the family, all but Cassy, had dark hair, almost black, and exotic features, possibly of Italian decent.

They weren't shy, quiet, submissive girls, that was for sure, Emma noticed, as she sat on the couch in the family room later that night after a dinner of pork chops, macaroni and cheese and beans. Lots of noise, she noticed, lots of laughing, and a little arguing between all the kids. Caitlyn was two years younger than Emma was, and just as beautiful as her sisters, with dark brown colored hair, and a smile that reflected perfect teeth. Emma observed that she was best friends, much more than sisters, with Carmen, something she had always dreamed of being with her own sisters. Caitlyn seemed softer than the two oldest girls did, but she certainly made herself heard and known during the bantering. Cassy had a different look from her sisters, and even her little brother, with blonde hair, similar to Mr. Rhodes, and so quiet you would almost miss that she was in the house. But Emma didn't miss her. She reminded her of herself—quiet—and suspected there was much more to the little girl. Will was the youngest member of the family, and had the same dark coloring as his mother and most of his older sisters. He was a cute little boy, and brought back memories of one of Emma's little brothers, Robby. He had a similar coloring and was just about the same age.

"Emma, what's your middle name?" Mrs. Rhodes asked with a laugh in her voice. "With two Emma's in the house, it might make things less confusing if we add on you girls middle names; otherwise you'll both come running if I call you." Emma noticed that Mrs. Rhodes seemed to laugh a lot, or be close to a laugh frequently.

"It's Claire," Emma answered, thinking, *I have gone from Emma, to Emma-Emma, and now I am Emma Claire, and she didn't mind.*

"Emma Katherine," Mrs. Rhodes called out to her daughter talking on the telephone in the kitchen, "we're going to call you Emma Katherine, and Emma—Emma Claire. Otherwise, you will both come running when I call out your name."

Despite her best effort, Emma smiled. It seemed she was getting a new name, even if it *was* her name, but no one called her Emma Claire, at least not with a grin on their face, not like Mrs. Rhodes. A new name and a new chance at a home, but she intended to move slowly this time, to protect her heart from breaking.

"Yeah—Yeah," Emma Katherine said with a smile, and turned her attention back to the conversation she was having with her new boyfriend, Jordan, on the telephone.

Late Sunday morning, Mrs. Rhodes suggested Emma Katherine take Emma on a tour of the property. As the sun shone down on the two teenage girls, and the warm breeze whipped their hair into their faces, Emma Katherine led Emma around to the back of the house lined by a field and prairie grasses. Then she led her around to the other side of the house, the side Emma had seen from the road when she had first arrived. They continued walking, and passed by the covered porch that stretched the entire length of the front of the house. Looking over at the porch lined by tall bushes, Emma noticed two columns at the top of concrete steps, and red brick that created the base for the railing. There was a window placed at the front of the house—on the first floor—that overlooked the yard and road from the living room, perhaps at one time more of a parlor, or fancy entry for guests. The porch looked like a nice place to while away a summer afternoon, Emma considered, as she followed Emma Katherine down a hill and crossed the gravel drive toward the barn and outbuildings.

"I have *two* horses," Emma Katherine said with pride shining in her eyes, as she opened the metal fence that led inside to a portion of the red barn.

Emma looked at the two beautiful horses with the shiniest coats she had ever seen, one with reddish colored spots on a white background and the other a brown in color. One of the horses made a snorting noise and stomped a foot, and Emma Katherine reached out a hand and rubbed its nose to calm him.

"This one here is, Shawna," Emma Katherine said, as she continued to rub the horse's nose. "And the one over there, being shy, is Tasha," indicating the brown horse. "Do you ride?" Emma Katherine asked, as she looked back towards Emma.

"No," Emma said quietly. "They sure are beautiful."

"They're my show horses," Emma Katherine shared. "I've shown horses for years…they are my love…" her voice trailing away.

"We used to have cows too," Emma Katherine said, leading Emma out of the barn and back into the brilliance of the day.

"Cows?" Emma asked curiously.

"Yeah," Emma Katherine laughed. "We used to have to come out and milk them every morning before dawn. It was a pain!"

The girls continued their walk—passed several outbuildings butted up to more fields as far as Emma's eyes could see—chatting about life in the country, school, and of course, boys.

The weekend passed quietly and quickly, without incident or anyone trying too hard to impress her, which was a good thing, because Emma was not ready just yet to be impressed. Audrey called Sunday afternoon to ask how the weekend had gone, and to let her know she would be picking her up soon to take her back to the Matthews' foster home.

"How did it go?" Emma heard Audrey, as she cradled the hand piece of the phone to her ear.

Unsmiling, Emma answered, "Fine."

"No problems?" Audrey asked.

"No," Emma said. "No issues. They seem nice enough. Kind of noisy with a house full of kids, but not in a bad way, really. You know, you can just go by the Matthews' house to pick up my bag…the black garbage bag near my bed. I didn't bother to unpack. I didn't see the point since I'm not staying there. After all, it's just another temporary home."

The school year would be starting soon and Emma wanted to be placed somewhere before classes started. Who knew how long it would take before another foster home opened up for her to visit, she considered. It had been a decent enough weekend, but not enough time to really know who the Rhodes family was. It had taken awhile for Sheila, her ex-foster mother, to reveal her true nature, so she knew a weekend wasn't really long enough to know this new family. Foster homes were like rolling dice, no guarantee that you'd roll a winning number, or winning family.

"Emma," Audrey said, "you don't have to stay at their house if you don't like it. We can keep looking." Audrey cared about Emma, knew life had dealt her a bad hand, and this time, if she had anything to do with it, she wanted to load the deck a little so Emma had a better shot at a decent life. If she didn't feel absolutely comfortable, then she wanted her to keep looking.

"It's okay," Emma insisted. "Besides, who knows how long it will be before another home opens up." She had no intention of budging. It didn't matter. Chances were this home would suck, and she was making no long-term plans, but she knew that she couldn't stay at the Matthews' house, so this home was as good as any, as far as she knew.

"Emma, are you sure?" Audrey asked in a skeptical voice. "This is the first home you have visited since the children's home. Are you sure you don't want to try a few more?"

Impatient to get off the phone, Emma said, "This is fine, Audrey. I don't want to have to pick up and move during school. That would suck. Let's just see how this works out."

Audrey had gotten to know Emma well over the last few years, and recognized the heavy note of resignation in her voice, and didn't like it. It worried her. "If you're sure," she said, thoughtfully.

Emma's voice reflected the emptiness she felt inside, as she said, "I'm sure."

One afternoon, after driving to town—that's what the Rhodes called the town of Largo, the town where Audrey lived, and where Emma had lived at several foster homes in the past—to shop for the school supplies she'd be needing, Mrs. Rhodes had taken Emma on the very quick tour of the town of New Point. The town of New Point was too small to have a grocery store, beauty shop, or even a library...so if they needed these basic amenities, it was to Largo they travelled...*to town*. She was catching on to the country lingo quickly.

Sitting on the passenger seat in the station wagon, Emma had liked what she had seen—liked the feel of the old town of New Point. It was a pretty town, Emma had to admit, with lots of tall old maple and oak trees, and sidewalks lining every street. Most of the homes were modest in size, but there were a few houses sprinkled around the small town that were reminiscent of miniature Victorian mansions from another era. It had been a sunny day, the day of the New Point town tour, and Emma had noticed that, strangely enough, the town seemed to have an over population of butterflies of varying colors, and chirping birds.

The downtown area consisted of one long block, with buildings lining either side. The architecture was really cool, Emma had noticed... *old*. Mrs. Rhodes explained that at one time, New Point had been a booming town, before people decided to move closer to jobs, to towns like Largo. Once upon a time, the streets of New Point had been hopping with people, walking down the sidewalks of the downtown area headed to restaurants, entertainment, and various types of shops. Now, many of the old brick buildings, with fading logos and store names, sat empty. It was surprising that one of the impressive structures still housed a bank and across the street from it, was the city building. There were a couple other businesses on the block, but Emma was more interested in envisioning the town during the height of its heyday. It was a shame, she had thought, that such a quaint and pretty town had been abandoned by so many of its people.

Prior to leaving the house for the town tour, Mrs. Rhodes had asked Emma if she'd like to open a savings account so she didn't have money lying about her bedroom, that and she felt it was important for Emma to learn how to save money. She knew most foster kids had little exposure to what they would need to get by in life, such as, a simple thing like knowing about banks and saving money. Emma still had money left over from her paychecks at the children's home, and Mrs. Rhodes thought it would be a great way to introduce her to her first banking experience.

Several months ago, shortly before leaving the children's home, Emma had used some of her money earned cleaning the Rec Hall at the children's home to have her long hair cut. Now her formerly long golden locks were resting just above her shoulders, and she'd used a portion of her earnings to purchase contact lenses. The state had an annual medical and clothing allowance for all wards of the court, but they did not cover contact lenses. Emma had wanted contact lenses, so she had saved her money and bought them herself. It had been worth every sweaty hour of hard work she had put in cleaning the Rec Hall. The natural green color of her eyes was now hidden behind tiny chocolate brown contact lenses. She thought the dark color gave her an air of mystery, and the added bonus was that she wasn't constantly pushing her thick-lensed glasses up on her small nose. The remainder of her paychecks was now held safely in the New Point bank, Emma the proud recipient of her very first savings account.

Two weeks later, Emma found herself sitting in the guidance counselor's office located in the basement of the New Point High School, sorting through the short list of available classes. The high school was the largest building in the small town of 330 people. She knew that was how many people lived in New Point, because there was a fancy, dark gray wooden sign with the name of the town and population count stenciled in white, just before you entered the town. You couldn't miss it as you drove toward town on the two-lane almost abandoned highway.

The New Point High School was an impressive blonde brick structure, and when Emma had arrived at the school over an hour ago, Mrs. Rhodes had led her up the stairs to the main entrance and then a quick left into the office. There, Emma had been introduced to Mrs. Green, the school's friendly secretary. She looked to be in her thirties, Emma had gauged, noticing as Mrs. Green smiled a greeting and said, "Hello."

"Hi," Emma muttered. She wasn't used to school personnel speaking to her, well, outside of the children's home that was. The home had been different, Emma thought. She had loved many of her teachers and cottage mothers, but she was in the real world again, where people were mean and looked down on her, treated her like trash because she was a foster kid. It was what she was used to, so this smiling thing that was going on was throwing her off. Maybe it was just a fluke she considered, just a strange nut for a secretary. She suspected the rest of the staff would be what she was used to, nasty and mean. Stranger yet, a few minutes later, Mrs. Rhodes had knocked on the principal's office door, next to Mrs. Green's office, and introduced her to the man himself, Mr. Parker. Again with the smiles and niceness. It was too weird, she had thought suspiciously.

And now here she was, a half an hour later, seated before the school's guidance counselor, Mrs. Craft. Mrs. Rhodes had left Emma at the school for the rest of the day, trusting in the ability of the high school staff to acclimate her to the high school. What were a few more strangers, strange building, and town, Emma thought sarcastically in an effort to squash her nervousness.

Emma was a junior in high school which had been an amazing feat to catch up an entire year's worth of course work the previous year. As a little girl, Emma had loved school. She had always loved reading, English class, and History class had been an extension of English, with the fascinating stories of people long since gone. And math, she had loved learning about numbers and how putting them together worked out. But eventually, due to the many sleepless nights of being ripped out of bed by her dad in the middle of the night, and the other—bad things—she had begun to fall behind in school. When her stepmother had left her dad, all attempts at routine and normalcy had ended. Then, when she had been taken from her dad, the court hearings had thrown her even further behind in her classes—her days of straight A's on her report card were behind her. Eventually, she began to give up, on school, on life; nothing mattered anymore because she came to realize that she didn't matter.

"Okay," Mrs. Craft said, as she studied Emma's transcript. "Last year was a busy year for you. I can tell by reading your transcript that you really worked hard. Frankly, I'm amazed you were able to do two years worth of high school work in just one year. This year shouldn't be too bad for you, but junior year *is* typically a challenging year." Mrs. Craft placed the transcript on her desk and looked at Emma.

"There are core classes that you are required to take this year, such as government class, and you need a math class," Mrs. Craft said, detecting a little slouching from her new student when she mentioned math. "You told me you have worked hard to catch up in math, but still worry you won't be able to keep up with your class, but I think you'll be fine." The guidance counselor couldn't remember a child seated in her office with such obvious lack of confidence, and tried to encourage her, "Emma, I think you will be fine. Let's try you in a regular algebra class and see how you do."

Emma's stomach churned, and she felt the room become several degrees warmer. Math, she thought, if only there was a way to get out of the class. Thinking back over the years, back to first grade, she remembered the little girl she had been—so full of confidence. She hadn't known yet, hadn't learned to fear everything, everyone, and even her own abilities. Then, school seemed like a fun little adventure, but now... *Ugh!* She dreaded math class, just knowing she was going to fail. *It would be so much better not find out.* She would prefer to avoid proving to herself and everyone else that she was going to fail, that foster kids were retarded...that she was a loser.

"Maybe I should take a different math class," Emma suggested. "Maybe an easier one."

"Emma, you need algebra to graduate." Smiling, the guidance counselor said, "You'll be fine. You just worked through two years of math, in one year! That shows me that you have the ability to be successful in this algebra class." Mrs. Craft noticed that Emma didn't seem convinced and said, "I could place you in a pre-algebra class, but that would mean two years of math for you. I really think you will be fine, and next year you can have an extra study hall...if you get this math class out of the way."

Sighing, Emma said, "Okay," not convinced that she would pass the class. She hated failing, and she had a bad feeling she was about to fail. She was sure she had algebra at some point in the last few years, but she couldn't remember any of it. She had missed so much school because she had been passed from home to home so many times in the last few years—the different schools, different curriculum, different levels…it had been impossible to keep up.

"Okay. Great. You need an English class. I think we will place you in an advanced English class; it's a college level class. There is one with a seat open. It focuses on writing, and you said you like to write and your grades were good last year." Looking up at Emma, Mrs. Craft asked, "Is that okay?"

Emma raised her eyebrows at the thought of an advanced anything class. "Okay," she said, worrying about the difficulty of her junior year.

"Now, one more class. How about a speech class this semester?" Mrs. Craft asked. "Speech is another requirement for graduation."

Emma groaned and tried not to roll her eyes in frustration, wishing she had completed the speech class the summer before. When she had lived at the children's home, she had been allowed to take a few summer classes off campus, and speech had been one of those classes, but since she had run away from the home, she'd been dropped from the class roster. That summer class had been as perfect an opportunity as there ever would be for speech class, with a very small group of kids. *But a speech class…here,* Emma panicked. The thought of standing up in front of a group of people and actually talking made her feel faint with fear.

Emma's eyes opened wide, as she asked, "I have to take speech?" Holy shit, she thought, this year was going to suck!

"Let's throw in an art class and a study hall," Mrs. Craft suggested, "easing your load a little. And you are all set." The guidance counselor looked across the desk at the sixteen-year-old girl with shoulder length, light brown hair, with gold highlights when the light hit the fine strands just right. Emma's foster mother had shared a few details about her life, knew she had lived in too many foster homes, and her most recent long-term home had been at a children's home. Moving to a new town, new foster parents, and a new school was another in a series of changes for the young girl. Mrs. Craft couldn't imagine what it would be like to live Emma's life, of living with strangers, the loss of her own family…never knowing if her current home would be for a few weeks or a few months, or longer. The insecurity of a life like that, the life of a gypsy, must be an incredible burden, the type no child should bear.

"Do you have any questions or want to talk about anything?" Mrs. Craft asked kindly.

Emma looked down at Mrs. Craft's desk, not looking her in her eyes, and answered softly, "No, I don't think so."

"Okay, then," Mrs. Craft said brightly, and stood up. "Let's get you to class. Are you ready?"

Slowly, nervously, Emma rose to her feet in the small office, and said, "Sure." Emma followed the guidance counselor out of the office and back up the stairs—back to the office.

"Hey, Samantha," Mrs. Craft smiled at a tall slender blonde girl with glasses as they entered the secretary's office. "Are you the office assistant this morning?"

"I sure am," the young girl bubbled.

Samantha, I would like you to meet, Emma. She's a new student. Emma, this is Samantha. She's a junior too," Mrs. Craft said. Samantha was one of Mrs. Craft's favorite students. It could not have been more perfect she realized. She could see Emma was scared to death, and Samantha was the perfect introduction to her classmates. Actually, you couldn't go wrong with any of the students at the school. It was a unique situation, made possible by the small size of the school, that and the fact that so many of the parents had attended the high school. The high school was the community focal point, the place everyone gravitated. With the small size of the town, it was possible for those living in town to walk to school events, and most did, to all the sports related activities, plays...and the old timers loved tractor day. The town was a farming town, with a good majority either farmers or having farmed at some point in their life. The school promoted agricultural education, and each spring, on a special day, the kids that lived on farms drove their family tractor to school. Tractors would be lined up in front of the school, with old timers milling about the tractors, reminiscing of their own tractor days. It was a nice small-town-feel, where everyone knew everyone, where you lent a hand to a neighbor in need.

Samantha was a popular girl, one of the cheerleaders, was in advanced classes, had a popular boyfriend, and came from a solid family. But solid and popular had a different meaning in the town of New Point. The town had a story-like feel in the unusual way they treated one another, and the guidance counselor hoped Emma would thrive in the environment, knew if anyplace could heal her, it was the town of New Point.

"Hi!" Samantha said with a warm grin.

"Hi," Emma responded softly, with a small smile.

"Yeah, I'm on duty this afternoon. Mrs. Green had to step out for a bit, but I'd be happy to show Emma to her class," she said, smiling at Emma. "What class do you have?" Samantha asked, sensing her new classmate's nervousness. It must be tough starting at a new school. She already knew all about Emma, most of the school did. There wasn't much a school of 95 kids *didn't* know about each other. Emma being the only foster kid in town…was something to talk about. Emma's foster sister, Emma Katherine, had filled them all in about her last week. They were excited to have a new face in town, and at school. The boys were especially happy, Samantha thought.

"Great!" Mrs. Craft said. "Emma you have missed a couple classes today, so," she said, as she looked down at the white piece of paper with her schedule printed on it, "your next class is, speech." She held out the schedule to Emma, and said, "Just hand this to the teacher when you walk into the classroom. Class has already started, but that's okay. Don't worry about it, and if you ever need anything, or have any questions, you know where my office is. Okay?"

Class had already started, Emma groaned. Oh God, she was going to have to walk into a class with everyone staring at her. She sighed. Reaching for her schedule, she said, with a quiver in her voice, "Thank you."

Samantha chattered away as she led the way up the staircase, glancing back at Emma to make sure she was okay. "You're going to love this school. The kids are all so nice and so are the teachers. Do you play any sports? I'm on the volleyball team. Do you play?" Samantha asked.

Volleyball, Emma considered. She had played at the children's home. "Yeah. I've played a little," she said in a quiet voice, scared to death as each step took them closer to her new classroom.

"You should try out!" Samantha said. We just started tryouts. I know I made the team, most kids do," she said with a smile. "That's one of the great things about a small school. You can be part of anything you want."

"Well, here we are," Samantha said, with her hand on the doorknob of Emma's classroom. Smiling gently, Samantha assured Emma, "You're going to be just fine. Come on," and she opened the door and stepped into the classroom with her new schoolmate.

"Hey Ms. Thomas, this is Emma. She's a new student," Samantha said with a smile.

"Hey, Samantha," Emma heard, and looked up to see a group of teens, all smiling and giving Samantha a hard time. She counted 18 teens, a mix of boys and girls, all white faces smiling. She didn't notice or hear any snickers as she handed the teacher the class schedule.

"Okay, class. Class!" Ms. Thomas said, raising her voice over the laughing and ruckus in the room.

"Who are you supposed to be," a blonde headed boy asked, "the school secretary?"

"Watch it!" Samantha said, with an ear-to-ear grin. "I'll tell Aunt Jean you weren't paying attention in class."

The classroom erupted in laughter.

"Yeah, Tom, she'll tell your mommy!" a dark haired boy with dimpled cheeks, said.

"Yeah—Yeah," Tom responded with a smile.

Handing her the class schedule back, Ms. Thomas smiled, and said, "Pick a seat. They're not assigned."

Emma walked toward a seat in the center of the room, passed her new classmates smiling faces, and sat down.

"Don't let them bother you," a girl with short dark brown hair said. "They're just having fun. No one around here knows how to be serious!"

"What's that you're saying?" the boy with dimples asked with a grin, as he turned in his seat toward them.

"Okay, class. Let's get back to work. Eyes up here…at the front of the classroom. Can anyone remember what we were talking about?" Ms. Thomas asked.

The day was a blur for Emma, and when her last class finished, and she followed Emma Kathryn to the yellow school bus that would drive them to the Rhodes' house in the country, she was light headed with exhaustion. It had been another in a series of new, of change, of learning names and temperaments—teachers, and classmates—and of learning the lay of the school, and new rules.

Weeks passed with Emma knowing that in three months time, she would begin to feel more comfortable at her new foster home and at her new school. It was the way it always was; if her stay at a home lasted longer than three months, the fog of discomfort of new and strange faded to a manageable level. She just had to go through the motions of her days, waiting until it was time to go to sleep at night, hoping the recurring childhood nightmare didn't find her, and then at dawn, start all over again. It was the three-month-rule.

As new went, it hadn't been bad, Emma had to admit. New Point High was one of the smallest schools she had ever attended—not the building, the student body. The school was in a two-story blonde brick building with a basement level. There was a very small library in the basement, right next to a large open room utilized for study hall. Most of the regular classes were held on the second floor of the building. P.E. of course, was held in the gym which was off the main entry of the school. The hallways off the main entry contained all the lockers where kids stored their jackets and books during the day. The art, industrial arts, and agriculture classes were held in classrooms at the far end of the school, accessed by walking through the gym, tucked away at the far end of the gym next to the wooden bleachers. When you walked from the gym through the door leading to the classrooms, you were met by two steps and at the bottom, a large room opened up with large tables where the art and industrial arts classes were held. An adjoining room was used for the wood working portion of the industrial arts class and the agriculture classes.

Emma liked the feel of her new school at New Point. She preferred old schools, with old wooden floors, original marble, or tile flooring, closets tucked away in alcoves and stairs found in unexpected places. At some point along her travels, Emma had become fascinated by the architectural design of houses, barns, schools, and courthouses, and New Point High had just enough unique features, old features, to be interesting.

Emma found both the staff and the students at New Point High to be weird, very weird. It was as if she had stepped into some sci-fi Weird-Ville, where everyone was...*nice*. It was *not* normal, she thought skeptically. "Hi, Emma," the secretary, Ms. Green would call out when she saw her in the hall as students joked and laughed, seemingly having a blast all around her. The other students tried to include her, but she wasn't buying the act. Cheerfully, her classmates would wave at her from the bend in the staircase as she waved back with a suspicious smile, saying softly, "Hello."

This was not reality, or perhaps she considered, they were so far out in the boonies they had no idea how the real world acted. She had never seen anything like it, and was not quite sure what to make of it. Her past had shown her that people were not always what they seemed to be, so it was best to give people time to show their true selves. She intended to keep her expectations low, very low, regardless of how perky the students, teachers, and staff seemed to be.

The weird friendly thing going on at the high school wasn't the only way the school was different, Emma reflected. The size of the entire student body was only 95. Standing out as a foster kid was not desirable but at New Point High, there was no way to hide in such a small group of kids, which was exactly what she wanted to do, blend into the crowd.

Emma had found her rhythm—a routine—finding comfort in the sameness of each day. They were long days, especially considering now that she lived in the country again, her school days were made a little longer. Each morning she had to be out of bed extra early to make the trek down the long gravel driveway to catch the bus for school, and then each afternoon, lulled into half-sleep, she'd be dropped off at the bottom of the driveway, and hobble back up the drive on her wooden clogs. Living in a house with three other girls, with only one bathroom, had necessitated an even earlier day for Emma. She chose her shower time, or in this case bath time, as they had no shower, for the early morning hours, rising early while everyone but Mrs. Rhodes was still sleeping. It was the only way to ensure she was first in line to use the hair dryer and curling iron.

Emma Kathryn always amazed her. By the time Emma had her bath, hair done, and breakfast of toast and heaping bowl of oatmeal eaten, there Emma Kathryn would be, crawling out of bed. Each morning Emma just knew Emma Kathryn would miss the bus, but she never did. The two Emma's had been assigned a bedroom on the second floor to share. In all the homes Emma had lived in so far, she had never stayed in a borrowed bedroom where the roof was slanted in a way that if you sat up quickly in bed one could possibly knock themselves out! She and Emma Kathryn's bedroom was at the back of the house, facing fields as far as her eyes could see. The small room was sprinkled with medals, ribbons, and trophies won by Emma Katherine for showing horses. Instead of flowery posters, or girly things, the room had a distinct cowgirl feel. Well, Emma thought, it was obvious the girl loved her horses.

Caitlyn and Carmen shared a bedroom at the front of the house. It was the same layout, with the same slanted roofline. The bedrooms were spacious enough to walk down the center of the rooms, with the beds off to each side where the slanted ceilings were. But then Emma considered, she really did not have a need to stand on her bed, and had no intention of popping up in bed in the middle of the night. It was just...different.

Emma Kathryn's bedroom, the bedroom Emma was sharing, was dark as a cave with one small light glowing at the far end of the room. They each had their own twin-sized bed, with Emma's closest to the door, her sweaters, and jeans neatly folded against the wall near her bed. The bedroom, just like Caitlyn and Carmen's room, had two steps right outside the door that walked down to a large room. It was a cool space, Emma thought. The room spanned the length of the bedrooms, passed Cassy's small bedroom, also accessed by two steps, just passed the red, carpeted stairs that led to the first floor of the house. On the wall of the large room, positioned between two windows, was a beautiful painting of a tree. Mrs. Rhodes had explained that the tree had been painted onto the surface of the white wall in bright shades of greens and browns for the trunk by one of their friends' years ago. Emma loved it. It was different.

Caitlyn and Carmen's room had a warm feel about it, perhaps due to the pretty lights hung near both beds. Caitlyn slept on a twin bed with a fancy white headboard, placed on one side of the bedroom, and Carmen had, what Emma considered, the best bed out of all the girls. Mr. Rhodes had constructed a built in bed nestled against the wall. He had built wooden drawers under the bed and a wooden platform where the twin mattress lay. It reminded her of an old movie she had seen where beds had been stacked one above the other, on a train, with curtains hiding them away. Mrs. Rhodes said that her husband spent as much time as possible in one of the barns where he had created a wood working shop and the bed had been one of his many creations. Carmen and Caitlyn's bedroom was her favorite. The lights in the room dispelled any shadow that might have crept to the corners, unlike the bedroom she shared with Emma Kathryn. Emma didn't like dark rooms with what could be hiding in the shadows. But even with the shadows in the bedroom she was sharing, she hadn't had the recurring childhood nightmare in months.

Mrs. Rhodes had assigned household chores to all the girls, Emma being responsible for dishwashing each night after dinner. It was quite the chore scrubbing dishes fast enough for the other three teens to dry, that and she was now in charge of vacuuming the red-carpeted living room, and stairs to the second floor. Emma Kathryn had laundry duty, which it seemed to Emma to be the worst end of the chore deal. *Who wanted to be cooped up inside on a Saturday doing laundry?* And of course, Emma Katherine had to take care of her horses. Cassy helped Will clean his very messy bedroom, which was on the first floor of the house, right next to Mr. and Mrs. Rhodes' bedroom, and she was also responsible for feeding the two dogs that roamed around the property. Cassy assured Emma that their dogs wouldn't bite her. She told her that she could tell nice dogs from mean ones because nice dogs wagged their tails and their barks were happy ones, which was a relief to Emma. When Emma was a little girl, her dad had told her that dogs could smell her fear, and that they attacked people they knew were afraid of them. Maybe that's why, she had considered, she'd been attacked by dogs in the past. Size of a dog didn't matter to Emma; the fact that they had teeth was enough for her to know they could rip her to death. So she held onto Cassy's explanation of dogs, hoping she was right.

After dinner and dishes were over, Emma hid away in her bedroom doing her homework or reading a book she had checked out of the school's small library. Then, after she picked out clothes for the next school day, by 9:30, she flicked off the light in her already dark bedroom, and fell into a dreamless sleep. The weekends were the most difficult for Emma, with hours of not knowing what to do with herself...but think. She spent time staring at the TV in the family room, the room with the fireplace, thinking about the girls at the home, her boyfriend Tanner, and her sisters, Amy and Katie. She missed them all...and wondered where they were.

It was one of those perfect Saturday mornings; the sun was shining, and there wasn't a cloud in the sky, Emma noticed as she looked out the bay window overlooking the gravel drive and barn. She saw Cassy off to the right of the driveway walking in the grass beside the two-story playhouse. Emma scrunched her face against the window and watched until Cassy disappeared into the weeds near the field. Movement caught her eye and she looked toward the barn. It was Emma Katherine with a bucket in her hand, feeding her horses. They sure are beautiful, Emma admired as she watched one of the giant beasts eat out of her foster sister's hand. She decided to go outside and take a closer look, and walked away from the window.

Slowly, Emma walked down the drive toward Emma Katherine and her horses. Emma Katherine looked up and asked, "Do you want to pet her?"

"I don't know," Emma said, leery as she watched Shawna nibble Emma Katherine's hand. It was okay to admire the horse's beauty and majesty, but touch her…she wasn't so sure about that.

"Oh, come on" Emma Katherine encouraged. "She won't bite."

Skeptical, Emma reached her hand up toward the horse and pet the side of her neck, snatching her hand back in surprise when the horse whinnied.

"Here…you want to feed her?" Emma Katherine asked, as she tried to hand Emma some fruit.

Try to feed her, Emma considered. *The horse had almost eaten her hand for petting it!* Emma Katherine, had obviously taken leave of her senses, perhaps wanting her appendage ripped off, Emma thought as her heart thudded in her chest.

"Oh come on, she doesn't bite," Emma Katherine said with a smile. "Here…just open your hand like this," she demonstrated, "and she'll eat right off your hand. She *can't* bite you."

Not wanting her to know just how terrified she was of the beautiful giant horse, Emma allowed her foster sister to drop fruit onto her hand and then stiffly, with her palm as flat as she could make it, presented her hand to the horse with reddish colored spots hoping it wouldn't eat her fingers. The horse's giant sized tongued glopped onto her hand, and its funny looking lips nibbled at her palm. When all that was left was horse drool, Emma pulled her hand back and wiped it on her jean shorts.

Emma Katherine had been right, the horse hadn't bitten her; she still had all her fingers, she realized in relief. *Actually, it had tickled her hand.*

"Do you want to ride her?!" Emma Katherine asked excitedly.

She hadn't expected Emma Katherine to ask her to *ride* her horse. *Was she kidding?* She couldn't just let anyone ride her horse, Emma thought in concern. What if, like her, they had no idea what they were doing!? The last time Emma had been on a horse, she had been in fifth grade when her dad and stepmother had taken the family down south to visit their uncle, their dad's brother. Her uncle lived on a ranch with dairy cows, and they had to have horses to get around to feed all the animals, which was way more than just cows. They had chickens, turkeys, and sheep too. It was a huge ranch with caves tucked away, creeks, and a river running through the property…and ticks! It had been a tick fest when they had visited that summer. Disgusting! Emma remembered.

Emma's uncle had sons that helped with all the cows, and of course, they all knew how to ride horses. Of all her uncle's horses, an off-white colored one had been Emma's favorite. One of her cousins at the time—sixteen, and an expert horseman—offered to give her a ride. She'd had complete faith that it would be a nice, easy ride. She had been so excited that August morning. As she had looked up at the horse, so much taller than her, her stomach had flip-flopped. Well, she had told herself, how bad could it be—she'd just sit in front on the saddle and hold onto the horn thingy while her cousin sat behind her. She'd watched her cousin swing his leg up and over the beautiful giant of a horse, wondering how she was going to get up there without his help and how she'd manage to scoot in front of him.

"Come on," he'd said, as he held out a hand to her. "Grab my hand and put your foot in the stirrup. I'll grab hold of you and swing you up."

She had done as she was told, but she hadn't found herself sitting in front of her cousin on the saddle holding onto the horn thingy, instead, she was sitting behind him, not seated on the saddle at all, but on the bare back, close to the ass of the horse, *behind* the saddle. As she had sat staring at the back of her cousins white shirt, Emma had wondered what she was supposed to hang onto. Seeing nothing but the back of her cousin and the brown leather saddle he was sitting on, she grabbed hold of the top part of the curved saddle as tight as she could and away they flew. Her scrawny little arms held on with all their might, her fingers burning as she grasped as tight as her puny strength would allow. She was so scared she was going to fall off she was half crying when her cousin finally slowed the horse to a trot—surprisingly, a trot was just as bad as a full run—then they came to a complete stop. It had been a huge horse with nowhere to put her feet and only the back of the saddle to hold onto, and she had flopped freely in the wind, like laundry hanging on a clothesline on a windy day. It had been terrifying and painful. Since that harrowing experience, where she half suspected her cousin was being mean and hoped she'd fall off, Emma had been too terrified to even think about riding another horse.

"I'm going to get a saddle," Emma Katherine said, much to Emma's alarm.

Sure enough, Emma Katherine was back in a few minutes, with what looked like a small wool blanket, saddle, and a rein looking thingy. Once the horse was outfitted with all its gear, Emma Katherine led it out of the barn, with Emma following.

"Okay," Emma Katherine said, still holding onto the horse, "you just put your foot in the stirrup and swing your leg over."

Emma shifted her eyebrow as she looked up at the horse. What a beautiful horse, she thought as she moved closer, and pet the enormous beast. And so very far off the ground...thinking about how hard the ground would be when she fell off the horse and landed on her head.

"I won't let go of her," Emma Katherine assured her. "We'll go around the yard, and then if you're comfortable we'll go out on the road."

The road...Emma thought nervously. "Should we take a horse out on the road?" Emma asked. "If a car goes by, won't it spook it?" knowing very few cars ever passed by the house.

"No, silly," Emma Katherine said with a grin. "We take the horses out on the road all the time. They're used to cars. If a car goes by, we just get to the side of the road."

Nervously, Emma inserted her tennis shoe clad foot into the stirrup and swung her leg up and over, lowering onto the leather saddle, her feet secure in the stirrups, feeling the warmth and strength of the horse on her bare legs. As Emma Katherine led the horse up toward the house, Emma held onto the horn of the saddle feeling the power of the horse beneath her. She looked down and saw the top of Emma Katherine's dark brown head, and the ground far below. For fifteen minutes, Emma Katherine walked her horse, as if it was a dog, with her foster sister astride, around the yard.

When Emma Katherine led the horse down the hill, back toward the gravel drive, Emma's stomach flipped as she leaned back in the saddle. Emma clutched the horn, her heart thudding in her chest fearing at any second she would flip over the horse's head, and be trampled.

"Okay," Emma said breathlessly, "I think I'm ready to head back to the barn."

Looking back and up at Emma, puzzled, Emma Katherine said, "But we haven't even gone down the drive yet."

"That's okay," Emma said, not wanting her foster sister to know she was scared to death of her giant horse. *Dammit! I'm afraid of everything!* Sighing, she looked at the horse's mane as Emma Katherine led her and the horse back to the barn. Such a beautiful, scary animal, Emma thought, wondering if she'd ever get over her fear of so many things. It was with frustrated relief a few minutes later that Emma dismounted and watched as Emma Katherine took all the accessories off her horse.

"Emma," Mr. Rhodes said in a deep husky voice. "It's for you."

Scanning the Rhodes family seated around the dinner table, Emma furrowed her brow wondering who would be calling her. She had been living at the Rhodes' home for several months now, but hadn't developed any friendships close enough to give out her phone number, and she hadn't heard from her sisters in that time. Swallowing the bite of creamy macaroni and cheese she had been chewing, Emma scooted her chair back, walked around the kitchen table, around her newest family, and took the handset from Mr. Rhodes outstretched hand.

"Who is it?" she asked.

"I don't know," he said with a smile. "Some, boy."

The telephone chord stretched from its position on the kitchen wall as Emma stepped into the laundry room and shut the door behind her. "Hello," she said into the receiver of the beige colored handset.

"Hey," Emma heard a familiar voice say. Emma had not heard the deep voice of her ex-boyfriend, Tanner, in over four months, so why now, she wondered irritably. Scowling, Emma wondered where Tanner had gotten the Rhode's telephone number.

A couple of the girls from her cottage had introduced her to Tanner—a cute boy with shoulder length dark colored hair, and a sweet smile—at one of the dances at the children's home. He had been such a kind boy, Emma had thought. Soon after the evening they had met at the dance, Tanner and Emma had become boyfriend and girlfriend, which at the children's home had consisted of writing letters to one another, cuddling at dances, and stolen moments...kisses hidden from the eyes of the cottage mothers and cottage fathers. Tanner had graduated from the program at the home before her, but had been in no hurry to leave the home. He had gotten into a comfortable routine at the home, liked the cottage parents, his teachers, his cottage mates, and his girlfriend... Emma. When the state had decided to close the home, during the process of determining where all the children would be moved, Tanner had run away, and he hadn't been alone. A girl from one of the cottages was from his hometown, and she had run with him. Emma remembered how she had found out Tanner had run, *with that girl,* and what they had done. One afternoon, when Emma had been cleaning the Rec Hall, a girl from one of the other cottages had run up to her and blurted it all out... he had run away with a girl and they'd had sex while on the run. Now, as she held the phone pressed to her ear, listening to his voice, it was the first she had heard from him since he had run...not even bothering to say goodbye.

"Hey," she responded softly, not sure what else to say.

"How you doing?" he asked. Emma heard the smile in his voice. Tanner had always seemed to have a cute grin pasted to his face.

"I'm okay," she said slowly, with a distinct chill to her tone.

"So how's it at your foster home? What are they like?" Tanner asked, detecting the annoyance in her voice.

Rolling her eyes, Emma leaned a hip against the counter in the cramped space, and said, "It's just fine."

Tanner knew she was mad at him and she had every right to be mad. He hadn't told her he was going to run away—it hadn't exactly been a long thought out plan. It just seemed to happen. Running with that girl had just happened too, and then...the other had just happened.

Trying to draw her out of her anger he pried, "How many kids live with you, and are there any other fosters there, or are you the only one?" He paused for a minute and then asked, "Are they treating you okay?"

Sighing, she thought about what she wanted to tell him, what he *deserved* to hear. What he deserved was a hang up, she thought, but she didn't hang up, instead she responded, "It's fine here. They're treating me fine. The mom and dad don't seem to be too weird. Kind of normal, actually. And I'm the only foster kid living here. They only take in one foster kid at a time, not surprising considering they have five kids of their own, four girls, and one little boy. The oldest daughter is away at college, which leaves four of us at home...*full house.*"

"What's the house like—are you in a city, or town...?" Tanner asked, trying to envision Emma's new life.

She snickered, "No. This is certainly not a city, or even town. I'm in the middle of nowhere. Their house is in the country surrounded by fields about five miles from a tiny town and the school is just as small, well not the building, but there are less than a hundred kids in the entire school."

She paused for a moment as she twined the telephone cord around a finger and thought, the last few weeks hadn't been too bad. There hadn't been any issues at the Rhodes' home. They seemed to be going out of their way to be kind to her. So far, she liked living in the country. It wasn't at all like the other foster home she had lived at in the country... actually neither of the foster homes where she had lived in the country. And school was still as weird as ever, but in a nice way with everyone being nice to her. Her P.E. teacher was a hoot! He was a short little man, with dark curly hair and was always laughing. She hated P.E., but...not Mr. Richardson's, P.E. class. Another weird...the class was actually fun. Mr. Richardson wasn't one of those asshole coach type P.E. teachers that blew their whistle and yelled at you as if you were a jock or something. She had found most P.E. teachers in high school were similar. It was as if they thought all their students were training for some big game. Even though Mr. Richardson wasn't super P.E. teacher or anything, there were still things she hated participating in, like dodge ball, a form of legalized child abuse as far as she was concerned. Who in their right mind would condone the pummeling by a rubber ball, by a group of schoolchildren? It was like a modern day version of stoning, but instead of stones, they used red rubber balls that stung like hell! She wasn't too keen on the little square scooters they used in class either. They used them at New Point High to play a weird form of hockey, and it never failed, she'd roll over her own fingers as she pushed herself across the gym floor. Jeez, she was afraid one day she'd roll over one of her fingers and find it lying on the shiny wooden gym floor!

Not all kids wanted to be or could be a school's star athlete. If she had the physical ability, she would love to be a jock, but it had been pointed out early on in her childhood that she was not the jock type. She'd tried to prove everyone wrong by trying out for track her eighth grade year… to disastrous results. After two weeks of running laps around the baseball field in the cold, she had barely been able to crawl around the school because her legs ached so badly. Sports career over, she had dropped out. Everyone was right, jock she was not. Her older sister, Amy, must have gotten her portion of physical ability, and she had gotten an extra dose of nerd. The library was where she belonged, she considered.

Then there was another one of her teachers that was really cool, Ms. Blake the art teacher. Ms. Blake dressed like what Emma thought an art teacher would wear, flowing skirts and big natural jewelry, some days a scarf draped around her neck, and she had free flowing curly auburn hair. Emma estimated that Ms. Blake was in her late twenties, not out of college too long. As schools went, New Point High was really not all that bad, she realized.

She wondered about Tanner—how life had turned out for him, and asked curiously, "How are things with you?"

"Oh…you know me," he said. I'm okay. I'll always be okay. My sister's letting me stay with her. Her apartment isn't as big as my old cottage at the home," he joked, "but it's someplace to crash. My bedroom's a couch."

That was Tanner, Emma thought, always making the best of things, even when it didn't seem that he had the best of anything. Emma had known several foster kids that were in such a hurry to grow up, to be on their own, but she was not ready to give up on the dream, the dream of being part of a family…a family that would be good to her. Emma's dream had meant life with her biological family, at least with her two older sisters. Months ago, she had finally come to realize that she would have to let that part of her dream go. But she still didn't want to be an adult. She wasn't ready. She wanted to be a kid…to *finally* be a kid. *What kind of life was that for a kid, living on his sister's couch…?*

"Is everything okay? Are you happy, Tanner?" Emma asked with concern.

"I'm okay," he said, his cheerful tone not so cheerful now. "I can come and go as I want with no one bothering me. Sis is cool." There was silence for a moment as the two teens thought about their current lives— paths so different—and the life they had shared at the children's home not so long ago, but feeling as if it were a lifetime ago.

"I think about you a lot, Emma," Tanner said softly. "I miss you."

Emma felt a tug on her heart, feeling sorry for Tanner and his life that sounded awful to her. Before she could respond, Tanner asked, "Do you ever think about the kids at the home?"

Sighing, Emma confessed, "Everyday."

"Do you think about me?" He asked hesitantly.

She felt uncomfortable and didn't want to hurt his feelings, didn't want to tell him she had gotten over him pretty fast. The shock of his running—running with that girl—had faded within a week. It wasn't that she hadn't cared about Tanner—she had—but with the home closing, her world had become scary, and breaking up with a boyfriend had been the tiniest of her worries.

He sounded so sad, so lost, and she said, "Of course I think about you," which wasn't a lie, she just didn't think about him in the way he wanted her to.

"You know, you could come down here...to my sisters. I bet she'd let you stay," Tanner said hopefully.

With those words spoken, Emma knew Tanner was not okay. But even knowing this, she did not intend to run several hours away, or whatever it was he was suggesting, so she could share a couch with him. At the Rhodes' home, she had her own bed in a warm, cozy house in the country, with a family that seemed to be what a family should be. Soon she would be at the three-month mark, and she didn't want to start all over again, didn't want to go through the uncomfortable, not fitting in, not belonging, new feeling, again.

Tanner's loneliness seeped through the telephone and covered Emma, bringing with it memories of long ago, of the little girl she had been, of others pain, and sadness. Struggling with the suffocating memories, Emma mentally clawed them away, and gasped, "Yeah, that would be great, Tanner. I just have so much going on right now, with school..."

"Yeah...I understand," he said sadly.

His sadness crashed over her. Emma struggled to catch her breath, squeezing her eyes tight as tears burned the back of her eyes. If only she could ease his sadness...but she knew she couldn't—there was nothing anyone could do. Who was she, but a foster kid, and Tanner...there was nothing she could do, nothing she could ever do to help anyone.

"Tanner," she said softly.

"Yeah," he said, trying to sound his usual happy self.

"I have to get going. I have to finish dinner with my foster family," she said feeling guilty.

"Emma, can I call you again?" he asked in a rush, afraid she would hang up on him.

"Sure," she said.

"I'll talk to yuh later," he said a little brighter.

"Okay. Bye," Emma said quickly.

"Bye, Emma," Tanner said softly.

Emma freed her fingers from the cord of the telephone, and slowly opened the door.

An hour later, as she washed dishes, Emma was quieter than usual. Her thoughts were filled with her past, of Tanner, her friends from the children's home...and of Amy and Katie. Were they all happy...were they all okay? As she placed a plate in the sink full of warm water, she wondered what Amy and Katie were doing at that very moment.

"So you did gymnastics at your old school?" Mr. Richardson asked.

Emma, dressed in a pair of navy blue cloth shorts with a white stripe down the side, watched as her P.E. teacher, Mr. Richardson, dressed in his typical uniform of sweat pants with a short-sleeved t-shirt tucked into the waist, swing a rope above his head, freeing the rings hanging from the high ceiling of the gym. Mr. Richardson had mentioned rings during gym class and Emma had told him they had a segment at her old school on gymnastics, rings included. New Point High didn't have parallel bars, a horse, or a balance beam, but they did have rings and he wanted her to demonstrate her ability.

Looking up, Emma watched as Mr. Richardson, suspended in air, raised his feet up so he looked like he was in a seated position, and then slowly, his hands clutching the rings, he extended his arms to the side of his body. Okay, I certainly *cannot* do that, but I *can* do something, she thought with a determined grin.

Emma heard and felt the thud when Mr. Richardson's feet hit the polished gym floor. "Okay!" Mr. Richardson said with a grin. "It's your turn! Show me what you got."

"Well," she said with a smile, "what I got is not what you just did. I don't have the strength in my arms to hold myself suspended like you just did."

She looked up at the rings and stretched her right arm up, wiggling her fingers, not quite reaching. "I can't reach," she said with a question in her voice.

He noticed the spark in Emma's eyes, and wanted to encourage the moment. She had been a tough kid to reach. Emma had been the topic of many meetings with staff and teachers over the past few months, of just how to help the lost girl. "I'll give you a boost," Mr. Richardson said.

I can do this, she thought as she stepped into position under the rings, looked up, and stretched her arms toward the rings. Mr. Richardson placed his hands on her waist.

"When I say jump, push off and I'll lift you, then grab the rings and I'll let you go. Okay?" the P.E. teacher asked.

She placed her hands over Mr. Richardson's hands, and then crouched a little, preparing to spring up toward the rings hanging just out of her reach.

"Ready?" he asked.

"Ready," she replied.

"Jump!" he shouted.

Her heart pounding, Emma kicked off with her feet, stretched her hands toward the rings, and grabbed tight when her palms met the smooth wooden rings. She felt the pressure ease from her waist and knew she was on her own, now hanging from the rings several feet above the floor.

During the last six months at the children's home, Emma had spent evenings working out, and had a ten-pound weight loss to show for her efforts. She had never been a heavy child, if anything, had always been on the thin side, but a year living at the home, eating all the starchy food prepared by the cooks at the dining hall, had taken a weight toll. So each night while the other girls watched TV, Emma had done sit-ups, push-ups, headstands, and combinations of floor exercises learned in her P.E. gymnastics class.

She pulled herself up, her body positioned above the rings now, and stretched her legs straight out in front of her as Mr. Richardson had done moments before. Her arms were tight to her body, knowing better than to try to extend her arms outward to the side, like Mr. Richardson had done, or she'd end up on her butt or head on the floor below.

"Whoa!" she heard, concentrating so hard she hadn't realized an audience had gathered. As the sound of clapping hands broke out, Emma released the rings and landed on her feet, a grin lighting her face. Still grinning, Emma turned, pivoting on her toe, and looked up into the brown eyes of a very tall boy with thick, almost black hair, dressed in a baggy pair of dark green slacks, dress shirt, and brown loafers.

"Nice!" the boy said.

"Thanks," Emma smiled.

"I think she just showed you up, Mr. Richardson!" the boy joked.

"I think she did, Jacob!" Mr. Richardson laughed.

"Now it's your turn!" Mr. Richardson joked with the six foot four senior, built like a linebacker. Jacob Garner was the senior class clown, a little rowdy, but a good kid. He was in Mr. Richardson's last period P.E. class. Mr. Richardson admired the fact that although Jacob's dad owned a bank in town, his parents insisted the teen find a job on his own without his father's influence, and worked most days after school. At a young age, Jacob's father had begun teaching him about financial responsibility, and that included earning his own money and then budgeting his money. Jacob's grandfather had taught *his* father a similar hardworking ethic, and he wanted the same for his son. Mr. Garner's father had taught him that respect for community was important, and one way to foster trust was by making one's own way. He felt handing a child everything took away the opportunity for a truly rich life to grow into a person of depth, and substance. He wanted his son to know as much as possible about life, and that included that although they had a nice house, cars, and perhaps more material things than other people, they were no different from anyone, no better and no worse. If anything, they had a responsibility to their community because of all they had.

Grinning, Jacob threw his head back, laughed, and then looked at the P.E. teacher, and still grinning, said, "You're not getting me up there. I'll fall and break my head!"

Smiling, Emma shook her head and thought, *funny guy*. She hadn't noticed this Jacob boy before. How was that possible in such a small school, she wondered. The bell, sounding like a fire alarm, rang; indicating students had three minutes before their next class began. Emma jogged toward the wooden bleachers, skirting three teen girls walking into the gym, as Jacob said something to her. Not hearing him, she whisked the stack of books off the first row bleacher and walked toward her art class, her favorite class of the day.

"Todd, can I squeeze in there to put some water in here?" Emma asked, holding a clear plastic container in the air for him to see. Todd, the short boy with light brown hair, and glasses as big as the ones she had tucked away in a drawer at the Rhodes' house, smiled and scooted over to give her room. The last bell of the day would be blaring any moment and she needed to get the paintbrushes she had been using during class soaking in a plastic container before she left for the day. Emma loved to paint, became lost in the process of bringing an animal, scenery, or a person to life with oil color or even a charcoal pencil. Mrs. Rhodes had discovered Emma's love and talent of drawing when she had seen a sketch she had doodled on a piece of notebook paper. Wanting to give Emma something within to develop, the next day, while Emma was at school, Mrs. Rhodes had purchased a small art kit for her to play around with. When Emma had arrived home from school, she had been thrilled to find the black leather kit lying on her bed. Inside the case she found four willow charcoal sticks, an 8 ½ by 11 sketch pad, and 16 tiny tubes of oil color paints, and several paint brushes, one a fan brush, not the cheap kind, but the kind with good bristles that didn't fall out.

The ringing of the last school bell of the day interrupted Emma's daydream. She was going to have to get a move on or she was going to miss the bus! Placing the brushes in the container, brush side up, she placed the plastic container back on the shelf where it belonged. Grabbing her sketchpad off the navy blue colored, long work desk with an eyeball painted in its center—a design for the table she had created and then painted—Emma rushed toward the door behind the rest of the students.

"Have a great weekend, Ms. Blake!" Emma said happily. She loved Ms. Blake's art class. It was her style of class…laid back, where creativity flowed freely and was encouraged.

"You too, Emma!" Ms. Blake called after Emma.

Emma rushed to her locker and gathered the books she would need for homework over the weekend and the Steven King book she had borrowed from the library to read on the bus. Next stop was the vending machine for Doritos.

"Hey!" a deep voice to her right, said.

Looking up, she saw Jacob leaning his arm above her head on the vending machine.

"Oh, hi," she said with a smile. Leaning over, she grabbed the small bag of chips out of the slot in the vending machine. Jacob was a boy she would never date, not in a million years, definitely just friend material, so with no pressure to impress him, she felt at ease.

Standing up with the bag of chips in her hand, Emma smiled up at him. Gesturing toward the door, Emma said, "I have to catch the bus," and took a step toward the double doors that served as the main entry into the high school. Jacob fell in step beside her.

"So what are you doing this weekend?" he asked with his usual wide grin spread across his face.

"Oh, the usual," Emma said, glancing over at him, the smile still tugging at the corners of her lips. "I have my date," she said, holding the Stephen King book up for him to see, "and homework."

"Awe, that doesn't sound like any fun at all," he said with a playful grimace.

As they approached the bus, Jacob asked, "Do you want a ride home?"

Surprised, she looked up and considered the idea, but didn't think Mrs. Rhodes would approve of her riding home in a strange boy's car. The Rhodes had been good to her and she didn't want to do anything to make them mad. "Thanks, but I'll just take the bus home." Standing a few feet from the bus, Emma noticed the driver, her foster mother, Mrs. Rhodes, wasn't ready to take off yet, and asked Jacob, "What are you doing this weekend?"

"I'm working tonight," he said easily, as if they had been friends forever, instead of strangers until that afternoon. "We should hang out sometime," he said, as if the idea had just popped into his head. "A couple friends and I hang out on the weekends sometime. We grab something to eat and sometimes just goof off at the mall. You know, hang out, and do what kids do here in the middle of nowhere. You should come with us."

"Like, cow tipping?!" Emma laughed. It was something she had heard about in one of her classes. The boys had been joking about it—knocking cows over. Emma had been skeptical, although they had never admitted whether they were joking or not, she didn't think it was possible that a small group of boys could really knock over a cow. And why they would want to knock over a cow was beyond her, but then, it was different at New Point. Fun for these kids seemed to be of the country sort...which did not include drugs or being mean to girls.

Jacob grinned at her and said, "Probably no cow tipping involved when hanging out with my friends and me."

Emma wrinkled her nose, grinned, and said, "Maybe...sometime."

"Emma, you ready?" Mrs. Rhodes asked, ever watchful over one of her daughters, especially when a teenage boy was nearby.

Climbing the steps of the bus, Emma looked back, and said with a grin, "See you Monday!"

He made a goofy face and waved at her. "Hey Mrs. R," Jacob said in a silly voice.

As Emma walked to her regular seat at the back of the bus, she peeked at her foster mother and Jacob chatting away by the door of the bus. Funny boy, she thought as she sat down and leaned back on her seat. Hearing a knock on the window by her face, Emma looked down through the foggy window and saw Jacob making a goofy face at her. He stepped back, grinned at her, and waved as the bus pulled away. She waved, smiled, and then settled back onto her seat.

The movement of the bus lulled her and she closed her eyes, thinking she loved having Mrs. Rhodes as the new school bus driver. The old bus driver, another woman, had quit a few weeks ago. She had been a real strange lady, with a three-year-old daughter that used to thunk her head on the backrest of her seat during most of the drive to school. Emma dozed for a few moments, waking when the bus came to a stop—the first stop—with many more to come before it was her turn to get off the bus. Reaching down next to her on the seat, Emma grabbed the bag of chips and tore the package open. She crunched a tangy chip, licked the orange off her fingers, and then picked the book up off the seat she had been reading in study hall earlier in the day. Opening the book to where she had her place marked, Emma lost herself in the horror of Steven King's novel.

A half an hour later, Emma walked into the Rhodes' kitchen, ready for a real snack. She was starving. Maybe a cheese sandwich she considered, but first she needed to put her schoolbooks in her bedroom, not wanting to trash Mrs. Rhodes' kitchen with her stuff. Placing the stack of books on the floor next to her bed, Emma picked up the small white envelope she assumed Mrs. Rhodes had placed in the center of her bed. Wondering whom it was from, Emma flipped the envelope over and read...*Cheryl*. It was from one of her cottage sisters from the children's home. Cheryl had first appeared in Emma's life over a year ago, at Audrey's foster home, and eventually she had been sent to the same children's home where Emma had been staying. Emma stared down at the small white envelope wondering how Cheryl had gotten her address, and where she was.

9

Over the next few weeks, the letter from Cheryl weighed heavily on Emma's mind. The time spent at Sheila's foster home had been tucked away in a corner of her memory, the sexual assault, and the hands…the bad stuff. Cheryl's letter brought it all back—memories washing over her like a wave, a crashing cold wave. Emma had ended up in a children's home a few months after confronting Sheila, her unmarried foster mother at the time, about what her son and her boyfriend had done to her. Sheila lived in the town of Largo, and as far as Emma knew, still did. George, Sheila's son, had been in his twenties, and had sexually assaulted Emma on numerous occasions, and not only that, he had driven her to the country, giving her the option of walking back to town, or taking a puff off a joint. Emma had feared what he would do to her if the drug had an impact on her, but had puffed quickly, hoping she would be okay. It was the only option she had, either that or face worse if she walked through the country back to her foster home…assuming she could find her way. Emma was sure the part of the confrontation that infuriated Sheila the most—to the point of shrieking to her son, *Hold her down, I'm gonna kill her*—was when she told her that Sheila's perverted forty-something year old boyfriend had tried to convince her to become a stripper.

Emma had been in and out of foster homes since she was a little girl, but had been made a permanent ward of the state when she was thirteen. In the last three years, she had been passed through eleven homes, in various towns throughout the state. Over the past few months, she had begun to, not forget, but to set her past aside, to consider that maybe here, at the Rhodes' foster home, she could try one more time, to give them a chance—a chance to be the family she didn't have, and so badly wanted. In her short time at the Rhodes' home, she had begun to feel happy, beginning to feel as if maybe she could be a kid after all, maybe belong…just a little. But a feeling of guilt clawed at her—that she dared be happy, that she could move on with her life not knowing how her sisters or the kids at the home were. Should she be happy…was it okay? A big part of her felt that to be a kid, doing the things she had dreamed of—being on the basketball team and a pom-pom girl—was a betrayal of her sisters. Cheryl's letter served as a reminder of who she was. It stirred the memories and longing for her sisters…pulling her in multiple directions.

Mr. Richardson and Mrs. Rhodes had talked Emma into trying out for the school's high school basketball team. It hadn't really been a try out at all, but more of a, *can I play,* the response being, *of course,* because as small as the school was, they didn't have enough players. Even if Emma were the worst player on the team, she would get to suit up and play for both the Junior Varsity and the Varsity team. Never in her wildest dreams had she thought she would play on a real sports team in high school, with a real uniform. Gold and purple were the school colors… her new colors. Her foster mother had also encouraged her to be part of the pom-pom squad. Emma couldn't believe it. She remembered the girls at one of her high schools that had been on a squad…and now she was going to be like them. A kid…she was finally getting to be a kid! But did she have the *right* to be happy, she wondered.

"Hey, Emma Claire and Emma Katherine, dad said he'd put up a basketball hoop for you in the barn," Mrs. Rhodes said.

A piece of the macaroni and cheese fell off the fork Emma held in her hand, as she paused her fork in mid-air, just about to place it in her mouth. The Rhodes family was packed around the dinner table, inhaling the fried pork chops that Emma Katherine had prepared, and chattering away about their day. With everyone talking at once, Emma was able to make out pieces about everyone's day, but when Mrs. Rhodes sprung the basketball hoop thing on the kids, conversation ceased.

Mrs. Rhodes intended to encourage anything and everything Emma Claire seemed to take even the slightest interest in, and lately it was basketball. She was behind the other girls in her skill level, even dribbling a ball. Emma had told her she had never played before, except what was required in P.E. classes, which was not a lot. Emma was such a timid girl—a beautiful girl—but had the lowest self-esteem and confidence she had ever seen in a child. She just needed some successes to know she could do something, and then she knew Emma would try at other things. Mrs. Rhodes had talked to her husband about putting up a basketball hoop in the garage, a warm place during the winter months where the girls could at least practice their shots. Since they lived in the country, the girls had to catch the bus immediately after school ended for the day, so there was no time to use the school's gym for extra practice. The barn seemed like the perfect solution. It was a full-sized barn so there was plenty of room; the only problem being that a space needed to be cleared. Mr. Rhodes had agreed with one condition...*Emma Kathryn* and *Emma Claire* had to help clear a space.

Emma rested her fork on her plate of half eaten dinner and smiled, saying, "Really?" She looked from Mrs. Rhodes to Mr. Rhodes in disbelief.

"Well, yeah, but he's not going to do it all by himself. You and Emma Kathryn have to help him clean up the barn," Mrs. Rhodes said, happy to be able to put a smile on Emma's face. Emma had come to her home a reserved, very quiet young girl, but slowly, ever so slowly, her reserve was slipping, and every so often, she'd say something funny, or laugh...not a soft laugh, but a laugh from her soul. Mrs. Rhodes suspected it had been a long time, if ever, that Emma had laughed like that.

"Sure, I'll help!" Emma said excitedly, as she looked across the table at Emma Kathryn to see what she thought of the idea.

"Emma Kathryn," what do you think? You interested in having a basketball hoop in the barn?" Mr. Rhodes asked with a smile.

"Well, yeah," she laughed. "As long as we don't have to clean out the barn on date night!"

Emma laughed as she thought about Emma Kathryn and her boyfriend. She was such a sweet girl, and her boyfriend, Jordan, was just as sweet as he could be. Emma considered Emma Kathryn and Jordan to be the young, unmarried, version of Joan and Ward Clever...wholesome.

"Don't worry, Emma Kathryn," Mr. Rhodes said with a grin, "we'll make sure we clean out the barn one night during the week. We wouldn't want to mess up your date night."

Emma Claire laughed along with Mrs. Rhodes and the Rhodes' children. A basketball hoop she thought...she could really use the practice. She hated being bad at things, and she knew she was the worst player on both the JV and Varsity team. She had never been good at anything as a kid, and for once, she would like to try not to be the worst or the last at something. Her coach, Mr. Richardson, had told her she was good, and with a little practice, she could be one of the better players on the team. It was something to shoot for anyway, Emma thought with determination.

It was decided that the next night, after dinner, the girls would meet in the barn and help clear a practice space while Mr. Rhodes put up a net. Emma wondered where and how he was going to achieve such a feat. What, she wondered, was he going to attach the metal frame of the hoop to?

10

"Emma! Catch!" Mr. Richardson shouted from across the gym.

Dropping the book she'd been holding to the polished gym floor, Emma caught the basketball, dribbled to the hoop, and did a neat layup, to the applause of Mr. Richardson and Jacob. Grinning, she sprinted to the ball, hustled to the free throw line, and easily swished it, holding the flip of her wrist for a moment. The hours of practice in the barn at the Rhodes' house was paying off and Emma knew it as she smiled with pride, and walked over to hand off the ball to her coach, who also happened to be her P.E. teacher.

"You *got* it!" Mr. Richardson said, pleased with her progress, not just on the basketball court, but also by the way she laughed easily these days—the pensive, distrusting Emma, now just a memory.

"Well golly," Jacob said in the goofy, high-pitched voice he used—when he wanted to make people laugh. "You'll be takin' my spot on the boy's team before too long!"

Emma laughed, knowing that was what the school clown—her friend—was trying to do, make her laugh. "Yeah," she said with a grin, "I'll be taking your spot as center on the boy's team. Somehow," she said raising an eyebrow, "I just don't think I'm a threat to you. Or, hey...I know," she said with feigned seriousness, "we can swap. You can take my spot on the girl's team—wear one of the cute girly uniforms—and I'll play center for you, and wear one of the boy's uniforms!"

"Hey…I have an even better idea," Mr. Richardson laughed. "Jacob you can take Emma's spot on the pom-pom squad! You have pretty legs. You could pull your hair into those pigtail things. We'd have to order an outfit for you…one of those sassy little skirts."

Jacob flung his head back and howled in laughter as Mr. Richardson slapped his knee and wiped a tear from his eye. Emma placed her hand on her hip and leaned over, laughing at the vision of Jacob wearing one of the pom-pom outfits she and her teammates wore, his hairy knees poking out from beneath the short purple skirt.

Emma swiped at her eye, and still laughing said, "I have to get to art class. Mr. Richardson," she called over her shoulder as she ran to grab the book she had abandoned off the gym floor, "see if you can get his skirt ordered!" She heard the older man and teen laugh as she ran away, still grinning when she walked into the art room, the last class of the day.

As part of the curriculum, Emma had been keeping an art journal of random sketches, her favorite being scenery—tree lined waterways—and any type of animal. Most recently, she had been experimenting with oil colors, liking the texture and look of deep, rich colors applied on her sketchpad. In the evening, after dishes were washed, and homework complete, if she didn't have a book to read, she worked on her art, sometimes getting lost in a piece for over an hour. Her weekends were spent in a similar manner, seated on the floor of her bedroom, sketching something.

Leaning her chin on the palm of her hand, Emma half listened to Ms. Blake, her art teacher. She was ready for the day to be over, planning to get a little basketball practice in before dinner, in the barn. It felt good not to suck at everything and now she wanted to be really good. She was willing to work hard to be as good as her teammates, and secretly wanted to be one of the better players on the team, and there were some good players.

Two hours later, with one of Mrs. Rhodes delicious homemade cookies shoved in her mouth, Emma hurried to her bedroom to drop her books on the floor, then she planned to head to the barn for a little B-ball practice. Still chewing the chocolaty treat, Emma stopped short when she saw a white envelope on her bed. She placed the stack of books on her bed, then sat on the edge and picked up the envelope. *Cheryl.* After receiving the last letter, Emma had asked Mrs. Rhodes how she thought Cheryl had found her. Through her caseworker, she had responded. Cheryl had found a way to contact Emma's caseworker, and since they had lived together twice, her caseworker had supplied her new address to her.

Emma ripped the envelope open, tugged the single sheet of lined paper out of its enclosure, unfolded the paper, and quickly skimmed the contents. Then she flipped over the letter and read it again, slowly this time. It was similar to the last letter Cheryl had sent…she was living on her own in a semi-independent situation. It was great, the letter read. A couple was letting her stay in their attic along with another teenage girl. Cheryl had a job and was going to school someplace, someplace that didn't sound like a real school to Emma, but a place she could still get her diploma. She could come and go as she pleased…blah, blah, blah, Emma thought. It was exactly the plan Cheryl had shared with Emma the year before when they had lived at Audrey's foster home together. She wanted to be on her own so she could do what she wanted, with no one to boss her around. It sounded crappy to Emma. She wasn't ready to be a grown up, doing…who knew what. Emma wanted the chance to be a kid…to go to a real high school, be in clubs with other kids, and now she was on a basketball team, on a pom-pom squad, living in a house on a hill in the middle of the country with a family that was good to her. She was…*safe.* Emma was sure her new life was better than the pretend grown up life Cheryl was living.

Emma let her hand, still holding the letter, fall to her lap. Slumping her shoulders, she looked up at the ceiling as she rolled her eyes. Cheryl's life was crap, Emma thought, worrying about her ex-cottage mate. What

16-year-old kid wanted to live on their own…trying to hold a job down—for that matter, find a job? Just what kind of job, Emma wondered, could Cheryl possibly find that would pay her bills, and why should any kid have to live the life of an adult, so soon. Who would be there for her, who *was* there for her, Emma stewed.

She fiddled with the small earring in her ear as she considered what Cheryl had suggested, that she should come stay with her. All was not that great in Cheryl's life, Emma realized with a sigh. Cheryl was reaching out; she needed her, Emma thought. Emma looked around the room she shared with Emma Kathryn. Not long ago they had swapped rooms with Caitlyn. Emma sat on the bed that Mr. Rhodes had built, with drawers that pulled out beneath the wooden flat that held the mattress she now sat on. Her bed was nestled into a corner of the room with a view out of the small window overlooking the road that passed by the house and of the field on the other side of the road. The field was empty now, but in the summer, it would be filled with a rich green color of either beans or corn that would blow soothingly in the wind…one of Emma's favorite sounds.

Just like the last letter Emma had received from Cheryl, Cheryl had written again that she wanted Emma to come visit her, to stay with her. The words Emma read were happy words, *You should come visit me. We will have a great time. You could stay if you want.* The words were happy, but Emma felt sadness, fear, and loss from the paper. *She was sure her caseworker could work it out,* the letter read. *No thank you,* Emma thought, but her heart was heavy as she shoved the letter back into the envelope and then under her mattress with the other letter she had received from Cheryl.

Thoughts of the children's home and her two older sisters crashed through her mind as Emma pulled on her tennis shoes. She pulled open one of the built in drawers, the first to the right, chose a purple t-shirt, and then closed the drawer. After carefully folding the red fuzzy sweater she had worn to school that day, she pulled open the second drawer to the right and placed it on the stack of sweaters, then closed the drawer.

She pulled the purple t-shirt over her head and then walked out of the bedroom, grabbing a jacket hanging on the round metal clothes rack in the large room that connected the three upstairs bedrooms.

Emma spent an hour in the barn shooting baskets, trying to work the memories and worry for those she had left behind out of her mind. Sweat trickling down the middle of her back, Emma stood still with the ball in her sore, burning hands and stared up at the hoop her foster father had hung for her and Emma Katherine. No matter how many times she threw the ball and ran after it, how tired she got, or out of breath, she couldn't forget.

When Emma stepped into the kitchen, she was met by the delicious smell of fried chicken, and the voices of her foster family. The table was already set for dinner. She was going to have to hurry and change out of her sweaty t-shirt, into a sweatshirt before dinner, she thought as she walked quickly through the room toward the stairs leading to the second floor.

"Emma Claire!" Mrs. Rhodes yelled after her. "We're eating in five minutes!"

"Okay," Emma called back, still in a funk as she continued up the red, carpeted steps to her bedroom.

Homework done, Emma passed the rest of the evening trying to lose herself in one of her mystery novels…a trick from childhood. In the worst of times, when she couldn't escape life's worst moments, she would pick up a book and let it take her away from reality, as she was doing now. A half an hour later, Emma walked into the kitchen for a snack and found Mrs. Rhodes sitting at the kitchen table.

"Emma Claire," Mrs. Rhodes said, "what's going on with you? You barely said two words at dinner, and since then you've been hiding away in your bedroom. Is something wrong?"

Stopping to stand beside the table, Emma looked at Mrs. Rhodes sitting at the white table. Mrs. Rhodes was one of the sweetest, most gentle women Emma had ever met. Her foster mother's soft, gentle, tender heart reminded her of her own, and had her considering that it was possible for those with gentle hearts to survive in the cold, cruel world. Mrs. Rhodes was a great deal older than Emma was, and it seemed that life had not hardened her tender heart. Emma found the most intriguing part of Mrs. Rhodes was how she interacted with her children, her husband, the kids at school, and even the teachers. Even if she raised her voice, it was never in anger; it was more to be heard over the exuberant voices of her children, and even the kids at school.

Mrs. Rhodes was one of the bus drivers for the high school, Emma's bus driver, and at times, as kids could be, kids on the bus would say cruel things to and about Mrs. Rhodes. Emma knew her foster mother heard the cruel things said, and knew it hurt her, but Mrs. Rhodes never said anything, her smile was just a little smaller. But Emma couldn't listen, every day, to the cruel taunts, and she *did* say something. She told the kids Mrs. Rhodes had never done anything to them, that it was a shitty person that would say mean things to such a nice person. The kids weren't mean to her after that, instead they smiled and said nice things to her when they got on and off the bus.

Emma pulled out a chair and flopped down on its cushioned surface. "Everything's fine," she lied.

"You don't look so fine," Mrs. Rhodes commented. "Did something happen at school today?" she asked.

Avoiding Mrs. Rhodes' eyes, Emma tapped the tips of her fingers on the table and said, "No."

"Well, what is it then? Your face looks as sour as sour grapes," Mrs. Rhodes noticed.

A ghost of a smile played on Emma's lips as she thought, her foster mother had the funniest way of saying things, and not just that, she noticed when something wasn't right with her. She cared *enough* to notice.

"Was it the letter you got in the mail today?" Mrs. Rhodes asked, suspecting when she placed the letter on Emma's bed earlier in the day that it would upset her.

Sighing, Emma answered, "Yeah. It was from Cheryl." Resting her chin on the palm of her hand, she said unhappily, "She wrote about how happy she is, but how can she be happy living on her own?" Looking up at Mrs. Rhodes, Emma shared, "She's living on her own, well basically anyway. She's living in some kind of semi-independent living thing…renting part of an attic from some people." Wrinkling her forehead, Emma asked, "Does that sound good to you…a kid living on their own…at my age?"

"Well," Mrs. Rhodes laughed uncomfortably. "It sure isn't how I'd like to live as a kid."

"Why would the state allow kids to live on their own, or even like Cheryl is living…in an attic of some people's house?" Even as Emma asked the question, she knew the answer. There just were not enough homes for all the kids that had nowhere to go.

"Is that the only thing bothering you, or should I say the only person?" Mrs. Rhodes knew Emma thought about her sisters quite a bit, worried about if they were okay, and she could understand the guilt she felt because of her new life. She knew Emma felt guilty, and as a result often had a difficult time just relaxing, and just being a kid herself—feeling responsible for her brothers and sisters, even though it wasn't her place to worry about them. She was just a kid and her job was to be just that…a kid.

Slouching on her chair, Emma said in a worried voice, "The letter made me think about Amy and Katie and my other sister and brothers. I mean, I think about them a lot, but Cheryl's letter got me worrying about them. What if they aren't okay? What if…"

"Emma Claire, look at me," Mrs. Rhodes said in as stern a voice as she could.

Emma looked up and looked across the table into the kind eyes of Mrs. Rhodes.

"Don't you feel *guilty* about being happy and safe. You deserve to be a kid. They'll all be okay, 'cause God's lookin' out for them." Mrs.

Rhodes looked across the table at Emma and noticed she didn't seem convinced and asked, "You believe in God don't you?"

Smiling, Emma nodded her head, and said, "Of course, I do." What a sweet, sweet woman, Emma thought, but she was *still* worried and she *did* feel guilty because she had so much and she was pretty sure her sisters and many of the kids from the children's home had very little.

"Pray for them," Mrs. Rhodes insisted. "God will hear your prayer. Do you ever pray...?"

Nodding her head, Emma assured her, "Yeah, every day. When I'm afraid or when I worry about my sisters."

"Well, you just keep praying for them, and I'll pray too," Mrs. Rhodes said.

Emma smiled at Mrs. Rhodes and said, "Thanks."

"I'm going to get ready for bed," Emma said with a yawn. It had been a long day and she was exhausted.

"Alright," Mrs. Rhodes said.

"Hey, why don't you see if you can spend the night Friday?" Janice asked Emma.

Janice was one of Emma's classmates from Nutrition class, and while cooking pancakes for the school's breakfast the next morning, they were planning their weekends. Emma felt comfortable with Janice; she was the only different kid, like her, in the entire high school. A tiny thing with short blonde hair from Chicago, Janice was now living with her grandmother in a small two story, two-bedroom house in the town of New Point.

"I'll check with my foster mom. I'm sure it'll be fine," Emma said.

"We can just hang out, watch a movie or something. My grandma and my uncle will be there, but they won't bother us," Janice said.

Flipping a pancake, Emma asked, "What was it like living in Chicago?"

"Cool," Janice said with a smile. "A lot better than this hick town. There was always something to do. I'd hang with my friends and boy-friend most weekends. This place," Janice said, waving a spatula in the air, "is driving me nuts! Just a bunch of farms with chickens and farm boys around here."

Emma grinned. She had never lived in a big city like Chicago and had no desire to…too many people. New Point was growing on her…the people, and she loved all the school activities. She had never lived with a family that was so involved in the local high school, attending all the basketball games, the boys, and girls. As the pom-pom girl's coach, Mrs. Rhodes had to attend all the games...not only that, she was the bus driver for the away games.

A few days later, lying on Janice's double bed, Emma held a picture of Janice and her friends from Chicago between her fingers. She listened as her friend explained the virtues of big city life. As she listened, Emma tried to picture in her mind the giant amusement park Janice told her about, the museums, and restaurants...the many places to go. But most of all, Janice shared that she missed hanging out with her boyfriend and friends.

Janice had gotten into a bit of trouble back in the city; that's why she had been forced to move in with her grandma...to get her away from the bad crowd. Since she had lost fifty pounds, trouble just seemed to find the sixteen-year-old girl, Janice explained with a grin. Emma, comfortable with Janice and the fact that she seemed to have a past, unlike the other kids at school, shared a few stories about her life in a children's home and as a foster kid. Janice was impressed by what seemed to be an edgy story...mysterious...different. The two misfits of the town of New Point had found one another, finding a place to fit, to be themselves... their past not a factor.

One afternoon, Janice didn't show up for Nutrition class. When Emma asked the teacher where she was, she was shocked to hear that Janice would no longer be in class—she wasn't coming back to school. Her teacher knew the circumstances of both girls and knew why Janice would no longer be attending New Point High and shared the details with Emma. Janice had run away, run back to Chicago to be with her friends. Another person she had grown close to...gone, Emma thought with a heavy heart. So often life changed without a moment's notice... and not for the better, Emma thought bitterly.

When she didn't see anyone headed toward the telephone, Emma scrambled off the couch and ran to grab it on the fourth ring. "Hello?" Emma said into the phone, surprised when she heard Cheryl's voice. Emma had responded to each of the letters she had received from Cheryl, and had provided the Rhodes' telephone number when requested in the last letter.

"I'm doing okay," Emma commented. She never gave specifics about her new life, just that she was living with a nice family and was attending a good high school. Cheryl's life seemed so awful to Emma that she didn't have the heart to share just how good she had it. The loss of her family was still a constant dull pain in Emma's heart, but she had finally accepted that life would never be as she had expected and dreamed. She and her sisters would never live together, and as far as her little sister and brothers, she would never see them…never really know them. It was a piece of her gone…like a puzzle that would always have several pieces missing…never whole.

"On the weekend?" Emma repeated. "Not much. I just hang out and do homework, read or watch TV. Nothing special."

"Oh man," Emma heard Cheryl, say, "if you lived with me, we could do whatever we wanted. I don't have anyone to tell me what to do. You should really leave, Emma. Me and my old man can pick you up some night. Just tell me how to get to you." Emma knew the old man Cheryl was referring to was her new boyfriend, not her dad. It was what Cheryl had always called her boyfriends…*old man.*

Inwardly, Emma groaned. How could she tell Cheryl that she didn't want to run away when she so obviously needed her? She pulled out a chair and sat down pressing her forehead into the palm of her hand. *What to say…?*

"I don't know, Cheryl. I have a lot going on right now," Emma said uncomfortably.

"Awe, come on. You would love it here. We would have so much fun. What do you have going on…*school?* You can go to school here. *I'm* going to school," Cheryl coaxed.

"Yeah, I have a lot of stuff going on at school. If I moved, I just don't think I could make all this work up. Moving to a different school...the graduation requirements might be different. I really want to graduate on time with my class. And I don't want to disappoint Mrs. Rhodes. She has really gone out of her way for me..." Emma's voice trailed away, hoping Cheryl would stop trying to convince her to run away.

"You are such a worrier. Of course, you will graduate on time if you move here. Stop worrying. You just need to have a little fun...live your own life," Cheryl insisted.

Emma didn't know what to say to convince Cheryl she didn't want to runaway, at least not without hurting her ex-cottage mate, and making her feel as if she were rubbing it in her face that she had a good home. She must be miserable, Emma considered, otherwise why was she trying so hard to get her to run. What could she do to help her, she fretted. Cheryl didn't want to live in a foster home, didn't want to live life like a kid should, so what could she say to help her?

Closing her eyes, Emma thought quickly, and said, "Cheryl, I just can't go right now. Maybe later...I just have too much going on. Have you talked to Audrey lately?" She hoped Cheryl would talk to Audrey, and that she could help her.

"Yeah, I talk to her sometimes. It's too bad she's not still a foster parent. I wouldn't mind living with her...but she's not." Switching topics back to running away, Cheryl said in an excited voice, "Emma, I'll have my old man drive me to your town, in a few days—just tell me how to get to your house."

Sighing, Emma said, "I'm in the country. You'd never find me."

"Can you get to town—meet me in town some night? Maybe you can catch a ride or spend the night in town somewhere. Just tell them you'll be sleeping over with a friend and then we'll come get you," Cheryl insisted.

"I can't. There *is* nowhere to spend the night. It's not like that here. They don't let their kids spend the night with people during the week," Emma said, thankful for the strict rules.

"You're kidding! That's nuts! You need to get out of there. Then… where are you? We'll just come to the house. What's it look like, the house? We can drive by—you'll know it's us—and you can walk to the road and meet us. We'll just park on the side of the road and watch for you," Cheryl insisted, as if the plan was all settled.

"Cheryl," Emma insisted, "you will never find me. The house is in the middle of nowhere!"

"What color is the house?" Cheryl demanded.

Giving in, Emma said, "Green."

"We'll find you," Cheryl assured her, determined to find her.

"Cheryl, I have to go. One of my foster sisters is bugging me to use the phone," Emma lied.

"Okay," Cheryl, said. "Don't worry. We'll find you. We'll be in town Thursday night. What time does everyone go to bed?" she asked.

Standing near the cradle of the telephone hanging on the wall, Emma wanted to hang up on her but didn't. What time did they go to bed, she thought…well, she was in bed by nine thirty, but knew everyone else in the house was up much later. "Ten thirty," she said.

"Then we'll be there at eleven. Just be outside," Cheryl insisted. "We'll find you."

"I have to go, Cheryl," Emma said, nervous about where the conversation had gone and that Cheryl was not taking no for an answer.

"I'll see you soon!" Cheryl shouted.

Emma hung up the phone and stared at the receiver. Eleven, she thought. She was never up at eleven on a school night! She didn't want to be up at that time of the night and didn't want to stand outside in the cold. No, what she wanted was to be snuggled in her safe, warm, bed! I'm not meeting her…anywhere, Emma thought, anger growing inside her that Cheryl wouldn't listen to her. Cheryl's life might suck, and she was sorry about that, but it wasn't fair to draw her into it too! Thursday night…two days away, she thought, as she walked back to the deserted family room.

The next two days passed too quickly, with Emma wondering if Cheryl would really show. *Nah,* she assured herself as she climbed onto the bus on Thursday afternoon. *It was nuts!* The girl lived two hours away. Why would she drive all that way to come get her? It made no sense, except she must be really miserable. But then what…what did Cheryl think she was going to do if she really ran away with her—get a job…go to school? How would she get to wherever she needed go? How would she eat? Flopping down onto the last seat at the very back of the school bus, Emma huffed, scrunched down, and rested her knees on the seat in front of her. She was tired.

Emma stewed all evening about Cheryl, wondering if she would be able to find the house, and if she did, what would she do if she didn't show up outside. Would Cheryl knock on the door, honk the horn maybe, or yell Emma's name, she worried? *What would her foster parents say if some strange girl and man sat on the side of the road at eleven O'clock at night and blared their horn, shouting, Emma!?*

It was getting late, and Emma was already in her PJ's, warm and cozy in her country home. She had no desire to go outside. It was cold enough outside to see her breath for heaven's sake! Maybe she would just fall asleep like when she was a little girl, when her sisters had wanted her to keep watch for an hour. She remembered all those years ago, in fifth grade, when she and her sisters had planned to run away from their dad and stepmom's house. Where they were going to go, had been Emma's concern. As little girls, they had no plan…just purses stuffed with clothes and nowhere to go. And *this* was just as bad a plan, she thought irritably, but she was worried about Cheryl. What was wrong with the stupid state, she scowled at the TV? Why hadn't they placed her in a good foster home…somewhere like the Rhodes' home?! At 9:30, Emma crawled into bed, still not sure what she would do when 11:00 O'clock arrived, not sure at all.

At 10:45, it was quiet in the house. The only sound was the breathing of Emma's foster sister, Emma Katherine, across the room. *Damn! Fine!* Emma thought angrily. She'd go outside for *just* five minutes, but if Cheryl didn't show up, she was going back to bed, she decided. She pulled on a pair of jeans, and then grabbed a sweatshirt, pulling it over her brilliant blue jersey, thigh length nightgown. Carefully, she pulled a jacket off a hanger in the middle of the common room and wadded it under her arm. Five minutes, she thought in annoyance, hoping Cheryl wouldn't show, and then she'd just hop back in bed. But, just in case she was found out by one of the members of her foster family, she'd say she hadn't been able to sleep and had decided to shoot a few hoops. Sounded like a reasonably believable lie, she considered.

Tiptoeing, Emma snuck passed Cassy's bedroom, down the carpeted steps and around the corner toward the kitchen—watching to see if Mr. or Mrs. Rhodes came out of their bedroom. Almost to the kitchen, she froze like a mannequin. *No sound in the house.* No parents coming out of their bedroom...Emma continued on to the kitchen, and then carefully opened the door and stepped into the enclosed area where greenware was lined up, like soldiers on shelves. She paused again, listening to the house. Hearing nothing, cautiously Emma opened the door, stepped outside, and pulled the door shut behind her.

Pulling the jacket tight around her, she zipped it to her chin, and then walked down the gravel drive, looking one way down the road then the other. No lights and no cars in sight. Sighing in relief, she walked quickly back toward the house, thankful for the warm bed that awaited her. Turning at the bend in the drive, she looked down the long drive to the road as a car sped by. Shoving her hands into the pockets of her jacket, she kept walking toward the house. Just five minutes she had decided, and five minutes were up.

Now, to get back to her bedroom before she was found out. She was hoping she wouldn't have to actually say her stupid lie out loud. Grabbing the doorknob in her right hand, as quiet as possible, Emma twisted the knob. It wasn't turning easily in her hand. It seemed to be stuck. She tried to twist it again, but...nothing. It wouldn't budge! Her heart caught in her throat as she realized the door had locked when she closed it behind her! Shit! Still staring down at the doorknob, her hand resting on its cold surface, Emma couldn't believe her stupidity. The door opened easily from the inside…but was locked on the outside. Those inside could get out, but those outside could not get in. *She couldn't get back in!*

Stepping away from the door—chilled—Emma crossed her arms over her chest and glared at the door, trying to think of a way into the house. The front door was always closed, so no entry there. Windows… no. Turning slowly, Emma scanned the yard, taking in the barn. Too cold to sleep in there, she thought as she shivered. *Shit! She was going to have to knock on the door, and wake someone up to let her in.* So, she was going to have to actually say her stupid lie aloud after all, she thought sarcastically…but would anyone buy it, she wondered. Well, it was a good thing she had her PJ's on under her sweatshirt, she thought. That would add a little credibility to her lie…she hoped, as she tugged at the blue fabric so whoever answered the door could see it.

Taking a deep breath, Emma stepped closer to the door, and balling her hand into a fist, raised it toward the window inset into the door. She paused for a minute, then throwing her shoulders back, took a deep breath, preparing herself for what was to come…lots of yelling she was sure. She knocked. Several minutes passed before Emma knocked again. As she was preparing to knock one more time, the door opened. Mr. Rhodes glanced at her and said softly with a small smile, "What are you doing out there in the cold?" as he opened the door wider to let her in.

"I couldn't sleep. I went to shoot baskets for awhile," she said. Well, part of what she had said was true, she thought, wondering why he wasn't yelling at her.

"Well, get on to bed. It'll be time to get up for school soon," he said.

Crawling under her blankets she considered, maybe tomorrow they would tear into her. She snuggled the blankets around her shoulder, warm and safe, as she fell into a deep sleep.

12

"Emma," Mrs. Rhodes called from the telephone hung on the kitchen wall.

"Yeah?" Emma said from the recliner in the family room.

"Audrey's on the phone for you," Mrs. Rhodes said.

Emma hadn't talked to Audrey in awhile, and smiling, she walked toward the hand piece lying on the table where Mrs. Rhodes had left it.

Picking up the phone, Emma said, "Hello."

"Hi, Emma," Audrey said. "How's everything going?"

"It's going okay," Emma responded. Emma loved talking to Audrey, had since her time in her foster home over a year ago. She was one of her favorite foster mothers and if she'd had a choice, she never would have left her home. "I'm real busy with school. It kind of sucks—not school—I mean all the work. I still feel like I'm behind, and there are days it seems as if I will never get it…never catch up."

"Well, you keep trying and you'll be just fine. You're a real smart girl," Audrey said.

Emma rolled her eyes, not quite agreeing with her, but appreciating the vote of confidence. "How are you doing?" she asked. "Are you still working out?"

"Oh, I'm trying," Audrey, said. She had shared with Emma while she was living at the children's home, that she had started a workout routine, but that wasn't what Audrey wanted to discuss right now. Audrey had heard that Emma's best friend, Janice, had run away and feared it might be weighing on her. Emma had more than her share of people leaving her. Actually, Audrey considered, she had the share of multiple adults when it came to abandonment and loss.

"Hey, Em," Audrey said, "I heard about your friend Janice running away. I'm so sorry. But don't you worry, you'll make other friends, you'll see," she encouraged.

Sighing, Emma said, "Yeah. I can't believe she just left like that. I didn't know she was thinking about running away. She never said *anything* to me. Seems as if everyone always goes away. Maybe it's more that she had someplace to go. It bugs me sometimes, Audrey. Don't get me wrong, I like the Rhodes I really do...but I still don't feel like I really belong anywhere. I feel so different from everyone. At least with Janice, I felt we were kind of the same."

Audrey understood what Emma was saying and how she felt, as much as she could anyway. She'd had enough foster kids over the years to understand the heavy weight of being abandoned by abusive parents and sometimes by parents that loved them but just couldn't take care of them. It was heart breaking to watch kids try to heal and find something in themselves that they thought someone would love, not realizing that there was nothing wrong with them. It was a sad, crazy world for foster kids, Audrey thought.

Hoping her next words would cheer Emma up, Audrey dug in and said, "Well, I have some exciting news for you!"

Emma's thoughts swirled as she wondered excitedly what could be up. "What is it?!" she asked excitedly. She immediately thought about Amy and Katie. She hadn't seen or heard from them in awhile. Maybe that was the surprise, she considered.

"Some of the kids that lived at the children's home want to pull together a reunion!" Audrey announced, thankful to have good news to share. She was certain Emma would want to attend. "They are going to meet at the home, this Saturday."

It felt as if her heart stopped as Emma leaned against the kitchen wall, the hand piece of the telephone pressed against her ear. "Who... who's going to be there?" Emma asked.

"Well, Cheryl is the one that coordinated the whole thing, so she will be there, and there is another girl that was in your cottage, Beth. A few other girls might be there too, and maybe a couple of cottage moms," Audrey said.

Emma shook her head, and thought...a reunion. Was it really just a reunion, she wondered.

"If you want to go, I'll drive you up for the afternoon," Audrey promised.

"Oh...I don't know," Emma stammered. "I have stuff going on. I'm not sure I'll be able to go," she said thoughtfully.

"Are you worried Denise won't let you go?" Audrey asked.

Denise was Mrs. Rhodes' name, but Emma heard her referred to at school so much as Mrs. Rhodes that she naturally thought of her that way. "Well, I'm not sure," Emma said. "We might have something going on."

"I'm sure you want to go, and she'll understand. I'll talk to her for you if you want," Audrey offered.

Emma knew there would be no way to get out of going—she didn't want to tell anyone what was bothering her. She missed her cottage parents and many of the kids at the home, but, as much as she liked Cheryl, she hadn't been one of the girls she hung out with. Nice girl but she wasn't her best friend, but Beth *had* been one of her best friends. Surely it would be okay, she assured herself. No way would Cheryl ask her to leave with her Saturday. Not with cottage moms and Audrey there. What could be the harm, she considered? And besides, she really did want to see how Beth was doing.

"No, I'll ask her if it's okay if I go," Emma decided.

"Okay. If it's okay, then I can be at your house at eleven O'clock. That'll give us plenty of time to get there," Audrey said. "We're going to meet everyone in front of the Rec Hall at the children's home."

"Okay," Emma said distractedly.

"Okay, Em, I'll call you tomorrow night to check in with you," Audrey said.

"Okay," Emma responded. "I'll check with her and talk to you tomorrow night."

"Talk to you then," Audrey said.

"Bye," Emma answered. In two days, Emma considered, she would be walking on the soil of the children's home.

Curled onto her chair in Art class the next afternoon, Emma thought about the conversation she'd had with Mrs. Rhodes the night before. Unfortunately, she didn't have one single problem with her going with Audrey to the children's home on Saturday...not one problem. Resting her chin on her fist, Emma doodled a picture of a green eyeball with a black center, and then flipping her pencil around, she erased a tiny spot to indicate a light reflection.

"Hey, Emma," George, a senior in her art class said. "Some girl was asking about you earlier this week. Did she ever find you?"

"Huh?" she asked, wondering what girl at school was talking about her. George, like most of the kids at New Point High was a real nice kid. He kind of looked like a clean cut hippy, she considered as she looked at his dark blonde hair that almost touched his shoulders. But he didn't act as she thought hippies acted. He was respectful to the teachers, and really, besides his hair, she thought, he looked real clean cut, with a big smile for everyone. Nice, she thought, he was just as nice as everyone else was. New Point was a strange school she thought. It was not like any school she had ever attended. She wondered if the teachers and students knew they were living in some alternative, nice universe...definitely not the real world.

"Some girl," George repeated. "It was real late one night. I was still at work in town at the grain elevator when some girl and guy drove up. They said they'd been looking for you. I told them where you lived. Did they find you?" he asked.

"No..." she said thoughtfully. It had to have been Cheryl, she realized.

"She said she was your sister," George commented.

"Huh," Emma mused, knowing it wasn't either of her sisters, surprised that Cheryl would pretend to be one of them. "No one came out to the house. Well," she said with a small, distracted smile, "I wonder who it was."

"Does your sister have kind of short, light colored hair?" George asked.

"No. It couldn't have been her. She has long hair," Emma shared.

"Well," George said with a casual smile, "I'll let you know if I see that girl again."

"Thanks," Emma said uneasily.

Saturday morning, Emma lay in bed longer than usual. It amazed Emma that during the school week, Emma Katherine slept in as long as possible, and almost every day Emma wondered if she would make it on time—but she always managed to catch the bus. Then the weekends would roll in and it was a different story. No matter how hard Emma tried, Emma Katherine was always out of bed first, starting her day long before Emma had even cracked her eyes open. This morning was no different from any other Saturday morning, Emma realized as she looked over at her foster sister's empty bed. Emma sighed and pulled her pillow over her head wishing she could get out of the reunion at the children's home. Ugh! She missed lots of people from the home, but...something didn't feel right, and she had enough not feeling right moments to know that it typically meant bad was coming. She just never knew what form the bad would come in.

"Hey, Emma," Emma Katherine called from the room off the kitchen.

Emma looked toward the voice of her foster sister, finding her amongst mounds of laundry. Laundry day was Saturday and Emma was thankful it was Emma Katherine's job and not hers.

"Yeah?" Emma responded.

"If you have any laundry, make sure you bring it down before you leave," Emma Katherine said in a sing-song voice.

Perhaps she should stick around and help Emma Katherine out, Emma mused. Rolling her eyes, she opened the refrigerator door, and cinching the belt to her red robe tighter, looked for the milk. With a huff, she banged the plastic jug on the table, twisted off the plastic cap, and trickled a little milk on her oatmeal, deep in thought about the rest of her day.

"Do you have any laundry?" Emma Katherine asked from the door of the laundry room.

"Huh? Oh, yeah. I'll bring it down in a minute," Emma said absently. She'd bring it down before hopping into the tub, which, as she looked up at the clock on the wall, meant she needed to be getting a move on or she'd still have wet hair when Audrey showed up.

Laundry, such an ordinary, normal thing to do, Emma considered as she watched Emma Katherine sort the family's dirty clothes, when a few minutes later, she deposited her folded dirty laundry on the floor of the laundry room. Emma paused, watched her foster sister, and wondered what it was like to be her, what it had been like to grow up with her family. She had seen photographs of the Rhodes family, some random, some taken during various holidays, and some formal. Emma Katherine owned two beautiful horses that she housed in the barn, just a walk across the yard from the house, one with a shiny brown coat and the other an appaloosa, white with reddish colored patches. Pictures of her showing her horses and medals were evidence of the love and hard work she put into the beautiful, but intimidating animals. It was like a fairy tale, like something out of a book, Emma reflected as she walked toward the bathroom to prepare for the rest of her day, the reunion at the home.

In spite of the butterflies in her stomach, when Emma saw Audrey's car pull up the gravel drive, she was happy to see her. Audrey would always have a very special part of her heart. If Emma had her way, she'd never have left the comfort of Audrey's home, but it was not to be. Audrey's home was licensed as a temporary placement foster home, and besides that, she was no longer a foster parent. She still called Emma from time to time to check up on her, and she never minded the random phone calls from Emma. The older woman had always been so easy to talk to, Emma thought with a smile as she walked to the door to greet her.

"Are you ready?" Audrey asked in her deep husky voice. "It's a beautiful day, not at all like fall."

"Kinda feels like an Indian summer, doesn't it?" Mrs. Rhodes commented.

Emma folded her jacket over her arm as, patiently, she watched her ex-foster mother and present foster mother shoot the breeze. Denise was taller than Audrey by several inches. Audrey was wearing a pair of light blue colored slacks and a short-sleeved, small floral print, blouse, while Mrs. Rhodes was wearing her typical jeans and sweatshirt. Audrey was right; it was a beautiful day, with the weather projecting almost 70-degree temperatures. Emma had chosen to wear a pair of dark blue jeans, a soft, white, three-quarter length top with ties at the elbows and waist, with just the tiniest v-neck for accent, and a pair of tennis shoes. She was ready for a beautiful day—but she was bringing a jacket just in case it was breezy on campus at the home.

She'd had her contacts for several months now, completely broken in and was excited to show them off to cottage mates that attended the reunion. Her eyes were no longer green; instead, they were made a chocolate color by the lenses. She looked a little different from when she left the home—slimmed down a few pounds, and her hair was shorter. She felt different...older.

"How are you doing, Denise?" Audrey asked with a warm grin.

"I can't complain," Mrs. Rhodes said with a grin stretched across her face.

Emma watched the exchange between the two women, both wonderful women, so strong, loving, and encouraging. While Emma had known Audrey longer than she had known Mrs. Rhodes, she cared about her new foster mother too, almost as much as her old foster mother and it confused her, wondering if it was okay to care about them both. Somehow, it seemed as if she were a traitor if she cared about Mrs. Rhodes too…her new fill in mom.

"What time will you have Emma Claire home?" Mrs. Rhodes asked.

"We should be back by dinner time," Audrey assured her.

"Well, alright. You two have fun," Emma's foster mother said.

"Bye," Emma said with a smile, not wanting to go, but happy to be spending a little time with Audrey.

As they drove along the country road, Emma forgot all about Cheryl as Audrey asked her about school and boys.

"I don't know," Emma said. "I guess there are some cute boys at school, which is surprising considering how small the school is. There're are some real cute boys in my class, but none of them even know I'm alive, well, except for the fact that I'm the foster kid at school. I just don't fit in, Audrey. I'm not like the other kids," she insisted.

"Nonsense!" Audrey protested. "You're a pretty girl. They're noticing. You just have to give them a chance…join some clubs or something, that way you'll make some friends, and get to know *everyone*," she said with a knowing grin. "What about that boy you told me about when you were playing basketball?" Audrey asked.

Turning in her seat, Emma stared at Audrey, watched her take a drag off her cigarette with one hand while the other rested on the steering wheel. Audrey stared straight ahead. "Jacob?" Emma asked wrinkling her brow. "We're just friends. He's fun, and goofy and all, but it is definitely not like that."

"Does he have a girlfriend?" Audrey asked.

Emma thought for a moment… "You know, I don't think he does. That's strange, isn't it? Well," she reflected, "the school is awfully small; maybe he's gone through all the girls already!"

"Maybe he's sweet on you!" Audrey said playfully and more than a little serious.

Emma laughed heartily. "Audrey, you are too much! That boy is not interested in me, and besides, he is the class clown kind of boy. Do I look like the kind of girl that dates the class clown?" she asked grinning.

"Well, just who *are* you interested in?" Audrey asked, suspecting Emma did have her eyes on someone.

With a thoughtful smile, Emma confessed, "There are a couple really cute boys—one in my grade, he's a junior, and there's this senior."

"And…," Audrey coaxed with a smile. She knew it, Emma was interested in a boy, and that meant she was starting to settle into her new home and school.

Turning even more towards Audrey, Emma shared, her voice becoming softer as if someone other than Audrey might hear, "The junior is really cute. He's about six feet tall, I think, with almost blonde hair." A sigh escaped her as she continued, "But he wouldn't be interested in me. He's a really nice boy. And the senior is just a few inches taller than me, blonde hair and real cute, really good at sports, but he wouldn't be interested in me either." Discouraged Emma whined, "Audrey, no one from that school will ever go out with me, because I'm a foster kid! They're all going to think there's something wrong with me, that I'm trash!"

"Oh, that's silly, Emma! Has any one of those kids at school treated you badly?" Audrey asked.

"Well…no," Emma allowed. "But none of them have asked me out," she smiled.

Emma turned around in her seat and looked out the window as Audrey exited off the highway. In less than ten minutes they would be at the home, she worried, but she was excited as well, excited to see who from the home would show up. She hadn't realized how badly she had missed her old home, cottage mothers, cottage mates, and well, so many things.

Audrey slowed her car as she approached the Rec Hall, right in front of a small group of adults and teens.

"Beth showed up!" Emma said excitedly, "and I see Mrs. Michaels, one of my old cottage mothers!"

13

Audrey knew Emma needed to embrace her old life, the memories of a time and people that had cared about her, kept her safe, and healed her broken heart, so she left her at the children's home with a promise to return in three hours to take her back to the Rhodes' home. The unusually warm and sunny fall afternoon passed quickly, with a handful of former residents from the children's home sharing lunch, a walk around the grounds, laughs, hugs, and catching one another up on their new lives.

Emma found her worries about Cheryl unfounded. Cheryl mentioned briefly that she had driven to New Point one night and tried to find her, and had even stopped and asked a boy where she lived—the boy in Emma's art class, Emma suspected—but she and her boyfriend had driven home after driving around for an hour to find her. Emma just shrugged her shoulders pretending she knew nothing about Cheryl's encounter with her classmate. Cheryl didn't push the subject; instead, she moved on to talk to one of the cottage mothers.

Emma felt the gentle breeze and warm sun on her arms—her jacket tied around her waist—as she walked beside Beth, similarly dressed in jeans, tennis shoes, and a navy blue colored t-shirt with white lettered numbers on the front. It was a beautiful day, Emma reflected, as she felt the concrete sidewalk beneath her feet and listened to her friend Beth chatter away about her new life. For the first time in months, Emma felt absolutely comfortable, not pretending, or exerting energy to put on a fake happy face, constantly on edge to fit in. She didn't have to pretend with the girls from the children's home. They knew her and accepted her.

Beth was happy in her new life—her new school, and new friends. She said she was staying out of trouble, and was really enjoying her teachers. Emma noticed that she was absolutely glowing, but then, that was Beth, Emma realized with a smile.

Lunch had been simple but delicious: cheeseburgers, fries, with lots of laughing on the side, and cake for desert. The only drawback to the day was that it was ending. Emma glanced down at the thin-banded watch strapped to her wrist...in twenty minutes Audrey would arrive to take her home.

"Hey, Emma, wait up," Emma heard Cheryl's voice behind her. Stopping, she turned toward her, admiring her pretty, short-sleeved blouse gathered at the waist and light colored blue jeans. Cheryl rarely wore tennis shoes, and today was no different. She was hurrying towards them as fast as her dark brown, round toed high-heeled shoes would allow. Squeezing beside her on the sidewalk, in a hushed voice, Cheryl said, "You should go home with me."

Emma stared at her, not believing her ears. Go home with her, Emma thought. Wrinkling her brow, Emma said, "Cheryl, I don't think Mrs. Rhodes will let me spend the night with you. For one, I have no clothes with me, and two, it's too far away. She's not going to want to come pick me up tomorrow. Not only that, but you sleep in an attic. There wouldn't be room for me." What a dumb idea, Emma thought. She knew there was no way Mrs. Rhodes would agree to let her go to who knew where, and not only that, she didn't *want* to spend the night with Cheryl!

Beth looked down at the two girls, and deciding to extricate herself from what she suspected was going to end badly, walked towards a small group of girls.

Grinning, Cheryl said, "No, Emma. I'm not talking about spending the night. I want you to come live with me. Just tell Audrey you're not going back with her."

Staring at her with her mouth open, Emma processed what she had just heard, then asked, "Tell Audrey I'm not going back with her?"

"Yeah, just tell her you're going with *me*," Cheryl insisted as she pointed toward her chest.

Emma brushed a stray piece of hair off her face. Squinting in the late day sun, she sighed and said carefully, "Cheryl, I'm going back with Audrey. I'm not going to do that to her."

As Emma stared at Cheryl, she recalled just how different they really were, *very* different. Emma recalled that her first encounter with Cheryl had been at Audrey's house over a year ago. One afternoon, Emma had come home from school to find a stranger, Cheryl, in her bedroom. Before Cheryl had arrived, Emma had the bedroom to herself. It was during their chitchat that afternoon that Emma had discovered they had little in common, well, aside from the fact that they were both foster kids. They had very different types of friends, Emma hanging out with the nerdy kids and Cheryl with, well, no one in high school. She had been excited to share with Emma her love of truckers, Peterbuilts being her favorite. Cheryl was a free spirit.

Emma caught the tail end of what Cheryl was saying, "Come on Emma, go with me!"

Shaking her head at the sixteen-year-old standing beside her on the sidewalk—touching her arm now, "Emma said gently, "No Cheryl. I want to go back with Audrey."

"If you go with me, you can do what you want…no adults telling you what to do…" Cheryl said with a smile, prancing around as she tried to convince Emma to runaway.

Emma looked into the dark eyes of her ex-foster sister and ex-cottage mate, knowing she could not be happy with her life, and suspected she wasn't trying to help her, but in reality, it was Cheryl that needed Emma's help. She had to be miserable, Emma knew. There had to be something going on that she wasn't sharing...something was wrong. Was she afraid of something, someone, she wondered. *Did she need her help with something?* That had to be it, Emma thought, otherwise why else would she be pushing her so hard to get her to runaway.

She looked lost, Emma thought, and not for the first time as she considered how miserable Cheryl's life must be. Emma knew firsthand how badly it sucked not to be wanted. Hell, she herself had been abandoned by her own mother not once, but twice; her stepmom had left her; her dad hadn't cared about her—he'd abused her almost to death and sexually abused her—and foster homes, she had lost count of how many strangers had thrown her away. The pain had been almost unbearable. Each time she had been thrown away, the scab was ripped from her heart. She had only been with the Rhodes family for a few months, and knew any day now they might want to get rid of her too, so she knew how Cheryl must have been feeling—alone—scared—lost. Cheryl *needed* her. Knowing how much she was hurting, how could she abandon her too, Emma wondered with a heavy, resigned sigh.

"Come on..." Cheryl said, as she glanced back at the small group of what used to be cottage mothers and children's home residents. "You don't belong at that home, anymore than I belong in a foster home. Adults don't know any more than we do. We're both almost eighteen, so there's no reason not to be on our own, *now*. Who's to say they're not going to get rid of you anyway, just like all the other foster homes?" she persisted.

Sighing, Emma walked away from her ex-foster sister, her voice still ringing in her ears and walked toward the small group. She had already given Cheryl her answer. There was nothing left to say. Yes, her guts were in turmoil knowing Cheryl needed her but she didn't want to go with her. She smiled up at Beth as she walked beside her toward the Rec Hall.

"Everything okay?" Beth asked.

"Yeah," Emma said quietly.

"Are you going with Cheryl?" Beth asked concerned.

"No," Emma said shortly. "I'm going back home with Audrey."

"Just remember all the stuff you learned at the home," Beth said in a worried tone.

"I know…" Emma said softly.

The two girls walked side by side on the sidewalk in the brilliant fall sun with just a hint of a breeze. Walking passed the dining hall, Emma looked across the street towards the Rec Hall and saw Audrey's car parked in front by the curb. Smoke was wafting from the open driver's side window.

"Emma!" Cheryl shouted, as she caught up with her.

Emma knew Cheryl saw Audrey's car too, and worried that she was about to start in on her again…she was one of those relentless people. She never gave up.

"Emma, Beth, wait up!" Cheryl puffed.

Beth and Emma stopped and turned toward Cheryl, waiting for her to catch up.

"So are you going with me?" Cheryl asked expectantly.

Emma stared blankly at her.

"Come on, Emma!" Cheryl said excitedly. "You'll be able to do whatever you want. Hell, you could even see your sister—Amy—whenever you wanted."

Amy, Emma thought. She hadn't talked to her in awhile…wondered how she was.

"Yeah," Cheryl continued, "maybe Amy could come stay with us. We could all get an apartment together…"

Shaking herself internally, Emma thought, *no way*. She had no way of knowing for sure what Cheryl's life was really like, just that something didn't seem to be right, and that was enough to know that Amy wasn't going there.

"Cheryl…No!" Emma said in a loud voice. She could feel anger beginning to rise in her as Cheryl continued to ignore her response. "I'm not going with you." Looking towards Audrey's car, she said firmly, "Audrey's here and I'm going home with her. I'm not just," she said, as she flailed her arm in an arc in the air, "going to tell her I'm not going back with her." Confronting Cheryl she said, "Just tell me how you think that conversation might go!"

That Cheryl could so easily hurt people that had tried to help her really pissed her off. How the hell had she gotten that way, Emma wondered as she looked down at the girl, a little shorter than she was. She didn't know a lot about her, just that she had run with truckers before being placed at Audrey's foster home, had a baby, and had gotten into a little bit of trouble before being sent to the children's home—some horrible thing. Her choices in boys, well, men for *her,* because she preferred men, was awful! *Of all the kids Emma knew from the children's home, Cheryl needed parents, adults in her life to teach her some boundaries… how to be a kid because she was not ready to be a grown up!*

"Chill out, Emma! God, you are so uptight. Just tell her she isn't going to tell you what to do. Just—Just tell her you're going to spend the night. You don't have to tell her you're going to live with me. Just tell her you're going to spend the night…where's the harm in that? Two old friends hanging out. No biggy! I'm tellin' yuh! She's not going to care!" Cheryl insisted, her body twitching with excitement and determination.

The girls continued arguing as they walked toward the small group now standing in front of the Rec Hall. Emma looked toward the group, saw the cottage mothers hugging each other and the former residents of the home, heard the laughter, and saw Audrey climb out of her car, then close the door behind her.

Cheryl continued her barrage of, "Just tell her you're spending the night. They're just going to get rid of you anyway. Maybe we can go get Amy…and you're old enough to be on your own! We'll have so much fun together…it will be so cool!"

Emma tried to focus on saying goodbye to Mrs. Michaels and Beth, hugging them as she smiled. She had missed them both…missed her home, and now Cheryl was ruining the last few moments she had with them.

"Emma!" Cheryl said behind her.

"Are you ready?" Audrey asked.

Emma looked at Audrey, and said irritably, "Yeah."

"What?!" Emma asked whipping around towards Cheryl.

"Aren't you going to tell Audrey?" Cheryl demanded.

"What, Cheryl?! Tell her what?" Emma asked in annoyance.

Cheryl, was really getting under her skin, Emma stewed. *What was wrong with her? Why couldn't she get off her case!*

"What's going on, girls?" Audrey asked with concern in her voice.

"She's not going back with you," Cheryl insisted, adrenaline making her voice louder than it should have been, her cheeks flushed, and her body twitching as it did when she was excited, as she was now.

"What is she talking about?" Audrey asked Emma.

"Nothing," Emma said quietly.

"Go on!" Cheryl insisted. "Tell her!"

It felt very similar to some of her days in the children's home, Emma thought, but this time, there wasn't a group of eleven cottage mates and a cottage mother to sit down and talk it all out with Cheryl, giving her a Bring Up for her shitty behavior. "Shut up!" Emma yelled at Cheryl.

"Come on," Audrey said. "Let's get in the car."

"There's my old man!" Cheryl said with a grin, as she watched an old hunter green, compact car pull in front of Audrey's car. "Come on!"

"Come on, Emma," Audrey said, as she began walking toward the two cars.

Emma watched as Audrey walked toward her car, seeing Cheryl prancing next to her with an excited grin, chattering away about her old man and how they were going to have so much fun. She walked toward the two cars, Cheryl by her side, grabbing her arm when they got closer. Cheryl opened the back door of her boyfriend's car. Then still grinning, she pushed Emma toward the car, saying, "Get in the car, Emma!" as if they were about to embark on a grand adventure.

Feeling far away, Emma heard Audrey's voice say, "Emma—Emma. Are you coming with me or are you going with Cheryl?"

Emma leaned into Cheryl's boyfriend's car, and then scooted onto the seat. *She just needed everyone to stop talking, to stop yelling at her!*

"Emma!" Audrey shouted.

"I told you, she's going with me!" Cheryl said with a grin, and closed the back door and then opened the passenger front door and slid onto the seat. She closed the door behind her and leaned her arm out of the open window.

"Audrey...Audrey!" Emma shouted, attempting to be heard over their voices. "I'm going with her."

Tired, she leaned her arm out the window, and looked up at her ex-foster mother. It felt as if a sledgehammer was smashing into her heart when she saw the hurt expression on Audrey's face. She loved Audrey and didn't want to hurt her, but Cheryl would not let up. Something was not right...she needed her. She had to go, as much as she knew she was disappointing Audrey...proving to her how unworthy she was, and that maybe she wasn't worth loving after all.

Projecting defiance she wasn't feeling, Emma said, "I'm going with Cheryl."

Staring down at Emma, Audrey asked, "What do you want me to tell Mrs. Rhodes? Have you thought about her...all she has done for you?"

Unable to look into Audrey's eyes, Emma pulled her arm into the car, looked straight ahead, and said, "Just tell her I'm spending the night with Cheryl."

"When are coming home? Are you going to call her? Call her Emma," Audrey insisted, as the car pulled away from the curb.

Emma felt sick to her stomach as the car pulled away from the curb, not knowing where they were going...what she had just gotten herself into...still seeing the disappointment in Audrey's eyes.

14

Several stops, and hours later, after stopping for gas and cigarettes, the hunter green colored car pulled up in front of a large two-story house in the country. Emma had no idea where she was, knew if she needed to she would never be able to find her way back to town, and even if she made it to town, she'd have no idea how to make it back to New Point. She was lost…somewhere in the dark, in the middle of nowhere, staring at a house that didn't look anything like Cheryl had described. The description Cheryl had given of the house she lived in, had been much smaller than this one, perhaps half the size and she hadn't realized she lived in the country. She wondered how she got around…without a driver's license or car. Still sitting in the car, Emma looked at the house and noticed the welcoming glow of lights in several of the windows on the first floor.

Cheryl turned in her seat. Emma could just barely make out her face in the dark. "You ready?" Cheryl asked.

Ready for what, Emma wondered and shrugged her shoulders.

Cheryl was waiting by the car by the time Emma closed her car door behind her. Emma wondered why Cheryl's boyfriend wasn't driving away or coming into the house with them, but she said nothing.

As they walked toward the house, Cheryl explained, "You're going to be staying with a friend of mine."

Emma's heart caught in her throat!

"He'll treat you real good," Cheryl promised.

Panicking, Emma asked, "This isn't where *you* live?" her eyes wide with fear and disbelief.

With a casual swat of her hand, Cheryl said, "Naw...I live in town. He's just a guy I know. He won't mind if you crash here for a while. Like I said," she said with a sly grin, "He'll take good care of you."

What the hell! Emma panicked. "But you're staying here with me... *right...?*"

"You're a big girl. You'll be just fine. Chill out, Emma! It's okay," Cheryl insisted as she knocked on the door.

"Cheryl...No! I'm *not* staying at some strange man's house...*alone!!*" Emma cried. "I'm going wherever you're going!"

"Emma, I've got to straighten things out at the house first. Just give me a little time," Cheryl whined.

"Why am I here if I can't stay with you? What's going on, Cheryl!?" Emma demanded.

"I just have to talk to the people I live with first. Stop freaking out!" Cheryl snapped.

Emma snapped her head toward the door and stared up at a burly looking man wearing a wrinkled white t-shirt and blue jeans. Glancing down at his feet, she saw he was wearing a pair of holey white socks. She looked back up at the man with a stern expression, taking in his dark brown hair badly in need of cutting, washing and brushing.

"Hey, Tommy!" Cheryl said with a grin, as she stood on her tiptoes and kissed him on his cheek, and as he bent towards her, he wrapped his arms around her.

"What do we got here?" he asked in a gruff voice, as he swiped his hand over the stubble on his chin.

Cheryl pranced passed her friend, Tommy, into the house and said, "Oh, she's a friend." She pivoted on her toe and motioned for Emma to follow her.

Hesitantly, and unhappily, Emma walked into a filthy entryway. Clothes were strewn on every surface. As she glanced about the small space, she saw full laundry baskets heaped with even more clothes. Peering into the room beyond, bathed in a soft glow from a lamp placed on a small table next to a couch, she saw an even bigger mess of pizza boxes, food wrappers, glasses, cans of pop and crumpled beer cans. Emma scanned the entryway, peered down the dark hallway to the right and tried to see as far as she could into the dark nooks and crannies of the lower level of the house, wondering what or who might be lurking in the shadows.

Emma watched as Cheryl and her friend Tommy walked down the dark hall out of view. So, Emma thought sarcastically, nice plan. What the hell was Cheryl thinking...her big plan, trying to convince her for a month to come live with her when it was quite obvious there was no place for her.

She turned quickly toward the sound of feet clomping on the wooden floor and voices, and saw Tommy and Cheryl walking back down the hall toward her.

"Emma, this is Tommy," Cheryl said, gesturing toward the tall man. Emma estimated Tommy to be in his late thirties, was over six feet tall, a little thick around the middle, and looked as if he hadn't shaved or showered in a few days.

"Hi," Emma mumbled.

The unsmiling man stared down at her in response.

"You're staying here with Tommy for awhile," Cheryl said with a grin and one of her little prances. Grinning up at Tommy, she said, "Tommy'll take real good care of you, won't you Tommy?"

As he looked down at Emma, he ran a hand over his face, as she stared warily up at him.

"Cool! I got to get going. My old man's been waiting long enough for me," Cheryl said with a broad grin, as if they were all sharing some fun secret. If there was some secret going on here, Emma thought, she wished someone would let her in on it.

Cheryl stood on her tiptoes, wrapped her arms around Tommy's neck and kissed him on the cheek, then walked toward the door. Emma panicked and hurried after her.

"Cheryl!" Emma hissed, as she wrapped her jacket tighter around her to ward off the chill of the night. "Where are you going?!"

Cheryl turned toward Emma, smile still in place, and said, "I've got to get going. My old man's waiting." She pivoted on her hip and cocked her head, saying, "Chill, Emma. You'll be fine. Tommy's a real nice guy. Just hang out here for awhile."

What the fuck!? Emma thought, staring at the smile that seemed glued in place on Cheryl's face. Did the girl ever take anything seriously, she wondered hysterically.

"You can't just leave me out here," waving her arms around as if she were showing off a fancy prize on a game show, "in the middle of God only knows where, with some man I do not know! What the hell is going on, Cheryl?"

"You'll be fine," Cheryl assured her frantic friend. "Just have a little fun. You're not a kid anymore. We...*you,* can do whatever you want now...with no adults telling you what to do."

Cheryl skipped down the steps to the sidewalk and pranced in a circle, and beaming, said, "Live a little...life's too short!" then turned and skipped to the car.

"Cheryl!" Emma ran down the steps and shouted at the car as it sped away.

As she wrapped her arms around her waist, Emma watched the lights disappear into the black of night. She looked around her, peering into the dark, trying to make out the various shapes. Trees, and more trees, she thought, that and a road that went...somewhere.

It felt as if Emma were carrying a heavy boulder on her back, pressing down on her entire body—her body heavy with exhaustion. Fear gripped her as she turned back toward the house. Her body was stiff from the cold and holding herself rigid. She stared at the porch, windows bordering the door, the lights glowing from the inside piercing the darkness.

The door creaked as Tommy opened it and called to her, "Come on in and get out of the cold."

Her arms folded stiffly crossed over her chest, Emma considered the large man in the doorway, wondering what hellish nightmare she had gotten herself into now. Forcing her legs to move, slowly she walked toward the wooden steps, climbed three steps, then squeezed past Tommy and walked into the entryway, not sure what would be expected of her next. Hearing the door close behind her, she turned and stared at the man she had met just fifteen minutes ago. Her heart raced as she realized there was nowhere to run.

Tommy walked passed her into the adjoining room and mountains of what looked like baskets of clean laundry. Standing in the doorway, her hands clasped tightly in front of her, she scanned the room for anything that would tell her about the man flopping down onto a rust colored recliner. A few pictures were placed about the room, and as she squinted, she saw that a much younger him was smiling at whoever had taken the picture, and his arms were draped loosely around a couple of young children. A dad, Emma thought. She wondered where his kids were…and his wife. Wherever they were, she considered, they really needed to get their laundry folded and put away. The room was a mess and he didn't seem too concerned about it. There was nowhere for her to sit, so she continued to stand where she was, not sure what was expected of her…terrified of *what* he expected from her. Well, Emma thought, if Cheryl and Tommy thought she was going to pay for her stay by having sex with the man…they were nuts!

Everywhere she went…sleazy men, Emma stewed. Avoiding rape was an art form…one she was sick of perfecting! Shit! She couldn't get away from groping, sick, twisted men! Damn you, Cheryl! Emma screamed silently.

"You can shove that laundry over and sit down," he growled.

Emma looked at the couch, the area closest to the lamp near his chair that he had indicated. Picking up a pile of white clothes, she moved it to the other end of the couch, adding it to the already huge mound. Exhausted, she flopped down on the couch, determined not to fall asleep, fearing what she'd wake up to.

"So...how old are you?" he grunted.

"Sixteen," she said quietly.

"You look a lot older," he grunted, and looked back at the TV screen.

Yeah, she thought, she'd heard that before. It was the way she was built that made her look older. She had filled out before her older sisters, and since then had just kept growing. Emma remembered when she'd gone through puberty, and long after, she had attempted to cover all the hideous places that girls tended to grow from prying hands and eyes by wearing a blue jean jacket.

Curling her feet under her, tennis shoes still tightly laced onto her feet, Emma glanced at the watch strapped to her wrist...10:30. If she could just close her eyes for a few moments...

Clunk! Emma shot up straight in her seat as Tommy pushed the footrest of the chair down and shimmied out of the over-stuffed recliner.

"I'm going out," he said, avoiding her eyes, and walked out of the room into the darkness in the hall.

Whew! Emma breathed. Thank you, Jesus! If he was out of the house she could breathe a little easier, but she still couldn't allow herself to fall asleep. The most terrifying sexual assaults she had suffered had been when she had been caught sleeping, either by her dad waking her in the middle of the night with his groping hands, or a foster brother doing the same thing. It was a horrible feeling of helplessness to wake and be pinned by a grown man with nowhere to go until he went away.

When she had lived with her dad, several years ago, she knew she had to sleep, so she tried to think of things to deter him from hurting her while she slept...like wearing a furry winter coat to bed. One night he had climbed into bed with Emma—snuggling close—rubbing his hand on her, but to his surprise, his hand had met a buttoned up coat. He had to get through the coat to get to her. Smiling, Emma could still remember that night, and how angry he had been because she had won, but she had been terrified he was going to pull her out of bed and beat her. It had been worth the risk, she considered with a frown, because she knew if he had gotten to her, he could have hurt her much worse than if he had beaten her. She figured he had been shocked, discovering his youngest daughter, living with him any way, was ready for him—just trying to find a way to keep his hands off her—and roughly, he had shoved her aside that night.

At one home, she had slept with a knife under her pillow, not knowing—fearing—what could happen while she slept. The father of the home had been a violent alcoholic and eventually she had ended up running through a cornfield to the police station for help and safety. Then, she had been placed in more foster homes, with more hands... more nightmares.

The door slammed and she jumped. Leaning forward on her seat, Emma strained her ear, listening for a car engine to roar into life. There it was, she thought...and soon the sound of the car or truck noise, she wasn't sure which, faded. Tommy was gone.

Emma looked around the room again. Shaking her head she thought, it looks like a house tornado has blown through here. It was apparent that no one had cleaned in quite some time. Where was his wife and kids, she wondered.

Slowly, she unfolded from her spot on the couch, and letting out a tired sigh, stood up and placed her hands on her hips. I'm not having sex with that asshole, she thought as she clenched her jaw in defiance. Scanning the room, she considered...maybe I can clean this shit hole up and that will be enough for him...my payment for letting me stay here. At least for now, wondering just how long, and how much she could clean before he took what it seemed all men wanted from little girls and girls her age. Well, she thought, as long as she could hold him off as long as possible, and when the time came...he wasn't taking it without a fight.

First, she planned, she'd clear out the garbage in living room. Looking around, she wondered where the kitchen was. She was going to need a garbage can or at least a garbage bag—paper sack—something. Walking to the edge of the room, Emma peeked around the corner into the dark hallway, just beyond the glowing lights. To the right, she saw what looked to be an outline of a table...dining room she considered. The kitchen might be the other way, to the left. Bracing her left hand on the wall, bravely she placed her right foot into the hall, and stopped. Fear crowded her thoughts as she wondered, did Tommy have a roommate or a dog? Trying to calm the panic building inside her, she reasoned, she hadn't heard a dog bark. If there was a dog in the house, it would have barked by now...*right?* Emma was just as afraid of dogs as she was people. Over the years, she had been the recipient of several dog attacks, teeth tearing into her legs. When she was growing up, living with her dad, he always had a dog, a hunting dog chained up in the back yard. The dog would bark and growl at her as if she were a stranger. Her dad had taken pride in showing off the aggression of whatever dog he had at the time...explaining in vivid bloody detail what a dog could do to a person's throat if it got a hold of them.

But she hadn't heard a dog...there wasn't a dog in the house she thought, trying to calm her fear. And if there was someone else in the house, she would have seen them by now, she reassured herself. She looked at her hand still clutching the corner of the white wall, willing it to let go so she could move into whatever was waiting for her in the dark.

Taking a deep breath, Emma released the wall and planted both feet in the center of the hall, staring and listening to the dark. Her heart was pounding as she forced her feet forward toward what she hoped was the kitchen and a garbage bag. Running her hand along the wall of a black room, Emma searched for a light switch, and finding it, flipped it upward. The room was bathed in light and Emma's eyes were met by a kitchen buried under filthy pots, pans, glasses, plates, silverware, empty beer boxes, and garbage spilling over onto the floor.

Shaking her head, she began rummaging through cabinets for garbage bags; she was going to need a fistful. Surely, she hoped, if she cleaned up the man's shithole, he wouldn't be expecting sex from her. He could get that from some other girl.

At four O'clock in the morning, Emma finally took a break, sitting down on the now cleared off couch. For hours, she had collected garbage from the lower level of the house, and now six bags were placed beside the kitchen door. The clothing that had been strewn about the entry-way, and in the living room, had been cleared away, and was now placed in piles ready for the wash. The kitchen dishes had been done, and the counters wiped down.

Placing her face in her hands, she yawned. Carefully, she rubbed her eyes. She hadn't brought her contact case and solution, nor her glasses, not realizing she would be needing them. It was a lucky thing she had crammed a twenty-dollar bill in the back pocket of her jeans when she'd left the Rhodes' house in case of an emergency.

It had turned out that Emma Katherine constantly had babysitting jobs lined up and she had asked Emma to fill in for her a few times. Happily, Emma had accepted every time. Liking how it felt to have money of her own, and living in the country had proven to be a great way to save money. She had stashed every penny she had made so far in the savings account that Mrs. Rhodes helped her open.

Cramming her hands in her back pocket, Emma felt for the bill. It was still there. Well this was certainly an emergency, she thought, blink-ing and squinting her eyes in pain. When Cheryl came for her—when-ever that would be—she hoped she would take her to a store to buy a case and solution for her contacts. Since she had broken in her contacts months ago, she had worn them every day, but she had never slept in them before. Now, as she sat slumped on the couch, she was afraid to close her eyes, fearing the tiny contact lenses would get stuck up in her sockets, that and Tommy could be home any minute and she didn't want to wake up to his hands trying to rip her clothes off.

Sucking in her breath in surprise, Emma sat up straight on the couch as Tommy walked into the room. So tired, she hadn't heard the noise of the front door opening, or his shoes as he walked across the wooden entryway floor. Standing, she watched him as he looked around the room, much cleaner than when he had left. As he sat down in the recliner, Emma grabbed one of the baskets overflowing with laundry and dumped it on the couch, hoping he got the clue…this was to be her form of rent payment…nothing more.

Emma was exhausted from working through the night. Her fingers were just barely functioning as she folded a load of white laundry…t-shirts, underwear, and socks. Tommy had disappeared about half an hour ago, probably to bed Emma thought, as another giant yawn escaped her. She needed sleep, but she didn't dare lie down on the couch…

That's it, Emma said to the empty room and the now folded laundry. Every basket filled with clean laundry was now folded. The house, at least the downstairs portion, was picked up, dusted, and wood floors swept. There was nothing else to do, Emma realized, as her stomach growled. She was so hungry she felt sick, and she was so tired. Collapsing at one end of the couch, Emma grabbed the TV remote and clicked through the channels. It was 7:30 in the morning, so nothing much but sleep-enhancing news was on. Curling into the corner of the couch, Emma propped her chin on the palm of her hand and stared at the reporter on the screen, talking about…

"Let's go!" Tommy said clapping his hands.

"What?!" Emma said, disoriented. Where was she, she panicked. Then she remembered as she looked around the room—the laundry—Tommy. She must have fallen asleep. Everything seemed okay, she thought as she looked down at her clothes—everything just as it had been when she dozed off.

"You need to use the bathroom before you go?" Tommy asked as if talking to a child. It just sounded funny the way he'd said it.

"Where am I going?" she asked sleepily.

"Cheryl is comin' to pick you up," he grunted.

Stumbling to her feet, Emma tugged her jacket down and in place and walked down the hall toward the bathroom. Well, she thought, he must have gotten the message, relieved that Cheryl would be there soon.

15

The sun streamed in through the window of the car, almost blinding Emma as she sat in the back of Cheryl's boyfriend's car. It felt as if someone was taking sandpaper and swiping it back and forth over her eyes. She considered taking her contacts out and popping them into her mouth just to give her eyes a break, and to moisten her contacts. If it didn't sound so gross, she would. Well, she thought on a sleepy sigh, she now knew she could sleep in her contacts and they would *not* get lost somewhere in her eye sockets.

"Hey, Cheryl," Emma said sleepily. "Can we stop somewhere so I can pick up some stuff for my contacts and a tooth brush and tooth paste?" Her mouth tasted like rot and she suspected her breath didn't smell any better. *Growl!* Her stomach grumbled. "And maybe we can pick up something to eat…"

Emma watched Cheryl turn her head towards her boyfriend for a minute. She wondered curiously, what Cheryl's boyfriends name was. Surely, it wasn't really, *old man,* but that's all she called him. He wasn't that old, she reflected sleepily, maybe twenty…something.

"Yeah!" Cheryl grinned as she turned toward Emma. "We can stop and get you some stuff for your contacts and some pop and donuts to eat."

"K…" Emma said as she closed her eyes for a moment.

"Emma!" Cheryl said, as she shook her friend to wake her up. "Come on. Let's go into the store."

Blinking a few times and wiping the crud from the inside corners of her eyes, Emma leaned forward and groaned. She had fallen asleep again.

It seemed unusually bright as she walked next to Cheryl on the sidewalk passing various shops and people. God, Emma thought, as she glanced out of the corner of her eye, where does the girl find her energy. She was always bouncing around. All Emma wanted to do was sleep, right after she got a case and solution for her contacts...and donuts.

An hour later, Cheryl's boyfriend dropped them off at the curb in front of a house and they walked up a long sidewalk to the door. Upon entering the house, Emma found herself in a generous sized living room. It was an older home she noticed as she looked around, and the furniture matched the house, old and worn. As she looked around, she hoped someone would direct her to where she could lie down and sleep for awhile, like for maybe the rest of the day and night.

An unsmiling older woman, about Emma's height, with short dark brown hair, walked into the living room, the room where she now stood. Grinning, Cheryl introduced the woman to Emma as her landlord. The woman and her husband were renting the space in their attic to Cheryl. Emma had envisioned Cheryl's room would be accessed from a discreet door in a hallway. When one opened the door, they would find a narrow staircase which would lead to an open room the size of a large living room. She pictured a rough room, perhaps with an old wooden floor, but room enough for a bed or two, dressers, and maybe even a couch. Maybe she could crash in Cheryl's room, Emma hoped, feeling as if she could fall asleep standing up, either that or she would collapse in a dead faint soon.

"Emma, this is Dana," Cheryl said with a smile, motioning toward the still unsmiling woman.

"Hey," Dana said in a deep voice, as she looked Emma up and down.

"Hello," Emma said uncomfortably.

"Follow me," Dana insisted, and Emma did just that. She craned her neck to see Cheryl and realized she wasn't behind her.

"You stayin' here," Dana growled, "means you gotta work. No work, no food. You got that?"

"Yeah," Emma said, as her heart began to pound. Work...work where, she wondered, not sure what the woman meant.

"I like a clean house, you got that?" Dana said, glancing back at Emma.

"Yeah," Emma said, wondering why she was telling her about her clean house.

Emma followed her across the living room, feeling a thin carpet under her feet, and looking down, she wondered if it was carpet at all but instead maybe just a threadbare wall-to-wall rug. The living room emptied into a generous sized bedroom.

"This is my room...me and my husband's bedroom. We don't sleep in. We get up early and get the housework done. I like my room clean. My bed," she barked, as she bent down indicating that Emma should bend down and look, "gets made with hospital corners." Briskly she walked over to the long, dark brown, worn dresser, and as she swiped her hand along its surface, said, "I don't like dust. We dust every day."

Half asleep, Emma began to catch on. She was to be the new house-keeper...maid, or whatever they were going to call her. Would they feed her, and let her sleep, she worried. God, she was so tired. Stop talking woman, she screamed in her head as Dana's voice buzzed in her ears.

Finally, the tour of the house and her duties as the housekeeper was over which was a good thing because Emma was so tired, that she only heard half of what she was told—mid-tour she had shut down. Once again, Emma had lost Cheryl. The girl was nowhere to be found. Maybe she was in her bedroom, Emma thought, wondering where that was. She sat down on the lumpy couch to wait for her return, and moments later fell asleep in a seated position.

Hours later, Emma woke to the sound of a blaring TV and voices shouting. Looking around, she saw the house had increased its occupants. From where she was seated on the couch, she could see into the dumpy looking kitchen. There was a man with a big belly, which she assumed was Dana's husband, Gary, and two younger kids, a boy and girl. But she didn't see or hear Cheryl's voice.

Knowing she couldn't sit on the couch forever, Emma slid off the couch, and taking her sack of contact lens stuff, walked to the bathroom. She stared in surprise at her reflection. Her eyes were so blood shot, they looked as if they were actually bleeding. After washing her hands, she prepared the contact case, filling first the right and then the left side with solution. After washing her hands again, she placed them in the case and closed the caps on either side. She folded toilet paper to make a compress and soaked it with cool water, then sat on the closed lid of the toilet and pressed the paper to her eyes. Sighing, she slumped over. She wanted to go home...

She soaked her contacts for several minutes, time enough to pee, then after washing her hands, she painfully placed them back on her eyes, groaning in pain as she did so.

She placed her sack next to the small end table beside the couch, then slowly, dreading to meet whoever had arrived since she slept, walked into the kitchen. Her stomach growled when she smelled food cooking on the stove, and hoped they would offer her something to eat. She smelled something else, and wrinkling her nose, looked over at Dana's husband sitting at the gray plastic topped, metal-sided kitchen table, and saw a joint hanging off his lip as if he were smoking a cigarette. Glancing across the small table, Emma saw two children she guessed to be maybe ten and eight year's old sitting with plates in front of them. It was apparent to Emma that the kids had witnessed their parents getting high before. *Adults getting high...and in front of kids.* Emma didn't know what to think, except maybe...she had just landed in Trashville USA... again. So this is where the state was allowing Cheryl, a sixteen year old, to live. Nice, Emma thought, real nice.

"Grab a plate," Dana snarled. "Get something to eat," she motioned from her position in front of the stove. "When you're done, you can help me get these dishes and kitchen cleaned up."

Hungrily, Emma picked up the plate off the counter near the stove Dana had indicated, and scooped green beans, corn, and chicken onto her plate. Shaking with hunger, Emma grabbed a piece of bread out of a bag on the table, and then dug in. *Slow down, she cautioned herself, or you'll choke to death, and from the looks of these people, they might just let you.* Dana placed a cup of water in front of her which she gulped down. Emma couldn't help comparing the food to Mrs. Rhodes and even Emma Katherine's meals. Maybe it was life in the country, Emma reflected, that made them such great cooks, but even so, she was thankful for the food Dana had given her. It had hit the spot and would be fuel for cleaning up the kitchen, she thought as she looked around at the cooking and dinner mess.

Her body still felt heavy from exhaustion. She needed more than a nap to overcome the tiredness she felt from staying up the night before, and not just that, but plowing through the crazy mess at Tommy's house. Deep in thought, Emma dried dishes. She wondered just who Tommy was, and how Cheryl knew him…and why she had taken her to him. Nothing was making sense about this set up, she thought, as she glanced over at Dana. *Where was Cheryl?* She hadn't seen her since that morning.

Later that night, as Emma sat with the family, *whoever they were,* in front of the TV in the dark living room, Cheryl bebopped into the house.

Where the hell had she been all day, Emma wondered grumpily. She was tired, pissed off, and really wanted to go home! She watched as Cheryl did the excited prance Emma was so accustomed to, with a big grin and then said she was going to bed. Emma sprang to her feet, with as much spring as her tired body would allow and followed Cheryl into the kitchen.

"Cheryl!" she hissed, once away from the family of complete strangers. "Where have you been all day?" She didn't know what else to say without sounding clingy and very un-cool. What she wanted to say, was, *where the fuck have you been all day? Why did you leave me here with these people I do not know, and who is this Tommy? Why did you take me there and just what, pray tell, did the two of you think I was going to do with him? And then remind her just who she was and the kind of girl she was...as in she was not having sex with some strange man...just because! And what was she supposed to be doing with her life now that she had gotten her there? Just what was the big plan?!*

Still with the annoying grin, Cheryl said, "Chill, Emma. I was just out. I had stuff to do. You know."

No...Emma thought. She didn't know.

Rolling her eyes in annoyance Emma asked, "Where am I sleeping tonight. I'm tired...I just need to sleep."

"I don't know," Cheryl said, finally making a concession that she had no plan for anything where Emma was concerned. "Dana will find someplace for you."

Wrinkling her brow in anger and confusion, Emma flung her hand on her hip and said, "Find someplace for me. What's that supposed to mean? Why can't I sleep in your room?"

"Oh, Emma. There's no room up in the attic for you, at least not right now!" Cheryl said, sounding as if Emma had taken leave of her senses.

Dammit! Emma thought. What was she doing here? Staring at Cheryl, she realized the girl didn't need her. She was fine. So why, she wondered, had there been such a tremendous push to convince her to come here? Both hands on her hips now, Emma wondered what she was going to do. She couldn't call Audrey or Mrs. Rhodes. She had *blown* it! The weight of what she had done, what was happening, collapsed on her shoulders. Where was she going to go from here, she wondered. Who would want her? She was a runaway. What was she going to do? She didn't want to live her life like this...like, she didn't even know what this was! Out of desperation, Emma did something she hadn't done in a while, silently she prayed, *God, please help me.*

After a few more joints were smoked and the ten O'clock news was over, Dana and Gary rose from the chairs they had spent the last few hours in, and walked toward their bedroom leaving Emma alone. The kids had gone to bed hours ago. Emma glanced up when Dana walked back into the living room. She was carrying sheets and a blanket, and plopped them onto the couch next to Emma.

"You can sleep on the couch. Make up your bed," she said. "Remember, we get up early to get started on housework." Grabbing the remote to the TV, she clicked it off leaving the room and Emma in the dark.

Over the next few days, Emma developed a routine of making beds, cleaning up the dishes, and whatever chore Dana had for her. She polished every polishable piece of furniture and folded every article of clean laundry in the house. Then finally, she was given a glimpse of Cheryl's bedroom, and Cheryl's attic roommate. It was another in a series of shocks for Emma.

One morning, before Cheryl left for wherever it was she went during the day, returning sometimes after Emma had fallen asleep, she showed Emma her bedroom. Emma followed Cheryl down the short hallway, stopping beneath a dangling string just within reach of Cheryl's fingertips. She tugged on the string, pulling down a narrow, metal ladder. Emma stared up into the square hole above.

"Come on!" Cheryl insisted.

Cheryl disappeared into the hole above Emma's head. Gripping the sides of the ladder, Emma climbed the rungs, curious to finally see the room Cheryl was renting and sharing with another girl. Emma had seen the girl only once, and it had been a brief encounter. It had been late at night; the only light in the living room was from the glow of the TV. The

117

girl had an exotic look about her, with black hair, pretty features, about her height, maybe sixteen years old. Where Cheryl seemed to be a bubbling energy bubble, her roommate was quiet and reserved.

Standing on the fourth rung from the top, elbows propped on the wooden floor of the space above, Emma poked her head into the room above. What met her eyes was shocking. Emma had never really been up in an attic before; all she knew of them was what she had seen on TV and read about in mystery novels. Attics, in her mind, were large spacious mysterious rooms with windows at either end of the room, with lots of stuff stored away...trunks with treasures hidden away inside. But Cheryl's attic was nothing like the ones in movies or books. No windows dispelled the shadows in the corners of the small space, and the ceiling was so low it was impossible, even for a short teenager, to stand up straight. Then Emma looked across the expanse of the small room, at the floor...where the floor *should* have been. There was no floor. They could *make* a floor she considered, if they sprung for some plywood and nails. As she looked across what should have been the floor of the room, Emma saw pink cotton candy looking insulation, neatly laid out between two-by-fours running the length of the room. She knew what a two-by-four and insulation was because of the years her dad had spent ripping out the old walls in their old farmhouse, replacing old slat board, and plaster with the pink rolls of insulation. But he had covered the insulation with drywall...and then painted the walls. And of course, they had floors in their house, in all their bedrooms. She had never seen a room with no floor. Looking to the left, she saw a soft glow illuminating Cheryl's roommate's space—a mattress lying on top of a big piece of plywood, or several pieces of plywood. Craning her neck to the right, Emma checked out Cheryl's space, similar to the one to the left.

"This is it!" Cheryl said in excitement. "My space!"

"How did you get over there?" Emma asked with concern. "To your bed, I mean."

"I just walked on the boards. You have to be careful not to walk on the pink stuff or your foot might go through to the ceiling below. It's kind of cool, don't you think?" she asked expectantly.

"Uh-huh," Emma mumbled.

Cool, Emma considered. It was anything but. Once more, she glanced around at the creepy dark space with the slanted ceiling, suspecting it was the roof, before gingerly climbing back down the ladder. As she clanked down the ladder, she wondered if that was where Dana and Gary were planning to stick her too. The far side of the room, she had noticed, seemed to have just enough space for one more mattress. Then she wondered, had Cheryl's caseworker actually seen her room, and if she had…what adult in his or her right mind would allow any kid to live in those conditions?

Standing in the living room, Emma hugged her arms tightly and scanned the room. What was she going to do? What was she doing here, she worried. How long were they going to let her stay in their house just being their maid? She was out of her element here. What family would allow a sixteen year old girl to live with them…just cleaning their house every day. What was next? This is not normal Emma, she silently screamed. Home…she just wanted to go home… but she had no home now. God help her, what had she been thinking when she got in that car with Cheryl, and how was she going to fix this, she wondered, knowing that nothing short of a miracle would get her out of there. She was stuck…just stuck. God, she whispered with desperate tears glistening in her eyes…*please help me. I need a miracle.*

16

As Emma stood next to the stove stirring a pot of green beans, she heard a knock on the kitchen door. She turned and looked at Dana sitting at the kitchen table smoking a cigarette. It had been the typical long day of cleaning, dusting, making dinner, and the family seemed to have an abnormal amount of laundry that Emma folded each day. Sighing as Dana walked to the door, Emma thought…*this is not how I dreamed my life would be.*

Turning the fire on the stove down, Emma, as quietly as possible, took a step away from the stove and stretched toward the door to see whom Dana was talking to. She saw a handsome boy with dark brown hair, clean cut in a nice collared shirt and dress pants, and dress shoes. Taking a step closer, she saw that the boy had a vacuum cleaner sitting next to him. It was an upright model, and looked new. He was a door-to-door vacuum cleaner salesman, she realized. Well, she thought with a smirk, he had come to the wrong house. These people had no extra money for a vacuum cleaner. As she eaves dropped, Emma felt sorry for the boy. He had explained to Dana that he was in college and selling vacuum cleaners was paying his tuition. Awe, Emma thought, how cool. He was working his ass off, humiliating himself in front of the likes of Dana just so he could go to school.

Detecting a little maliciousness in Dana's motives, Emma watched and listened as she invited the boy inside to show her the vacuum cleaner. His discomfort seemed to ease as a grin replaced his serious expression. Poor thing, Emma thought, knowing he hoped he was about to make a sale, but she knew better. Over the few days she had been staying with Dana and Gary, she had seen and been the brunt of Dana's malicious nature and knew she was now toying with the college kid. She had no intention of buying a vacuum cleaner. Nope, she was just looking for a little fun and he was it.

Several hours later, after the family had eaten dinner and Emma was doing the dishes and depositing the leftovers in the refrigerator, college boy had disassembled the vacuum cleaner, per Gary's request. Large and tiny pieces were strewn about the kitchen floor for Dana and Gary's review. Rolling her eyes at the fiasco, Emma sat down at the table, becoming part of the audience. The salesman was much more casual now, his shirtsleeves rolled above his elbows and talking to Dana and Gary as if they were old friends.

Gary walked over to a drawer in the kitchen and pulled out a baggie crammed with pot and carried it back to the table. Emma looked from Gary, to Dana and then to the college boy, watching closely for his reaction. The grin on his face slipped a little. She knew he was just now figuring out that they had been playing with him…wasting his time. After rolling pot in white paper, Gary lit up and then offered it to the kid. They were testing him, Emma knew. This, Emma thought, would be what her sister Katie called, an alternate universe, where the life she had known just a short while ago…had gotten lost or merged with some other world. Her shoulders slumped as she watched the boy take the joint and put it to his lips. After he was done, he offered it to her.

"No thanks," Emma said with a fake smile.

"Go on, Emma," Dana insisted.

Emma looked over at Dana, and holding her breath, said softly, "That's okay. I'll pass," This was an uncomfortable first. Dana had never asked her to get high with them.

"Come on, Emma. Take a hit," Dana persisted.

"Maybe later," Emma responded, as she looked over at the college boy, watching him as he looked around the table at Dana and Gary. She didn't want to get high...didn't want them to ask her to get high and so badly wanted to be somewhere that no one asked her to get high! Placing her hands beneath her legs on her chair, Emma looked down at the table, hoping and praying they wouldn't ask her again.

"Here you go, Gary," the college boy said.

Emma looked up and caught the boy looking at her, and silently tried to convey thank you with the intensity of her stare.

His eyes broke away from Emma's, and with a smile, he said to Dana and Gary, "I've got to get this cleaned up and get going. I have a few more houses to stop at before I head home for the night." He glanced down at his watch and said, "Actually, I may only be able to fit one more house in tonight."

As Emma watched the college boy put the tiny pieces of the vacuum cleaner into a plastic bag, she wished she were in college...wished she had somewhere to go...anywhere else, feeling as if every dream she had ever had, would never happen. This was it, she reflected as she looked around the small kitchen, over at Dana and Gary, and watched the boy close the door behind him.

Later that night, Emma was curled up on the couch, her jaw resting on her fist—the smell of pot heavy in the smoke filled room—when Amy and Katie's faces swam before her eyes. Sighing, she sat up a little straighter and crossed her arms over her chest. A small smile played along her lips as she thought about some of the things Katie used to say. So often, her oldest sister would know just the thing to say when she was scared, and she wished she were here now. What would she say about the situation she had gotten herself into, Emma wondered, and smiled when she thought...Katie would probably say something like, *Gawl, bunch of freaks,* in her silly, trying to make Emma laugh, voice.

"Emma!" Dana shouted.

"What?!" Emma said, as her heart pound in her chest. She had been so deep in thought she hadn't heard her.

"Here," Dana said, holding a joint near her.

"I'm good. Thanks," Emma said uncomfortably, as the smoke drifted into her face.

"Go on," Dana insisted. "Take it."

Emma looked up into Dana's determined face. "Just—Just once," she said softly.

Over the next few days, it seemed to Emma that Dana was smoking pot non-stop and asking her to join her. She was relentless, standing in front of her until she took the joint. What else was she to do, Emma wondered—she had already tried the old, no thank you, and walk away routine. Dana would just light up another and follow her as she dusted, or folded laundry. There was an obvious shift in the expectations of Emma. Since her arrival, Dana had cracked the work whip. She had kept Emma busy from the time everyone got up for school and work, until the dinner dishes were done in the evening. Each night, Emma fell onto the couch exhausted after a day of cleaning, cooking, folding laundry, organizing dresser drawers, kitchen cabinets, and cleaning out the refrigerator. But over the last few days, there had been an uncomfortable and noticeable shift in her workload expectations. Dana was spending less time cracking the work whip, now insisting Emma sit with her on the couch and smoke pot. While Emma was glad for a break in the physical labor required of her—her body needed a break—she didn't want to be like them. She didn't want a foggy muddled mind, and she wondered at the change. It didn't make any sense to her...working her like a dog all day, then abruptly changing the routine. Dana didn't seem to care to have Emma clean her house all day anymore, instead, she wanted to keep her mind in a foggy muddled state all day. Emma preferred to work her ass off cleaning, at least her mind was clear and she could think. When her mind was foggy after smoking with Dana, she felt numb...memories of Katie, Amy and life at the Rhodes...fading away.

Emma stumbled around the kitchen putting the dishes away, her movements slow after smoking a joint with Dana. The light seemed dimmer in the kitchen than usual. Her mouth felt dry and she smacked her tongue on the roof of her mouth trying to find some saliva.

Slowly, she walked into the living room and found Dana, Gary and their kids already watching their evening TV program. Her spot on the couch was open she noticed in her pot fog induced mind, and she walked across the room.

"Emma," Dana said, "here."

Emma fumbled the joint out of Dana's hand and took a drag off of it, then slowly extended her hand—seeing the joint between her fingers—and offered it back to her.

"Take another toke," Dana insisted.

Her mind numb, Emma did as she was instructed, then extended her hand toward Dana again. This time, Dana took the joint from her.

What seemed like hours later, but in reality was less than twenty minutes; Emma heard a pounding on the door across the living room, near the TV. Foggily, she watched Gary open the door.

She looked up at two police officers. They were looking down at her…saying something to her, but she didn't understand.

One of the men walked across the small room and stood in front of her in the swirling mist of pot smoke. He wiggled his hand at her. Through the fog of her mind, she realized they were there for her. They wanted her to go with them.

As if in slow motion, Emma climbed off the couch, and without looking back, followed the officers out the door and down the sidewalk into the cold night air. One of the officers had the door to the back of the car open and silently she climbed onto the seat, her mind so numb she was not registering anything, except that she was getting into a police car.

17

Within a few minutes, Emma was standing in the foyer of a brightly lit house watching a perky woman with short black hair, wave her hands in the air, and smile up at the officers. She bobbed her head up and down in response to something they had said to her while Emma stood waiting for whatever it was they were going to do with her.

About an hour later, after the pot fog receded, Emma looked around her new surrounding knowing she was in another foster home.

"Hey Emma," the lady with short black hair said, as she breezed into the living room where Emma was watching TV.

"Hey," Emma said unsmiling.

"I'm going to make up a bed for you on the couch," the lady said with an easy smile.

Emma nodded her head, letting the lady know it was okay with her.

The next morning, Emma woke to hushed voices and a door closing. Lying on her side, she looked at the fuzzy outlines of the room she was in, and the adjoining room. She knew the layout of the two rooms, the clear vision memory from last night before taking her contacts out, and then falling asleep. It was a cozy house, at least the small section she had seen.

"Oh, you're awake!" the lady said perkily. "Are you hungry?"

Emma sat up and rubbed her eyes, and answered in a shy, uncomfortable voice, "Yeah."

"Well, why don't you go clean up and I'll get you some breakfast. I've got some spare tooth brushes in the downstairs bathroom," she said, gesturing to the half bath down the small brightly lit hall. Come to think of it, Emma thought, everything in the small house seemed bright, noticing the white sheers pulled open on the windows in the small dining room and in the room she was sitting in.

Over breakfast, the lady cheerfully explained that her husband had a basketball game at the gym nearby. She shared with Emma that typically, she worked out on Saturdays at the gym too, but she was staying home with Emma that morning. Emma felt bad that she had messed up the lady's day, curious that she seemed so cheerful to have some strange kid disrupt her plans.

"Your friend Audrey will be here in a couple of hours to pick you up," the lady said gently.

Emma looked up at the lady in surprise. She wasn't sure what she thought would happen to her next, but she hadn't expected Audrey to want to come get her, not after she had run away. She was confused, wondering why she would want to come get her after she had been so horrible to her. Then, there was the other thing...how had the police found her, Emma wondered.

Sitting across the table from Emma, a cup of coffee in front of her, the lady said, "She's going to take you back to your foster home. To the Rhodes' home...I think that's their name," she said uncertainly.

"Yeah," Emma said. "That's their name."

"Do you like it there?" the lady asked.

With a sigh, Emma answered, "Yeah. They're real nice. I really like Mrs. Rhodes," she said, as she looked down at her hands. How was she going to explain running away, Emma wondered. She was sure they wouldn't listen anyway. It was a stupid reason, she thought as her heart began to pound anxiously. How could she have thought Cheryl had needed her, and so what if she had...which she now realized she hadn't.

What was wrong with her? Helping people or standing up for people just got her in trouble. You are so stupid, she chastised herself. She pictured what was about to happen to her...Audrey probably hated her now, and Mrs. Rhodes was probably going to have her pack her things in a garbage bag and make her leave. *Of course she would, you idiot!* She worried where she would end up next.

It was a quiet drive back to the Rhodes' house. Emma just knew Audrey hated her, of course, she did, she thought for the hundredth time as she stared quietly out the window watching empty fields whiz by. A few stomach-churning hours later, Emma was resting her chin against her hand, staring out the passenger car window as Audrey pulled her car onto the Rhodes' long gravel driveway. Emma watched as the dogs ran up to Audrey's car, barking and wagging their tails...almost as if they had been expecting her.

Emma was terrified. She knew the Rhodes family were nothing like Sheila's foster home, knew they wouldn't yell at her, or beat her for running away, but she just knew they were going to send her away. She didn't want to leave, hadn't wanted to go with Cheryl, but Mrs. Rhodes wouldn't believe her if she told her that. And even if she did believe her, it just made her sound like some stupid, messed up girl.

She didn't know what to say as she walked into the warm kitchen, the smell of baked pudding pleasantly in the air. Mrs. Rhodes was waiting for her alone in the kitchen, standing by the sink. She looked like she always did, Emma thought—not mad or anything. Emma shifted her eyes around the room looking for her garbage bag filled with clothes. When she didn't see it, she thought maybe it was in the other room.

"Are you okay?" Mrs. Rhodes asked.

Wanting to cry, Emma shook her head up and down. Standing next to the kitchen table, she trembled with fear as she wondered what was going to happen to her.

"I've got to get going," Audrey said.

Emma snapped her head around and looked at her, realizing she was staying. They weren't kicking her out.

Turning back toward Mrs. Rhodes, Emma asked, "I'm staying?" needing to be sure.

"Well, do you want to stay?" Mrs. Rhodes asked with a smile.

"Yeah," Emma assured her, shaking her head up and down.

"Okay, but no more runnin' away. I was worried about you," Mrs. Rhodes said sincerely.

Who the hell was this woman, Emma wondered in disbelief. She wasn't kicking her out… and she was talking to her…like she didn't hate her.

All of sudden Emma felt as if she might throw up. *What if Mrs. Rhodes changed her mind?*

18

For the next month, Emma felt as if she were walking on eggshells, each day wondering if today would be the day she was to be sent away. All the kids at school knew she had run away. Of course they did. In a school of less than one hundred kids, everyone knew everyone's business. They all hated her, she assumed. She had just proven she was exactly what they all thought foster kids were...trouble. Facing the kids at school had been difficult, but facing the Rhodes' extended family for Thanksgiving dinner was even more difficult.

Since she could remember, Emma had tried to do the right things, even when so many people around her were doing the wrong things. There had been so many bad things and bad people in her life, it had disgusted her, *they* had disgusted her. Her short life had been spent waiting for God to send someone to save her, and it had seemed more often than not, that no one ever came, so she saved herself. But God *had* come... she realized. The Rhodes' were good people, so why had she run, she stewed. *What was wrong with her?* Still, even after running away, they were treating her just fine. They weren't being mean, or anything.

Right now, the biggest problem Emma had, was Emma. She couldn't forgive her actions, couldn't forgive herself for running away, for destroying everyone's trust in her. Here she was, with an opportunity to be a normal kid...and she had run, and why...she struggled to understand. Cheryl hadn't needed her—no one needed her. And then when Cheryl wouldn't shut up, saying over and over to come on, Emma had just cracked. She had felt like a little girl again, and needed everyone to be quiet for a minute. Maybe, she considered, that was the reason she panicked and had gotten in the car. She just needed the noise to stop, the shouting, the intensity of the situation, and maybe she had thought Audrey would follow her, or call the police or…something. Maybe she had thought someone would come pick her up at Cheryl's place. They had known where she lived…hadn't they? Emma had thought her case-worker would just contact Cheryl's caseworker and someone would come get her. But it had taken awhile, too long, for someone to come get her. Emma still couldn't make sense of why she had run. Pressure and panic—Cheryl needed her—she had thought someone would come for her…but they hadn't. She had thought they didn't want her anymore.

Emma was sunk into Mr. Rhode's recliner in the family room. It was the most comfortable spot in the room with a perfect view of the barns, a few of the outbuildings, of the long driveway, and even part of the road. Placed right next to the fireplace, it was the coziest spot in the entire room. Her feet and several textbooks were tangled on the foot-rest, and her government textbook, spiral notebooks, old tests, and notes were strewn on her lap. Surrounding her on the floor were papers that had slid there over an hour ago.

Tears of frustration glistened in Emma's eyes as she stared out the large bay window at the barn, lit by the the yard light casting its light on an otherwise dark yard. She was never going to remember all this shit, she realized. She was going to flunk the class. *God, she was a screw up in every way imaginable!* Her world was, piece by carefully taped together piece, falling apart. It wasn't fair, she screamed inside her head! It wasn't as if she was one of those cute girls that had lots of friends, spending their time playing around. She was the girl that, for as long as she could remember, just wanted to read, get good grades, and have nice friends, she sniffed. But that's not how it had turned out, she sighed. *She was stupid.* She couldn't remember anything, didn't understand any of this, she thought in anger at herself, as she looked at all the papers on her lap. She wanted to crumple them up and throw them across the room! I can't do this, she told herself as she swiped away an angry, miserable tear from her cheek. I don't want to be a loser, she thought miserably...*but I am. I should just give up.* Audrey was wrong, she thought sadly. *I will never be anything.*

Turning a page in her textbook, Emma tried to read through her tears. *Grrr!* she cried. Grabbing one of the pieces of papers off her lap, she wiped snot on it, then crumpled it and threw it across the room. "I can't catch up, Audrey," Emma said to the empty room. Being out of school for a week had been a serious setback for Emma, and she knew she couldn't blame that on anyone but herself. She could blame many of her academic issues on the adults in her life—the fact that she had missed a great deal of school over the past few years because of court hearings, missed school due to moves from various foster homes, changing schools in the middle of school years—and just trying to survive her daily life. It had all impacted her schoolwork. But this...*this,* the fact that she had missed a week of school this time, was her fault, and she knew it. Tears coursed down her cheeks and neck as she cried, *I don't want everyone to be right...I don't want to be nothing.*

A half an hour later, Emma was sitting on the couch, just having finished a snack, flipping through the channels on TV. Her brain felt fried. She couldn't think straight anymore...needed a break. Glancing out the window behind her, she saw Mrs. Rhode's car pull up. She got up, walked into the kitchen, and placed her cup in the deep sink. Carmen, the Rhodes' oldest daughter, and Mrs. Rhodes walked into the kitchen. Emma looked over at them as they placed large plastic bags on the kitchen table. Carmen was home from college for the holiday break.

"Why aren't you studying?" Mrs. Rhodes asked, looking over at Emma.

"I was," Emma said shortly. Emma knew Mrs. Rhodes wasn't trying to be mean. She was never mean, but right now Emma was suffering from severe loser meltdown and Mrs. Rhode's question seemed an accusation to Emma's very short fuse.

"Doesn't look like your studying," Carmen stated.

"You need to be studying, not messing around, Emma. You don't want to fail do you? You need to pass this class if you want to graduate high school," Mrs. Rhodes said reasonably.

"S-H-U-T...U-P!" Emma shouted, more in anger at herself than anyone.

"Don't you talk to mom that way!" Carmen said angrily, as she stepped between Emma and Mrs. Rhodes.

"I'm not talking to you, Carmen!" Emma shouted, as the fear and confusion of the last month bubbled over.

"I *know* who you're talking to!" Carmen shouted back. "I'm not letting you talk to mom that way!"

Knowing they didn't want her...were going to kick her out anyway, Emma totally lost it and shrieked, "I'll say whatever I want to the bitch!"

Emma felt and heard the sting from Carmen's hand when she slapped her cheek. And just as quick as Carmen had slapped Emma, Emma slapped Carmen!

"Stop, you two!" Mrs. Rhodes shouted. It was the first time Emma had ever heard her foster mother raise her voice in anger. She was stunned and horrified at what had just happened, that she had called Mrs. Rhodes such a name...and then slapped Carmen. *Of course, they will want me to leave now, she thought. What the hell is happening to you, Emma, she wondered in an exhausted daze.*

"Emma Claire," Mrs. Rhodes said shakily, "go to your room. We'll talk about this later."

Emma wanted to escape the family room, and with tears in her eyes, walked quickly over to the recliner and scooped up her books, papers and the materials that had fallen to the floor. She brushed past Carmen on the way out of the room. Studying was over for the night, she thought with an exhausted sigh. As she hurried up the carpeted steps to her bedroom, she wondered what Mrs. Rhodes would have to say to her about her horrible outburst.

Twenty minutes later, Mrs. Rhodes knocked on the outside wall of Emma's bedroom. "Can I come in?" she asked tiredly.

Emma was sitting at the end of her bed, curled against the wall worrying about what was going to happen to her, wondering if Mr. and Mrs. Rhodes would want to get rid of her now. "Yeah," she said miserably, looking down at the blanket on the bed.

"Emma Claire, do you want to tell me what that was all about?" Mrs. Rhodes asked softly.

Shaking her head back and forth, Emma said, "I don't know. I guess I'm just so stressed out from studying...I can't remember everything. It's like my brain won't take anything else in."

Emma looked up at her foster mother and said sincerely, "I'm sorry...for what I said and for slapping Carmen. I feel awful."

"Well, it wasn't a very nice thing to say," Mrs. Rhodes said, "and I think you need to be apologizing to Carmen, not me for slapping her."

"Yeah," Emma said softly.

"Emma Claire," Mrs. Rhodes insisted, "you're going to do just fine on your tests. You just have to have more faith in you. *I* have faith in you."

To Emma's mortification, she felt hot tears spring to her eyes, and she gave Mrs. Rhodes a watery smile. Sighing, she said, "I sure wish I had the faith in me, that you have."

"Well, it's going to be just fine. Why don't you take a break and get some sleep. Everything will seem better in the morning," Mrs. Rhodes suggested.

"I will. I'm pooped," Emma admitted.

Emma's eyes followed Mrs. Rhodes as she walked out of the bedroom. She shook her head in bewilderment. The woman hadn't yelled at her, called her names, hit her, or threatened to kick her out. Who was this woman, Emma pondered, and how did she get the way she was? So...so gentle?

19

"Emma! Pass the ball!" Tara shouted from across the floor.

Emma dribbled the ball, looked to her right, and then passed the ball to Tara. It was Emma's fourth basketball game of the season playing on the Junior Varsity team. So far, the New Point High girls' basketball team hadn't won a single game. The school's boys' team was great, but the girls sucked! Emma wasn't surprised. After all, New Point High was the smallest school in the region with the smallest girls' basketball team. Just once, Emma thought as she ran to catch the ball, she'd like to win a game. Catching the ball, she raised her right elbow and wiped the sweat trickling down her brow.

A girl from the opposing team tried to wrench the ball from Emma's grasp, but Emma hung on with everything she had, thinking, girl, you have no idea but you just picked the wrong person. I may be small, but I'm not lettin' this ball go, she thought in determination, as she hung on with all her might. She held tight and swung the ball to the right with the girl still attached. The girl fell to the floor.

"Whooooo!" Emma heard the crowd chime.

She heard the ref whistle and shout, "Foul!"

"What?!" she said with a scowl. "Bullshit!"

She watched with anger as the ref made a "T" symbol with his hands and said, "You're out of here for the rest of the game!"

"Whooooo!" the crowd shouted again.

Emma stormed off the floor, flipping off the crowd as she walked past the referee. She fumed as she changed from her uniform to her street clothes, and then waited in the locker room for the game to be over.

The following week, one night after school, Emma found herself sitting in the dark waiting room of a therapist's office. Mrs. Rhodes was worried about Emma, first running away, then the aggression on the basketball court—flipping off the crowd...her anger. Emma had been suspended from school for a few days because of her antics, and it was then Mrs. Rhodes insisted that Emma had to talk to some stranger about what was bothering her. Mrs. Rhodes had tried to get Emma to open up, to talk to *her* about why she was so angry—but Emma couldn't talk to her because she wasn't quite sure what was wrong...what to tell Mrs. Rhodes. She was a jumbled miserable mess. After a lifetime of wanting to be loved, have a family—with her sisters—she just couldn't seem to let it happen. At the children's home, she had been able to open the door to trust and have people care about her...but at the Rhodes' home, she just knew the minute she let her guard down, let them in, they would throw her away just as everyone else in her past had. She didn't think she could do it again...open her heart, and then withstand the blow of knowing she was so unlovable, and so unwanted, when they sent her away.

Emma knew Mrs. Rhodes was just trying to help, but as she sat in the therapist's office, he asking prying questions, she with so much pain and fear swirling around inside her heart, she just couldn't get it out. Instead, she just sat on the soft couch in silent pain, wishing she were any other kid...but her. She wished she could rip away whatever it was that made people throw her away.

After two wasted trips to visit the therapist, Mrs. Rhodes knew it wasn't helping Emma. Having Emma clam up in a therapist office wasn't helping her and it wasted her evenings. Through the grace of God, something else was going to have to reach Emma.

Tuesday night, ceramic night, Emma thought as she walked into the family room after dinner. Mrs. Rhodes had a small picnic table set up, placed against the far wall of the room with a view of the driveway and barns through the bay window across the room. She watched as her foster mother placed things on the table in preparation for her students.

Mrs. Rhodes noticed Emma watching her, and asked, "Have you ever done ceramics before?"

Emma shook her head no, she hadn't, but she was curious as to how it was done. It looked like a neat craft.

"Well, stick around and you can see how they do it," Mrs. Rhodes said encouragingly.

Emma waited for the students to arrive, curious to see what they were going to do with the figures that were on the table, that and the tools, water, and sponges.

Standing a short distance away from the table, staying out of Mrs. Rhodes way, Emma watched the students scrape away rough edges and wipe clean their work with wet sponges, explaining what they were doing all the while. It looked like fun, she thought. She wanted to be a ceramic student too.

After class was over, Emma followed Mrs. Rhodes, carrying small bowls of used water to the sink, and then carried the small tools to the workbench in the room off the kitchen, which at one time had been the garage. It was in this room that Mrs. Rhodes had shelves higher than Emma was tall, filled with what she called greenware—greenware being what one cleaned, painted and fired, or baked in a kiln to create the final ceramic piece. Emma was fascinated as her foster mother explained the process to her. Carefully Emma moved greenware around to examine the various pieces, from small hearts that one could make into pins to larger pieces that could be used for decoration and even cups and plates. As Emma looked at the various shapes, her imagination went wild in wonder at the various colors one could paint and the various glosses and textures the art could become. Ceramic Christmas trees, Mrs. Rhodes told her, were very popular this time of the year with Christmas just a few weeks away. She showed Emma several that she had created with colorful lights set inside the holes. Wow…Emma thought, as she touched the glossy green surface of the small ceramic tree.

"I've got to pick up some more greenware Saturday morning," Mrs. Rhodes said offhand. "You want to come with me?"

Did she ever! "Sure," Emma said with a smile, feeling excited for the first time in over a month.

"This stuff I have," Mrs. Rhodes said, sweeping her hand toward the shelves, "is nothing compared to this one lady I know. She has an entire room full!"

Emma's eyes opened wide at the thought of an entire room of greenware to choose from. Jeez, she thought, it must be awful to have to pick.

Saturday morning, Emma looked at aisle after aisle of shelves filled with different types of figures…greenware that would one day be plates and cups, and doll heads, cookie containers…*my gosh…so many things.*

Standing next to Emma in the small warehouse, Mrs. Rhodes suggested, "Why don't you pick something out."

Pick something out, Emma considered as she looked around the room. How would she ever choose?

"Really?" Emma asked in surprise.

"Yeah. Go look around," Mrs. Rhodes replied, as she watched Emma scan the room.

Meticulously, Emma picked through the greenware on each and every shelf, and then she found it….the greenware that she would make into an artistic masterpiece. It was a planter the shape of a running shoe. It looked similar to the tennis shoe that was part of her pom-pom outfit. It was a little bigger than her actual shoe…but it looked just like her tennis shoe, at least it would once she was done painting it. Carefully, she carried it to Mrs. Rhodes, planning how she would paint it to make it look weathered and time worn.

"Did you find something?" Mrs. Rhodes asked.

Emma handed the piece of greenware to her foster mother, a little embarrassed by her choice, thinking she would think it silly that out of the hundreds of pieces, she would choose a shoe. But...a shoe was what she wanted. *She couldn't wait to get to work on it!*

20

Clad in her PJ's with her red velvet robe wrapped warmly around her, Emma said with a grin, "Merry Christmas!" She walked into the family room overflowing with Christmas gifts—crammed into every nook and cranny of the room. Beside her, Emma Katherine said a cheerful, "Merry Christmas!" to the family.

"Merry Christmas!" Mrs. Rhodes said, with a delighted grin.

"Merry Christmas!" Mr. Rhodes said, with a small smile.

"Merry Christmas!" Carmen, Caitlyn, and Cassy chorused.

"Merry Christmas! Look what I got!" Will, Emma's foster brother said, holding up a small car.

Emma gave the six-year-old little boy her attention, and grinning, said, "From the size of that stocking, I think you could fit your entire body in there!"

"Yeah, Will," Emma Katherine laughed, "be careful or you'll get lost in that giant stocking!"

Emma watched as Will dumped the remainder of the stocking on the floor in front of the fireplace. Emma glanced at the warm crackling fire, and then over at the Christmas tree twinkling with multi-colored lights. She walked over to the couch and squeezed in next to Emma Katherine, laughing as she did so, trying to avoid crushing the presents that were impeding the room, and her cramped space.

Emma looked over at Emma Katherine, and asked, "Is it always like this at Christmas?"

"If you mean, does Christmas take over this room? Yup!" Emma Katherine said with a grin.

Emma looked in wonder at the Rhodes family, everyone still dressed in their pajamas, at their smiles, and listened to their excited voices as they opened presents.

"Here, Emma," Cassy said with a smile, as she handed Emma another present.

"Thanks!" Emma grinned.

Looking down in surprise at the pile of presents on her lap, and stacked on the arm of the couch, Emma had a feeling of self-consciousness engulf her. Her eyes flitted around the room to see if anyone was watching her, and then carefully began to tear the tape from the beautiful wrapping.

"Wow!" she mouthed. She held in her hand an art kit, with pens, pencils, charcoal, paper, and special erasers. Caressing the case with her hand, she looked across the room at her foster mother, seeing that she was watching her, and smiled.

"Thank you!" Emma said, wishing she could express to everyone in the room, just how beautiful and special a moment it was. The fire crackled to the right of her in the fireplace; the adults sipped hot cups of coffee, and love was thick in the room. Picking up another sparkly paper wrapped package with a beautiful blue bow, Emma thought of Katie and Amy. She hesitated as she looked at her foster family, and hoped her sisters were somewhere warm, safe, and happy.

"Hey, Emma Katherine!" Carmen shouted. "I think one of your horses is loose!"

"No, it's not!" Emma Katherine laughed.

"She's serious," Mrs. Rhodes said laughing, as she looked toward the barn. "You better go get her."

"Oh, good grief!" Emma Katherine said with an annoyed smile.

Emma craned her neck to look out the bay window overlooking the red barn, and sure enough, the horse with spots was outside the gate. She followed Emma off the couch. How exciting, Emma thought...a Christmas horse adventure!

Emma Katherine walked from the kitchen into the room with all the greenware. A few minutes later, Emma watched as Emma Katherine walked toward the horse, her nightgown billowing about her legs in the Indiana wind. She had taken time to throw on an old pair of muddy boots and a coat, but hadn't taken time to zip the coat and it too flapped in the wind. Brrr! Emma thought, as she watched her foster sister corral the horse back into the barn. She rubbed her arms as if she were the one outside in the cold as she watched Emma Katherine walk back up the hill toward the house.

"That was so cool!" Emma said excitedly, when Emma Katherine walked back into the kitchen.

"Cool! No, it was freezing!" Emma Katherine joked.

The rest of the Christmas break was spent eating all the cookies, breads, and cakes that Mrs. Rhodes and Carmen had baked, and dinners at grandparents. Emma filled in the rest of her free time by reading a few books, and working on her ceramics project. She welcomed the new year by listening to the count down on the radio—it was the passing of one year to the next, of a new semester and new classes. With the passage of time, Emma was becoming more comfortable at the Rhodes' home. This year, she was determined to make it the year of possibilities.

She was still finding that she was playing catch up with some of her classes, but felt she was entering the new year a little more academically confident. Driver's Ed class was one of her classes for the new semester, a class she was both nervous and excited to take. The summer before, while living at the children's home, Emma had signed up for a driver's Ed class but had been dropped from the class when she had run away from the home. Now, here she was taking the class, not with her junior class, but with a bunch of sophomores. It could be worse, she speculated; she could *never* get her license, and besides, she had sophomores in some of her classes, on her basketball team, and on the pom-pom squad. *No biggy.* The written portion of the class didn't concern her, but the driving portion did, because she had never driven a car before. She didn't even know how to turn one on!

Suspension from the basketball team had lasted only three games and Emma was back on the team. While sitting out the three games, Emma made good use of her time. She got in as much practice off the court as she could, at home in the barn, and during P.E. at school. When her suspension was over, she was thrilled to be back in the gym practicing with her team, and began the new year as a JV starter.

Emma finally began to feel a little more secure at the Rhodes' house—feeling that she might just have a place to stay, at least until she graduated from high school. The house was comfortable, with plenty of space. The basement was the coolest place ever, with two kilns, a table for pouring molds, and for working on Emma's ceramic projects. When Emma wasn't performing with the other pom-pom girls during half time at the boys' basketball games or playing basketball on the girls' JV team, she got in as much ceramic time as possible. She had completed the ceramic tennis shoe Mrs. Rhodes had bought her already. It was now a glossy light blue, worn looking, ceramic shoe and one day would hold a small plant. She had used one of the ceramic tools to scrape her name and date on the bottom...commemorating her first piece.

The family had also started attending Bible study with several of Mrs. Rhode's friends. They met at a home in the country with three other families. Emma loved it. It was the perfect way to end her weekend and begin her week, with a message of hope...something to ponder.

21

Emma was hurrying through the throng of noisy teens to get out the door to the bus, when she heard a deep voice call her name.

"Emma! Wait up!" Jacob shouted with a silly grin.

She turned toward the tall boy, looking more like a linebacker than the center of the boys' varsity basketball team, and smiled.

"Well hey there!" she said, returning his silly grin. "Where are you going in such a hurry?"

He looked at her with a sheepish grin, and said, "Oh, I wanted to catch you before you got on the bus."

"You caught me!" she laughed, as she turned sideways and resumed walking toward the door.

She noticed the stack of books he held casually curled in his arm as he caught up and walked with her across the lobby of the school and then into the windy Indiana winter air. The bus was waiting at the end of the sidewalk with Mrs. Rhodes standing next to it, corralling the kids inside.

"Hey, I was wondering if you would go out with me and some friends some night. Just hang out...maybe grab a sandwich and go to the mall or see a movie..." he said quickly.

Pulling her purse strap onto her shoulder, and hiking the books she held under her arm a little higher, Emma thought for a moment...it would be okay, as long as there were other kids around. Boys made her uncomfortable. What if one touched her or tried to kiss her...or something. She wasn't ready for those types of situations, not ready to push a boy away when he tried to get her to do things she didn't want to do. As she looked into Jacob's smiling brown eyes, she realized she had no idea what his intentions were. More than likely, she reassured herself, he was the funny boy in school taking pity on the new girl and just wanted to be friends.

Squinting and smiling up at him, she said, "Sure! I'll ask Mrs. Rhodes. But I can't go out during the week. Maybe some Saturday. Is that okay?"

With a whoop, he said, "Sure! How about this Saturday?"

She laughed and said, "I'll ask. I'll talk to you tomorrow at school," and climbed the steps of the bus.

"You have her back by midnight," Mrs. Rhodes insisted protectively. Emma smiled as she watched Mrs. Rhodes and Jacob banter back and forth. Mrs. Rhodes was making him squirm just a little, Emma noticed, and she wasn't letting up, not until Jacob assured her he would return her safely by midnight.

"I know, or she'll turn into a pumpkin, right? Oh, wait...my car will turn into a pumpkin," he giggled.

Emma laughed at his silly joke as Mrs. Rhodes gave him the look that meant, *I'm serious.*

Emma was still smiling when she scooted into Jacob's tiny car, a silver colored Chevy Chevette, such a small car for a very tall boy. She glanced over to see if his head was hitting the roof of the car, and was surprised to see at least an inch or two of clear space. Amazingly, his six foot four frame wasn't squashed into the small space of the car, instead, he looked quite comfortable as he grinned at her and giggled.

She laughed. He had a way of making her feel comfortable...with his goofy expressions and silly giggles he created. Jacob was a boy that didn't care what people thought of him, secure in who he was...just loving life. If only she could bottle that joy, goofiness, and self-confidence, she thought with a grin, as they sped down the country road to pick up Jacob's friends.

Hours later, sitting in the car with windows fogged by the four teenager's breathing, Jacob handed Emma a can of beer. Fiddling with one of the small earrings in her ears, she stammered, "No thanks."

"Okey-Dokey," he joked, and took a swig of his opened can of beer, handing her unopened can back to his best friends, Doug and Judy. Emma had found it interesting that although Doug and Judy were Jacob's best friends, they weren't a couple. They each had a boyfriend and girlfriend...but not each other. The threesome had grown up together, gone to school since grade school, and had been best friends ever since. It was cool to Emma, because right now she really just wanted a group of kids to hang out with—with no boy complication.

"Excuse me!" Jacob giggled after letting loose a long obnoxious burp. The car exploded in laughter.

"Ready, kids?" Jacob laughed, as he opened his car door and pulled his seat up so Doug could climb out of the car.

Opening the door, Emma was met by a brisk wind, and pulling her rabbit skinned coat tighter, she pulled the seat forward allowing Judy to climb out. Jacob had planned an evening at the movies, which was located inside one of the malls, half an hour from New Point. The silly group joked and giggled as they walked through the mall occasionally posing with a random mannequin.

"Fifteen minutes until movie time!" Jacob called out, and then ducked when patrons of the store they were in turned to stare at him. Snickering he said, in a more subdued voice, "We should get going."

Emma was just about to walk away from a rack of blouses, a soft fabric of blue in her hand, when she turned her head with a smile on her face toward Jacob's voice.

"Oh!" she said in surprise to see him leaning over her. Unexpectedly, he had planted a wet kiss on her lips, and just as quick as the kiss had begun, he pulled back and gave her one of his big grins. It had happened so fast her mind was still trying to catch up, to register what had just happened, as she reached up and wiped his spit off her lips. Yuck! She thought, and then…what the hell!? Where had that come from? It must be the beer, she justified as she followed beside Judy into the movie theatre.

"So," Judy asked when they were alone in the lady's restroom. "What do you think about Jacob? Do you like him?"

"Sure?" Emma said, staring in the mirror at her reflection as she applied clear lip-gloss to her lips.

"No…I mean, do you *like* him—like him, silly?" she grinned.

Surprised, Emma paused, her hand in the air as she reflected about what Judy had just asked. Did she *liiiike,* Jacob. Wow! She had never thought about it before. He was funny. Screwing the top back onto the lip-gloss tube she thought, now Doug…he was a cute boy. Jacob…she reflected, was funny. He was nice.

"He's nice," she responded.

"Well, *you* are all he ever talks about!" Judy confided.

The girls walked up to the two boys waiting at the ticket counter, one with hair so dark Emma thought it might be black, and at least a foot taller than she was, and the other, a few inches taller than her with blonde hair. Sighing, she pondered, did she like Jacob—*like* him…

Emma was thankful that there were no more mushy, wet kisses, that night. She had a lot to think about…such as, did she *like* Jacob… like that.

A few weeks later, Emma rode along side Jacob on the passenger seat of his Chevette, so nervous she thought she'd puke. It was the first time she was sitting in his car…as his date. *What if she said something wrong, or did something stupid?* It had been so much easier, and simple, when they had just been friends.

"I thought we'd go hang out with Stacey and Doug, at his sister's house," Jacob said, as he glanced over at Emma. He and Emma had been friends for months so it seemed ridiculous that he felt so nervous being alone with her in his car, but he was. Few things had Jacob tongue tied, but being alone with Emma had done it, so he had called Doug and asked him to help him out…be a good friend—and be a crutch. Doug had never let him down. He and Stacey were already waiting for them at his sister's house, twenty minutes outside of New Point.

"Okay," Emma said, relieved that they wouldn't be spending the entire evening alone.

It was a quiet drive through the country, and then through the bustling town of Largo. Largo was the town where Emma had lived prior to the children's home. Audrey lived in Largo, as did Sheila, the foster home where so many bad things had happened. Largo happened to be the hang out for the kids that lived in New Point. It was the nearest town—much larger than New Point—with restaurants, shopping, the church that Emma and the Rhodes family attended, and her hairdresser. One of the men from church owned a hair salon and it was where Emma had her hair cut; a real treat considering she'd only had her hair cut once professionally during her year at the home.

Jacob led the way through the small house to the sound of Stacey and Doug's voices. He had explained that Doug's sister had left a few minutes ago for work so they were just going to hang out, order a pizza and watch a movie, if that was okay with her. No problem with her, she had responded, feeling relieved to have a little pressure off her shoulders. The more people the better, she thought thankfully, hoping no one noticed what a nerd she was…how quiet she just knew she would be. There were a great many times Emma wished she could magically turn into someone else, like her sister Amy maybe, or even Emma Katherine. So often, she wished she could be more like both of them, carefree, outgoing, confident…pretty. Ugh! But God seemed to have forgotten to gift her with anything useful, at least when it came to boys and…social settings.

Glancing to the right, Emma saw Doug and Stacey standing by a small table, and craning her neck, she saw bottles of alcohol and a few glasses on the table.

"Hey, Emma," Stacey said with a smile, as she turned toward her, "do you want something to drink?"

Something to drink, Emma thought blankly...yes, yes she was going to have something to drink. She refused to have her nerd-like traits exposed so early in her dating experience with Jacob. "Sure," she said, as she walked closer to the old, white table.

"What'll you have?" Stacey asked.

What indeed would she have, Emma speculated as she scanned the table and the glass in Stacey's hand.

"What are you having?" Emma asked.

Stacey held the clear, short glass up to the light, and said, "I'm having a little Vodka mixed with Sprite."

Trying to appear confident and cool, Emma smiled, and said, "I'll have the same thing."

"What's everyone want on their pizza?" Doug asked from across the room.

"Sausage and lots of cheese!" Jacob boomed.

"Girls...?" Doug asked.

"Fine with me," Stacey agreed.

"Me too," Emma smiled, and took a sip of her iced drink, trying not to grimace at the bitter taste.

After Doug ordered a couple of pizzas, he, Stacey and Jacob refilled their drinks, and headed toward the small living room to watch TV. Emma promised to be right with them. Looking down at the floor she realized, she didn't know Stacey and Doug, and really, how well did she know Jacob? She didn't belong, she fretted. They had all known each other their whole lives. What was she doing there, she wondered as she placed her hands on her hips and stared at the ceiling. Shaking her head, she looked down at the table crammed full of various bottles filled with alcohol...stuff she had never seen before.

Emma looked up when she heard Jacob say her name. "Emma, do you need another drink? Want something else?" he asked.

"Sure," she said, with a crooked smile.

"How 'bout," he said, as he moved bottles around, "rum? I'll see if they have any Coke, or Pepsi."

She watched as he opened the fridge and pulled out a can of Coke. Popping the tab, he added it to the brown liquid in the glass. After drinking half the concoction, Emma asked Jacob to direct her to the bathroom, and then she walked unsteadily toward it.

The last thing Emma remembered about her date was nibbling on a piece of pizza and then, with her mind in a fog, she was throwing it right back up. She had no recollection of just how many drinks she'd had, or even what she had drunk, or even if she had made it to the living room to watch TV. Later, as Jacob drove her home, Emma pressed her cheek against the cold window, praying she wouldn't throw up all over his car.

"Okay, this is what we're gonna say," he instructed her, as they sat in his car in front of the Rhodes' house. You just ate some bad pizza. Okay?" he asked, trying to get a response out of her.

Emma shook her head up and down and wondered, had it been bad pizza, feeling like she might puke again. Jacob had pulled over several times—on what had seemed like an endless drive home to Emma—so she could puke on the side of the road and not in his car. It felt like she had the worst flu ever.

Mrs. Rhodes was waiting for them in the kitchen. The lights were too bright and it felt as if the floor was moving beneath her, Emma agonized, as she looked up at the clock. Eleven, it read. She was home awfully early for a Saturday night, and realized Mrs. Rhodes probably wondered why she was home so early.

"You're white as a sheet," Mrs. Rhodes said in a surprised voice.

"I think she ate some bad pizza," Jacob shared.

"Pizza, huh." Mrs. Rhodes said skeptically.

Emma weaved on her feet, feeling as if she might topple over. Lurching forward, she banged her hip on the kitchen counter, grateful for something to hold her up.

"Well, you should get on to bed," Emma heard Mrs. Rhodes say through the thick fog in her head.

"I'll see you later, Emma," Jacob said softly

"Bye," she mouthed.

"Get on to bed," Mrs. Rhodes repeated.

Praying to God for a miracle, to *please don't let me throw up...* Emma stumbled as gracefully as she could to her bedroom and fell onto her bed. Kicking her shoes off, she pulled the covers over her head and kept praying to the *Don't Let Me Puke God* for another hour, as the room spun dizzily.

Riding in the back of the station wagon the next morning, Emma was sure little people had somehow climbed into her head the night before and were now chipping away inside with little axes. All she wanted to do was lie down and hold her pounding head, but instead, she sat through an extra long Sunday school class and then church service.

*Dear God, she vowed, I will never, ever, ever drink again....*and meant it.

"Emma *Katherine!*" Mrs. Rhodes snapped. "Stop slamming your door!"

"Oh sure! Yell at me for slamming a door, but don't yell at Emma Claire for coming home drunk!" Emma Katherine asserted.

"Emma Katherine!" Mrs. Rhodes chided sharply.

If there had been a rock big enough, and if she had been strong enough to lift it, Emma would have crawled under it. Emma Katherine was right, her mom *hadn't* yelled at her and she should have. It hadn't been bad pizza that had made her throw up...it had been everything, whatever that was, that she had drunk last night. She deserved to be yelled at, way more than Emma Katherine had been for slamming her car door. As she walked miserably to her bedroom, she thought, *Emma, you idiot, you have fucked up royally this time. You juuuussst can't seem to stop fucking up, can you?* She crawled under her blankets and spent the rest of the day, miserable in bed.

The next day, Emma had to face Stacey, Jacob, and Doug at school. She was mortified that she had thrown up in front of people she didn't know very well, cool kids, actually anyone for that matter. She had to force herself to walk into the school building, feeling eyes on her, hearing snickers. The entire school knew! It was one of the drawbacks of a small school, she stressed. In almost every class, one kid or another teased her about the big puke fest at Doug's sister's house. They had all the gory details, about how much she had drunk, the pizza she had thrown up, all in explicit detail—filling in much of what she couldn't remember herself.

Strange, Emma realized, they weren't really making fun of her… more, in a weird way, she felt they were accepting her, and Emma Katherine was still talking to her too, joking along with everyone else. It was okay, Emma realized. And she had a funny feeling that Mrs. Rhodes knew she had learned her lesson about drinking…just how awful it could be. Mrs. Rhodes hadn't felt sorry for her one bit, instead, she had made Emma get up with the rest of the family and go to Sunday school, pounding headache and all. Emma vowed never to drink again. It was one more thing she didn't know how to do right, knowing that throwing up could not be the goal. Drinking had been something she had done to cover up her fear and embarrassment of not feeling like she fit in, but she knew she was just going to have to figure out a different way of dealing with her fear, because she loathed throwing up!

22

Thankful to put the winter behind her—including the mortifying puking incident—Emma was ready for spring. One sunny, windy, March afternoon, Emma waited with Mrs. Rhodes in the kitchen for Jacob to pick her up to take her to dinner for her birthday...*on a school night.* Mrs. Rhodes must be slipping, Emma thought with a grin as she looked at her foster mother.

Jacob had called her the night before and asked her if she could go out to eat with him after school for her birthday. "Um. It's a school night," Emma had pointed out in surprise. She had insisted that, no, she could not. Clearly, he knew that Saturday was date night, or sometimes they switched nights and Friday night was date night. But *never* was date night allowed during the week, on a school night!

That morning, in honor of her seventeenth birthday, Emma had carefully selected an outfit to celebrate the occasion. Emma Katherine had generously loaned Emma her fitted, red painter's pants, and a white blouse, and thin gold colored belt. She had paired the ensemble with a white turtleneck, and brown clogs with little buckles on the side. Looking at her reflection in the mirror, Emma had felt very grown up.

Standing in the kitchen waiting for Jacob to arrive, with a curious grin, Emma pointed out to Mrs. Rhodes, "You do realize it's a week night, don't you?"

"Yeah, I know," Mrs. Rhodes, said mischievously.

Oh, Emma thought, as she squinted her eyes, and smiled. Those two were up to something. But what? Out on a school night. *Who did such things…well, not in this house!* It was a very clear rule in the Rhodes' house—no dates during the school week. So what the heck was Mrs. Rhodes grinning about—letting her go out tonight. It was a world gone mad! Emma and Jacob had been friends for six months, had been dating for over two, and today was her birthday, and he had planned a birthday surprise for her, and from the look on her foster mother's face, she was in on the surprise.

Emma wondered where Jacob was taking her to dinner—someplace special she was sure given the excited secrecy. Emma sat snuggled on the passenger seat of Jacob's car, her spot, as the countryside whizzed by—winter empty fields—as music streamed out of the special speakers he had installed. He loved singing along with the radio, loudly. That was Jacob, Emma thought as she looked at him with admiration and envy, so free and full of life! He looked handsome tonight, Emma smiled, as she admired his new dark blue jeans, fitted knit shirt with a collar, and tennis shoes. Not long ago, he had allowed her to tag along to the mall to buy a new wardrobe for him. Out had gone the old brown tasseled loafers, too big dress pants, and in had come some style, and over the last six months, he had shed at least forty pounds, she estimated.

They were so different, Emma considered; he with a tremendous amount of confidence; she with so little; he so carefree, and she still finding her way. The acceptance from the kids at school and unconditional love of the Rhodes family had helped provide the safe environment Emma needed to begin finding her way out of the depths she had tucked herself away. There had been no cruel taunts from any one of her peers. To Emma's confusion, it had been quite the opposite. At New Point High, she was treated as if she belonged, by her peers, teachers, principal, her new family, and even the parents of her peers. It had taken months for Emma to trust her new world, trust that it would not one day just vanish as things and people tended to do in her life. She laughed often now, and was one of the goofy kids in many of her classes, no longer fearing that anyone was watching her just waiting to make fun of her, to humiliate and hurt her.

As she glanced at Jacob she wondered, as she so often did, how he had grown so confident, to be the boy that feared nothing and was loved by so many...and she knew the answer. It was his family. Sometimes date night had consisted of grabbing fast food and then heading over to his parent's house to cuddle on the couch as they watched a movie or football on TV. Emma had felt instantly comfortable with Jacob's parents, Virginia and Brent Garner, with their easy laughs and warm smiles. They had asked Emma to call them by their first names, which seemed strange to Emma and a little disrespectful, but she knew it was a reflection of the warm people they were and their effort to place her at ease. Their home felt like a second home to her, a place of acceptance.

Jacob looked like a much taller and bigger version of his tiny mother, and had the same bundle of fun loving energy. Where Jacob and his mom had dark complexions, and dark colored hair, his dad was fair, and had what looked like blonde hair with a bit of red sprinkled in. They were a stunning couple—regal—yet never making her feel less than they were. Jacob's dad owned a business in town, and his mom had always been a housewife and stay at home mom, taking care of Jacob and his two older sisters—until his sisters graduated from high school and moved into homes of their own. As a business owner's wife, Virginia's life was not that of a typical housewife; in many ways she was her husband's partner, and not just in their marriage.

Jacob and Emma had gotten into a comfortable routine with each other. Sometimes, if he wasn't scheduled to work at the gas station, he would give her a ride home after school. He respected the house rules, which were no boys allowed at the Rhodes' home without a parent present. Emma loved the structure and house rules, loved to fall back on them and did often. Getting too close to any boy, Jacob included, scared the hell out of her, and the one night a weekend date night, and no boys in the house rule, minimized any difficult situation that she might not want or know how to handle. For too long, Emma had been forced to deal with avoiding men's hands. With Jacob, for now, she just wasn't ready to deal with it—sex—and he hadn't pushed the issue. The fact that he had only kissed her, and nothing else, had Emma feeling safe with him. She trusted him. Her boyfriend, built like a football player, was gentle, sweet and funny…and he made her feel safe.

They had turned right out of the Rhodes' driveway, which Emma knew meant that they were going toward the mall, away from the town of New Point. The Rhodes' house sat high on a hill in the middle of the country, with fields as far as the eye could see on all sides of the house, even across the road. The small town of New Point was five miles south of the Rhodes' house, and if you kept driving through town, and continued south, you'd run into the town of Largo, with a population of approximately fifteen thousand people, offering much more as far as entertainment and shopping were concerned. If you drove north from the Rhodes' house, through the country, you'd run into a town of about twenty thousand people, and that was where the mall was that kids from New Point hung out at. As Emma watched, she saw Jacob turn right… toward the mall. Hmmm, she considered. Typically, if it was dinner, they headed toward Largo. She was curious to know where was he taking her to eat. It must be somewhere pretty special, she realized.

A half an hour later, driving through town, Emma wondered if they were actually going to eat at the mall, becoming more curious with the passing of every block. He was pulling into the mall parking lot, she realized, surprised, as she scanned her memory for all the restaurants at the mall. Fancy did not come to mind.

"Are you ready?" he asked, a grin spreading from ear to ear.

"Yeah…" she said with a crooked grin. She guessed they were eating at the mall. She didn't want to hurt his feelings, but she was kind of disappointed that they were eating dinner at the mall for her birthday, so instead she pretended it was the best idea since…well, she didn't know when, but went along with it. After all, he had gone out of his way to convince Mrs. Rhodes to let her go out on a school night. That was pretty special in itself, she thought with an appreciative smile.

Emma walked with her hand clasped in Jacob's hand, and with her free hand, she pulled her jacket closer. It might be spring, she thought, but the Indiana wind could whip up quite the chill. Tilting her head up, Emma squinted her eyes in the bright sunshine, and asked, "Are we eating at one of the restaurants in the mall?

"I have to pick something up first," he beamed.

It was probably an errand for his mom, Emma suspected. He had a very close relationship with both his mom and dad, but he was especially close to his mom. Jacob towered over his mom, yet, he was still her baby. Emma saw the love sparkle in his mother's eyes when she talked and laughed with him…and his mom was sharing her son—their lives—with her, a foster kid. She loved being in their home, playing cards, watching movies, or just talking. They laughed a lot, she had noticed. It was a happy place. She loved that Jacob shared his special time with his family, even now, running an errand for his mother.

They took the escalator to the second floor and walked passed various shops, and finally Jacob led her into a jewelry store. Hmmm, she considered. It wasn't his mother's birthday, or mother's day.

Jacob turned toward Emma, and smiling down at her said, "I'd like to buy you a sweetheart ring for your birthday."

The surprise of his announcement took her breath away. When she finally found her voice, she grinned, and looking up into his puppy eyes, said, "Oh my, gosh!" Placing her hand to her heart she continued to look up at him, her eyes sparkling with surprise and love.

"It's kind of like a pre-engagement ring," Jacob said, knowing Emma wasn't like most girls. There was a chance she wouldn't understand the significance of the ring he wanted to give her, and he was correct, she had no idea what a sweetheart ring was. "I love you," he said sweetly, as he leaned toward her and kissed her gently on her lips. It was a kiss of tenderness and promise, born of new, young love.

"Jacob," she said, "I love you too."

For a half an hour, Jacob encouraged her to be sure to choose the ring that should be hers, the one that shouted out her name. And then there it was; a silver heart ring with a diamond nestled safely in its center called her name. It was the most perfect, beautiful ring, and gesture of someone's love that Emma had ever seen and worn. When she tried it on, it was as if it had known she would arrive for it that day. She wiggled the ring onto her ring finger. It fit perfectly…it was meant to be hers.

"Well let me see it!" Mrs. Rhodes said in an excited voice, an hour and a half later when Emma walked into the kitchen.

Happiness glinted in Emma's eyes as she looked at her foster mother in surprise, her mouth open wide, and exclaimed, "You knew! You knew where he was taking me!"

"Well, of course I did," Mrs. Rhodes, laughed. "You don't think I'd just let you go out on a date on a school night without a real good reason, do you?"

Emma laughed until tears sprang to her eyes. Then she placed her hand in Mrs. Rhode's hand so she could examine her new ring. As Mrs. Rhodes looked down at the ring, Emma watched her, feeling such love for the amazing woman God had placed in her life to care for her, to believe in her, and keep her safe. Emma wished she was the kind of girl that could just let go, could open up and tell her foster mother how much she loved her for not throwing her away. Emma had arrived at the Rhodes' home broken, believing that no one would or could ever truly love her, or want her, but every time she had pushed the Rhodes family away, they had held on. When she had runaway, when she had gotten suspended from the basketball team, and from school, and even the horrible things she had said…they hadn't thrown her away. She wished she could tell her…

"It sure is sparkly," Mrs. Rhodes said with a smile.

23

"You ready?" Mrs. Rhodes asked Emma.

"Sure!" Emma responded with a nervous grin.

It was the big day—the most highly anticipated day in a teen's life—driver's test day! When school had resumed in January after Christmas break, Emma had been excited for her class schedule change, and one of the most exciting—although scary—classes had been Driver's Ed. After passing the classroom portion of the class, Emma had quite nervously joined two other kids—sophomores—for the on-the-road portion of the class. Her very first time behind the wheel of a car was with her Driver's Ed instructor—her basketball coach—Mr. Richardson, the best possible teacher. He was laid back, and even cracked jokes during her nerveracking turn driving. She felt that every time she got behind the wheel, she was tempting fate with three other people in the car, any moment a possibility that she could careen the car off the road. Of course, the damage to the vehicle and occupants might be slight considering Emma was so scared to drive that she couldn't press the accelerator beyond thirtyfive miles an hour. Driving, so far, had been a white-knuckle, steering wheel gripping, slow driving experience for her.

After signing Emma out in the school's office so she could take her driver's test, Mrs. Rhodes smiled, and asked, "Do you have your permit with you?"

"Here!" Emma said, waving the paper in the air.

"Good! Cause you're driving to town," her foster mother declared.

Round eyed, Emma followed Mrs. Rhodes to the station wagon, and using the opportunity as a driver's test dress rehearsal, commenced the driving procedure by checking her tires, and mirrors.

Hours later, Emma sat on the passenger seat with tears burning her eyes, and no driver's license in her purse. Her primary drive time had been during class at school, and she hadn't felt terribly confident driving then, but she had hoped she'd be able to pass the test. But she hadn't. She had totally screwed up the parallel parking portion of the test, and then made a big mistake when making a turn...she had not been in the turn lane when she had turned. The man had said turn, so she had! Now she was on the way back to school and when the kids asked to see her crummy license with her picture, she wouldn't have one to show them. She just knew she was the first kid in New Point High history that had failed their driver's test!

Mrs. Rhodes pulled her car up in front of the school, turned off the ignition, and then turned toward Emma and said, "Now listen, we'll try again in a few weeks. Okay...?"

"Oh my gosh," Emma cried, "I can't believe I failed! I bet I'm the only kid in school that has ever flunked the test!"

"Oh, I doubt that you're the first or will be the last person that has flunked a driver's test. You just need a little more practice, and then you'll pass. You'll see," Mrs. Rhodes assured Emma.

Emma exhaled tearfully.

"Are you going to be okay?" Mrs. Rhodes asked, concerned for her very distraught foster daughter.

"Yeah," Emma said miserably.

Emma opened the passenger door and climbed out of the car as her foster mother called out, "Don't let anyone upset you! Have a good day!"

She turned back toward the car, smiled, and waved. That woman, Emma thought—still smarting from flunking her test—sure made it difficult to be totally miserable. Walking up the sidewalk toward the school, Emma continued to think about how even during the crappy times, life wasn't quite as crappy with someone cheering you on. Opening the heavy school door, she smiled and walked toward the office to get a pass to excuse her tardiness for her next class.

Later, during the afternoon school assembly as Mr. Parker, the school's principal, paced slowly back and forth across the gym floor speaking to the student body and teachers, Emma shared with Jacob her failed attempt to get her driver's license.

"Don't worry about it," Jacob said with a smile. He grabbed Emma's hand in his and gave it a squeeze. "We'll just practice. I'll take you in my car, my much smaller car next time," he emphasized. "Taking a driver's test in a station wagon was probably not the best idea," he insisted.

Doubtfully, she said, "Sure. I'll ask Mrs. Rhodes if you can take me out driving."

"Let's go this Saturday. We'll go driving around town, practice your parking, and get you driving in some traffic. You actually need to practice driving in *Largo,* because that's the type of driving and traffic you're in during your test. I'll take you back to the office where you took the test...*after* you practice in some quiet neighborhoods," he assured her, "and you can get a feel for turn lanes and stuff."

"Okay," she smiled, knowing that it would probably help to drive in city traffic if she was going to pass the test. Practice driving in the small town of New Point had not helped her master what she needed for the test. Odds were, the instructor was not going to have her drive down Pole Cat Hill, one of the pieces of road she had to master during Driver's Ed class—a big hill in the middle of nowhere, near the town of New Point.

Saturday morning, Jacob arrived bright and early to pick Emma up for their driving date, and after the twenty-minute drive through the country, he found a quiet, seemingly deserted neighborhood in Largo. He pulled the Chevet over, shut off the car, and announced, "The car's yours!"

After they swapped seats, Jacob reviewed the workings of his car with her, and then they were off. While the town's people slept in, Emma and Jacob drove around town, practiced turning and parallel parking, even on a hill, until Emma felt comfortable. Finally…she was ready.

Several hours later, Emma ran into the Rhodes' kitchen shouting, "I got it! I got it!" as she waved her driver's license in the air.

"Well…" Mrs. Rhodes said with a grin, "I told you, you could do it. Let me see your picture."

Proudly, Emma handed her little plastic Driver's license to her foster mother.

"It's a pretty picture," Mrs. Rhodes said, just as proud as Emma, as she examined the license.

"I want to see!" Cassy cried, as Mrs. Rhodes handed her the plastic card.

"Well, let me see too!" Emma Katherine said, as she took the card from Cassy's fingers.

"Hey," Emma Katherine joked, "nice picture of my sweater!"

"Emma Katherine!" Mrs. Rhodes said, as Emma and Emma Katherine laughed.

Emma sat in the kitchen listening to Emma Katherine talk to her mom in animated tones about the upcoming prom. Over a week ago, her boyfriend Jordan had asked her to go with him. Of course they were going, Emma thought with a smile. *They were so sweet—he was so sweet—the kind of boy a girl should marry.* As she listened in on her foster mother and foster sister's conversation, she caught various pieces of what they said—a color for her dress, dress patterns, and what Jordan was going to wear. Emma Katherine had chosen a beautiful cornflower blue fabric for her dress, one of Emma's favorite colors. Mrs. Rhodes was excited and already planning the dress she was going to make for her. Emma knew it would be beautiful. She was an amazing woman—an expert at so many things. Mrs. Rhodes had a gift of doing just about anything that required creativity, whether it was baking, ceramics, or making clothes for her children. She had an eye for beauty and fashion. The tops she had made for Emma were better than anything she could buy in a store, and unique. Emma was so proud to wear her foster mother's creations. It seemed there was nothing Mrs. Rhodes could not do.

Sunday morning after church, Emma sat next to Jacob on the passenger seat as he drove her home. Sometimes Jacob would swing by on a Sunday morning and take Emma to church. After a late Saturday night date, it was a lot to ask of him because going to Emma's church required an extra early morning. The three families they had participated in Bible study with had grown into a house filled with people, and now in a large rented space. Their little Bible study group was officially meeting as a church group now, with over one hundred people. The congregation was growing so fast there were plans for a new, much larger building for services and even a space for a school. Emma loved her church and the families that attended. It was an extension of her foster family.

Before church service, Emma met in one of the small classrooms with a small group of teens her age to discuss all things spiritual, and even their personal daily struggles trying to live in a Godly fashion. It was tough as a teen to do the things you knew you should do, and not do the things you knew you shouldn't. So far, Emma and Jacob had steered clear of the taboo sexual things. He hadn't pushed her, and that was how Emma knew he loved her…that he really cared. She had never met a boy, and for that matter, many men, that hadn't persistently put the moves on her, and in most cases, left her terrified and fighting to save her virtue. Jacob was different.

Emma loved getting dressed up—any occasion to wear a dress—probably because of the years she'd had so little, and going to church was a great dress up occasion. She was wearing one of her favorite dresses this morning, a long, beige colored t-shirt dress with three dark brown leather covered buttons at the neck, and at the hemline of the dress. It was synched at her waist with a matching multiple string belt that hung almost as long as the knee length dress.

Emma sat with her legs crossed, smoothing the hem of her dress, covering her knees, when Jacob asked, "Do you want to go to prom?"

Her heart beat with excitement as she snapped her head around and said, "Sure! I mean…do you want to go?"

"It's my senior prom…my last prom, so I'd really like to go," he said, as he glanced over at her and offered her one of his beaming grins.

Oh my gosh, her thoughts swirled. She'd need a dress!! Excitedly she considered, she had shoes…but she wondered if Mrs. Rhodes would have time to make her a dress too…would she mind making a dress for her? It sure seemed like a lot of work.

It was going to be the best night ever! She just knew it. The junior class was responsible for planning the senior class prom and Emma's class was really smart. The entire class, which consisted of twenty kids, was kind of nerdy smart, but they didn't seem like nerds. She just got lucky she realized, that in this small town, all the kids were just—well—good. As a junior, Emma sat in on all the prom-planning meetings and knew exactly what the plans were going to be. They had a building rented, and decorations and party favors purchased—things for everyone to keep forever…and even had money left over. They were trying to find extras to buy just to get rid of the money. The junior class chose a beautiful, sparkly, silver and blue theme, with clouds and…*just heavenly.*

Jacob drove up the long gravel drive, and parked next to Mrs. Rhode's car. Emma tried to reign in her enthusiasm as she tiptoed to the door in her high heels.

"You look like your bursting," Mrs. Rhodes said a few minutes later.

"I'm going to prom!" Emma shouted excitedly, as Jacob stood grinning beside her.

"Well, guess I'd better buy some more fabric," Mrs. Rhodes laughed.

"You'll make me a dress?" Emma asked excitedly.

"Well, I guess," she said still smiling.

"You better get busy, mom," Emma Katherine said with a smile.

"I guess I had," Mrs. Rhodes said happily. "So what color do you want?"

"I don't know—Um—maybe something delicate…with sprinkles of tiny blue flowers," Emma considered thoughtfully. She was picturing a long flowing gown, with flowers like you'd find mixed in with blowing prairie grass. Sighing, she thought…beautiful.

"Well you know you're going to have to match your tux to Emma Claire's dress, Jacob. Maybe a light blue…" Mrs. Rhodes commented.

Emma's eyes lit up! She had never been to prom…the one she had *almost* gone to her freshman year just a vague memory. Jacob would be so handsome in a blue tux to match her dress, she grinned as she looked over at him sitting at the kitchen table.

"Oh, I'll be so perty," he chuckled.

"Yeah, you might be prettier than Emma Claire," Emma Katherine teased.

"Maybe she should buy *you* a corsage," Mrs. Rhode kidded.

Jacob placed his hand to his mouth, pretending to be a girl, and giggled.

"You'd be awfully pretty with pigtails," Emma grinned as she stood behind him, and pulled his thick hair into her hands, separating it into two large pigtails.

As he batted his long lashes at the two teen girls and Mrs. Rhodes, the room broke out in ear splitting laughter.

After Emma changed out of her dress and into jeans and a sweater, she invited Jacob upstairs to hang out in the common room off the girl's second floor bedroom. The girls' bedrooms were strictly off limits, and the rule enforced, but they *were* allowed in the common area, which was a controlled area where little mischief could be had since one of the girls was constantly breezing through. So far, Emma Katherine and Emma Claire were the only ones, besides Carmen, old enough to date, and the only ones with boys visiting the house.

Jacob sat in the black recliner near the bookshelf, with Emma snuggled on his lap sharing a few innocent kisses, as Cassy walked through the area, snickering. Emma looked up and smiled as Cassy disappeared into her bedroom. She was such a sweet, sensitive little girl, Emma knew. Cassy helped fill the gaping hole of the loss of her own sweet little sister, Laura.

Emma snuggled into Jacob's shoulder and he wrapped his arms around her and pulled her closer. He made her feel small, and feminine. Although Emma was a slight young girl, at five foot three and one hundred six pounds, what she saw in the mirror was someone different, someone ugly and fat. She liked having a boyfriend much taller and built like a football player. He made her feel tiny and safe, and in reality...she was exactly that.

Later that evening, after kisses and a long hug at the front door, Emma watched Jacob drive down the driveway, watching until he turned left out onto the country road. Sighing, she walked back into the kitchen, closing the door behind her.

"What are you sighing about?" Mrs. Rhodes asked playfully.

"Cause she was upstairs making out with her *boyfriend!*" Cassy teased.

"I was not!" Emma said, with an embarrassed laugh. "We were just snuggling."

"Sure is a funny way to snuggle with your mouth on his," Cassy grinned.

"Yeah—Yeah!" Emma said, as she rolled her eyes knowing Cassy was teasing in good fun. There had been a time, not long ago, that teasing hadn't been meant as fun, but had been cruel, meant to hurt her. But that was a long time ago...a different life. The Rhodes were different. They were teaching her how to laugh, how to joke, and know that everyone wasn't trying to hurt her...not anymore.

As she snuggled into the corner of the couch with the family in the family room, Emma sighed with contentment, thinking, *it had been the perfect day.*

24

The tall brunette slammed the bird across the net at Emma. "Did you get a dress for prom yet?" Tara grunted.

Emma ran for the bird, stretching her badminton racket in front of her. She flicked the bird over the net at her teammate, and exhaled, "Yeah! Mrs. Rhodes is almost done with mine."

Slamming the bird back over the net, Tara, grunted, "She's making you one?"

Running backward with her racket held high above her head, looking up to make sure her racket and the bird connected, Emma shouted, "Yeah!" and missed the bird entirely.

Tara was in Emma Katherine's grade, a sophomore. She, Emma Katherine, and Emma Claire, had been teammates on both New Point's JV and Varsity basketball teams. Now that basketball season was over, Tara had talked Emma into joining the high school's badminton team. At first, Emma hadn't been real keen on the idea, because just as with basketball, and even when she had joined the school's pom-pom squad, this was another new for her, never having played badminton before, except for whacking a bird around a little with a racket as a kid, but there had been no rules, and no net. She didn't want to make a fool of herself in front of all the kids in school, or the schools they would be competing against. But Tara had convinced her it would be oodles of fun, so here she was, practicing for their first match.

"Did you buy a dress yet?" Emma asked.

"I picked one up last weekend from the mall. I'm gonna go all princess-like," Tara joked with a silly grin.

Emma laughed and shook her head as she bent over and grabbed the bird she had missed, again. Snapping the tip of her racket on the wooden gym floor, she tossed the bird at Tara. God, she sucked at badminton, she thought as she sighed. Tara was yet another class clown, or should she say, school clown, Emma thought, as she ducked under the net joining Tara on her side of the court.

"What are you and Jacob doing this weekend?" Tara asked.

"Seeing either a movie at the mall, or a movie at his house," Emma commented, as the girls placed their rackets in the rack with the others. "How 'bout you?" she asked.

"Probably hanging out with Deena. Just hang out and see what kind of trouble we can get into. You should come out some time," Tara offered.

Emma thought about Tara's invitation, about going out with the girls some time. It would mean sacrificing a night with Jacob. Time with friends consisted of one night on the weekend—date night—which was typically Saturday night. Of course, she thought, it *would* be nice to go out with other couples. It would be a great way to get to know other kids better, to make more friends. But she didn't want to give up time with Jacob.

"Yeah, I'll have to do that," Emma agreed.

"Emma Claire, can you babysit for the Thompsons tonight?" Mrs. Rhodes asked as Emma walked around the corner into the kitchen.

She stopped abruptly, mentally scanning her Friday night plans, and then said, "Sure!" Emma never turned down a babysitting job—it was easy money. The Rhodes' girls seemed to be the prominent source of babysitting service for the town, and with Carmen away at college and Emma Katherine and Caitlyn busy lately, Emma had been picking up most of the jobs. The Thompsons' lived just down the road, five minutes away on the outskirts of town in a large two-story, white, old house with a wrap-around porch. Riding home from school, Emma always looked at the house that sat on a hill nestled beneath tall trees—on a sunny day, so inviting, and magical looking. But there were times when Emma was at the house babysitting—after the sun had gone down, when shadows crept into the corners of the house—that Emma was reminded of a different house, the house she had lived in when she was a little girl.

After putting the two children that she babysat to bed on the creepy second floor of the house, Emma would sit downstairs in the living room watching TV. The house would be quiet but for the voices coming from the television, the occasional branch brushing against the house, and creaking from settling floors. It was definitely not the best babysitting job after watching scary movies, like the movie she had watched about the girl babysitting in a creepy house, late at night, when the phone kept ringing and a voice on the other end whispered, *Have you checked the children.*

Shivering Emma said, "Yeah, that's fine. I can babysit tonight." Typically, Jacob worked or went out with his friends on Friday nights, which left babysitting, ceramics, or a book to pass Emma's evening. Sometimes she babysat for one of the teachers at the high school, her Biology teacher...a funny man. It was the easiest babysitting job of all time because his son rarely came out of his bedroom, and if he did, it was just for snacks. Their home was in the small town of New Point, in a small one-story house, with no creaking floors or branches brushing against the house...nothing to remind her of her dad's house, of the nightmares of her childhood.

Hours later, Emma Katherine slept soundly snuggled under the blankets on her bed as Emma Claire, lying across the room on her own bed, a blanket pulled tight to her chin, twitched in her sleep as she struggled to free herself from a nightmare, one that hadn't visited her in over a year. Emma's eyelids twitched and her head jerked. She could hear the footsteps, closer as she stopped mid-run and snapped her head back and forth looking for a place to hide. She darted to the right, between what looked like giant bolts of fabric secured to the scuffed, dark brown wooden floor. As she ran, wispy pieces of pastel colored cloth caught at her arms and brushed her cheek. Her heart was pounding in her ears so loud she feared whoever was trying to catch her would hear. She was panting from running and fear, as sweat trickled down her face. Her hair was soaked and matted to her cheeks and neck.

She could feel him closer now. She could hear him, his breath so close she could smell him. She stopped again, frantically looking for somewhere to hide but as she spun in a circle, she could see only color, and cloth, everywhere the color. She looked up, up as high and as far as she could see, up toward the heavens. No matter how far and how fast she ran, she couldn't get out of the forest of flowing fabric. As the faint breeze blew, the wisps of gauzy fabric, like the sheer scarves women wore on their heads to keep their hair neat on a windy day, blurred together.

Emma caught a sheer baby blue fabric as it lifted in the breeze feeling the softness, looking at how delicate it was. A magical breeze blew through the fabric forest, but it had no impact on her hot sweat-soaked body. She turned her head, looking back the way she had run moments before. Colors of sheer blue, varying shades of green, orange, red, and yellow were lifting slowly, hypnotically up in the air. The colors swirled toward Emma, and as she looked down at a soft yellow, it caressed her hand. Her head snapped up as the sound of pounding footsteps became louder, and she sprinted to the right, past another bolt of blue.

Carefully, Emma draped the gown over one arm, and felt the rough fabric with the tips of her fingers. Beautiful, Emma admired. Somehow, Mrs. Rhodes had managed to create exactly what Emma had envisioned. She had managed to find fabric with a white background patterned with tiny bouquets of baby blue, yellow, and pink flowers, sprinkled about. A formal gown, Mrs. Rhodes had designed the dress with narrow straps instead of sleeves. There was a generous ruffle framing the bottom, with a baby blue satin strip separating the ruffle from the base of the dress, then, at the waist, another ribbon. It was the most beautiful gown Emma had ever seen or touched, and it was hers to wear to her prom. But Mrs. Rhodes had yet another surprise for her; a wrap made of the same fabric, framed with lace, and a satin ribbon that synched at the waist.

"It's beautiful," Emma said in awe. "It's just beautiful. Thank you." Emma looked up into Mrs. Rhodes face to see her smiling self-consciously at her. She looked embarrassed, Emma thought in wonder. Mrs. Rhodes was one of the most amazing women she had ever known—gifted—and yet she didn't brag or anything. Instead, she was constantly brushing away the things she could do, saying things like, "It's not me. It's just the gifts God gave me."

Emma had taken a scrap of fabric with her to help Jacob select his tux, a little darker color than baby blue, with navy accents, and a bow tie to match. His white ruffled shirt would be a nice accent to the lace on Emma's wrap. Emma pictured the two of them walking into the dance, and sighed, knowing they were going to be beautiful.

25

"You're beautiful!" Emma said sincerely, as Emma Katherine stood next to her boyfriend Jordan. Emma was standing out of the way, watching Mrs. Rhodes snap pictures of the couple posed in front of the fireplace in the family room. Emma Katherine was beautiful, wearing her spaghetti strapped, cornflower blue gown with her almost black hair resting just below her shoulders. The dress was the perfect color choice for Emma Katherine's coloring. They were so sweet, Emma thought with a smile, and if she didn't know better, she would think Emma Katherine and Jordan were brother and sister because their features were so similar.

They had all oohed and aahed over the wrist bouquet of flowers Jordan had given Emma Katherine. It was a lovely bouquet of white and blue flowers with a matching satin ribbon, which Emma Katherine had slipped over her wrist. Shyly, with a self-conscious grin, Jordan wrapped an arm around Emma Katherine as Mrs. Rhodes snapped another picture. For a moment, Emma thought of Amy, her older biological sister, and how their lives should have been. It had been difficult to accept that they would never share these kinds of moments, these memories with one another, nor would Emma share these moments with any of her biological brothers or sisters. They were living their lives separate from her, somewhere else, doing…who knew what at that very moment.

Emma stood inside the family room and watched through the bay window as Mrs. Rhodes snapped a few more pictures of the cute couple in front of Jordan's car, and then watched as they drove down the gravel drive. Smiling, Emma walked upstairs to her bedroom to finish getting ready. Jacob would be arriving in fifteen minutes and she still needed to put on her dress, shoes, and do a little last minute primping before her glorious evening began. He was taking her to dinner at a fancy restaurant before prom began. She hoped she didn't spill anything on her beautiful gown, she considered, as she stepped into her dress. Jacob had bought her a bib as a joke after their homecoming dance because she had dropped a big glop of pasta sauce on her top, in front of a table filled with their friends. Lasagna, she had noted was not an appropriate dinner selection when on a date. Unknown to Jacob, this evening she had already eaten, and would be having salad for dinner, something easy. No red messy stuff would be falling onto her beautiful gown, she thought with a smile as she smoothed her dress down her hips. Placing her hands on her hips, she twirled in a circle. I feel like a princess, she thought, and hugged her waist...*a princess.*

"Emma Claire!" Mrs. Rhodes called from the stairs. "Jacob's here!"

Holding the hem of her dress in her hand so she wouldn't fall or step on the delicate fabric, Emma walked carefully down the two stairs outside her bedroom, and then down the red carpeted stairs. She paused in front of the full-length mirror and turned looking at the back of her dress, then did a quick twirl facing the mirror again as Mrs. Rhodes and Jacob walked in and watched her.

"You look beautiful," Mrs. Rhodes said.

Emma looked up with a smile and said, "The dress is gorgeous! Thank you so much!"

"I wasn't talking about the dress—I was talking about the girl wearing the dress," her foster mother said.

Emma had a tough time accepting compliments. She didn't really know why, just that they made her squirm uncomfortably.

"Isn't she pretty, Jacob?" Mrs. Rhodes continued.

"She is darned perty," he exclaimed, in his goofy voice.

Grinning, her eyes sparkling, Emma looked at him, so handsome in his blue tux and said, as regally as she could, "Why thank you, sir."

"Come on you love birds," Mr. Rhodes smiled. "Let's get your picture taken."

Jacob giggled behind his hand as Emma dug her elbow into his ribs. She shrieked when he grabbed her around her waist. It wasn't that she didn't like being cuddled by Jacob, she did, but not in front of her foster parents. Pulling his hands down from her waist, she caught his hand in hers and followed her foster parents to the family room for pictures.

A half an hour later, Jacob held the door of his father's Lincoln as Emma carefully scooted onto the plush leather seat, clumsily pulling the bottom of her gown in with her. "Are you all in?" he asked with a grin.

Emma laughed at the silly production of hobbling to his car over the rocks in the driveway, then trying to figure out how to climb into the car, maintaining the fantasy that she was an elegant princess.

"I'm in!" she exclaimed, as she smoothed her dress down, sitting with as much pretend elegance as she could muster, thinking how fun it was to play dress up.

She glanced across at her prince as he slammed the door, and chuckled, "I feel like a blue penguin!"

"A very tall, cute, blue penguin," she laughed, not realizing how radiant she looked as she smiled at him.

Tilting her head down, she sniffed the corsage Jacob had given her. He had ordered a beautiful corsage, created to match her dress perfectly, with several white roses nestled against baby blue ribbons and white lace. Jacob had been horrified to find the beautiful white roses had yellowed over night in the freezer, not realizing his safekeeping, the freezer, would damage the petals. The once white petals of the roses were now an almost yellow color. It had been with mortification that Jacob had presented her with the corsage, explaining how his stupid mistake of placing the corsage in the freezer had ruined it, turning it yellow. What he didn't realize was just how much she had loved the corsage. It didn't matter what color the flowers were. What mattered was how much thought and care he had put into planning the evening. That he cared enough to try so hard to give her the perfect evening, and the perfectly beautiful corsage, she thought as she sniffed again, inhaling the scent of the roses pinned to her gown. Emma wore the lovely smelling corsage with pride.

As the song *Stairway to Heaven* streamed through the beautifully decorated hall, Emma wrapped her arms around Jacob's neck, and snuggled into him as his arms wrapped around her waist, pulling her close. It had been a magical evening, beginning with long photo sessions, first at Emma's foster parent's home and then at Jacob's home. After picture taking had ended, they had scrambled to get to the restaurant and eat dinner as quickly as possible so they would make it to prom on time. Then, they had more pictures taken, this time at prom amidst silver moons, stars, and steamers. The hall was decorated beautifully, with tables covered with white tablecloths, and adorned with tall hurricane glasses inscribed with the prom's theme and date, one for each guest to keep forever. The day before, Emma and the rest of the junior class had hung shiny silver and blue streamers, moons, and stars. They had converted the hall into a magical place of promise and dreams.

Doug and his girlfriend, Stacey, had saved two seats for them at their table, and the evening had passed with a great deal of loud laughing, dancing, and memory making.

"You guys going to any after-hours parties?" Doug asked.

Emma looked across the table at Jacob's best friend, Doug, his arm draped casually across the back of Stacey's chair. They were such a beautiful couple, both with blonde hair, he the high school star athlete in basketball and baseball, and she, the darling of the girls' basketball team and cheerleader. They were the *it* couple of New Point High. Stacey, a junior like Emma, had grace and etiquette—she had it all, Emma thought. Emma admired girls like Stacey, knowing that time was not on her side to learn all she needed to be like them. It just seemed as if there would always be a great divide between foster girls and girls like Stacey.

"I'm not sure yet," Jacob said.

"Emma, like Emma Katherine, had been granted an extended curfew, but even so, church was still an expectation in the morning. She planned to be awake all night, church or no church. It would be fun telling her friends at church about her night!

Were they going to an after-hour's party, Emma wondered? Jacob hadn't mentioned where they might go. She had assumed they'd end up at a party or two, like most of the other kids. Jordan and Emma Katherine were going to an after prom party. Emma Katherine had shared the details with her. They were going to a friend's house after prom, along with a bunch of other kids, where they would be playing cards, charades, baking, and the parents were making pizza for them. It was going to be a blast! Emma hoped Jacob had a similar evening planned for her. There was nothing she'd like better than to get to know some kids better from school, and to play some games until it was time for church. Nothing would be more fun, she thought, as she watched girls—princess' for the evening—dressed in beautiful gowns, and boys so handsome in their tuxes, dance amongst the shimmering streamers on the dance floor.

Emma glanced down at the watch strapped to her wrist. Fifteen minutes and her first prom would be over, she sighed. It had been everything she had imagined, with fancy gowns, dancing, boys acting like gentlemen, well…most of the time when they weren't being goofy, she smiled.

"You 'bout ready to get out of here?" Jacob asked, leaning close to her so she would hear him over the pounding base of the music.

She nodded, wondering where they were going next. The plan was to stop at Jacob's house to change into their after prom clothes. Emma was almost as excited about her after prom outfit and party as she had been about prom. For the past month, Emma had saved her babysitting money and had bought a pair of jeans, a light green color, and a soft, fuzzy green top with hunter green accents to wear to the after-hours parties.

Thirty minutes later, Emma was smiling at her reflection in the guest bathroom mirror at Jacob's parent's home. Standing on her toes, she pivoted on her heel, looking over her shoulder at the back of her jeans. Cocking her head, she grinned at her reflection and wondered, too much green, wondering if perhaps she looked like some green kind of creature, like maybe a frog. Smoothing the soft green top down in place, she gave herself one more look over, and then smoothing her hair in place with her hand, quietly entered the hall. She was ready for the after-hour's parties!

Guided by the light over the kitchen sink, Emma found her way back to the family room, and Jacob. Stepping down the two steps into the family room, a room that at one time had been a garage, Emma smiled when she saw Jacob, now in jeans and a shirt, lying on his back on the couch, his arm draped across his forehead, and his eyes closed. Poor guy, she thought. He had put in a full day already, working an eight-hour shift at the gas station. Tiptoeing, she crept across the room and gently sat next to him, then shyly brushed his lips with her own. Peeking beneath his long black lashes, Jacob reached his arm toward her and pressed his hand against the small of her back, pulling her gently toward him. Their lips met, gently at first, and then teasing.

Emma pulled back and smiled down at her sleepy boyfriend, and he smiled back. Chuckling she commented, "You're exhausted."

"I'm alright," he insisted weakly.

Shaking her head, with a good nature smile, she said, "You don't really want to go out, do you?"

"No...no...I'm fine," he insisted, as he sat up and ran a hand across his eyes.

"We don't have to go anywhere," she said softly. It had already been a beautiful night surpassing her most beautiful dreams and expectations.

Whether the rest of the night was spent in a crowded house filled with loud kids, or in a cozily lit living room quietly snuggled next to Jacob on his parent's couch, didn't matter to Emma. It had been a day, and evening forever printed on her memory. The day had meant more than just a dress up date with Jacob…so much more. Mrs. Rhodes and Emma Katherine had captured her in their web of excitement; the fitting for her gown; parents waiting downstairs as she dressed for her special night waiting to tell her how beautiful she was; belonging somewhere, and being part of a healthy, normal teen passage.

"Scoot over," she said gently.

He shimmied back against the couch, lying on his side, giving her room next to him and the small pillow to rest her head. Emma snuggled into him as he draped his arm around her waist. Their hands clasped together, Emma drew his hand to her chin, and together they spent the prom after-hours in one another's arms…sleeping.

26

In the mist of early morning, Emma had walked a few rows of the bean field across the road. One of the farmers from town owned the field across the road and then another down the road, and during alternating years, when the fields were planted with beans, the Rhodes' girls were offered the job of clearing the fields of weeds. It was hard, dirty, hot work. Hours were spent in the sweltering sun using a tool—a long sharp bladed flattened in order to cut and tug the root as low as possible attached to a long wooden handle, similar to a hoe, but with a sharp blade—to clear out the weeds. Now, sitting at the old worn table in the cool cramped space of the basement, a can of pop next to her, a cassette of Amy Grant playing softly in the background, and the tiny TV across the room sharing a soap opera drama, Emma worked on her soon to be masterpiece. The Rhodes' kids were upstairs, involved in whatever they did on hot summer afternoons, talking on the phone to friends, reading, or watching the same soap opera on the much larger TV in the family room.

With no air conditioning, the basement in the Rhodes' house was the perfect place to while away an afternoon on a hot summer day. Turning the ceramic soap dish in her hand—at least it would be a soap dish once she completed painting, glazing, and then firing it in the kiln—Emma considered the design possibilities. She intended to enter a few ceramic pieces in the art competition at the county fair in a few months and this was to be one of them. Such a simple piece, but she intended to use various paint and techniques to make it complex. It was a whimsical piece, a soap dish with pieces of a pretend beach sprinkled around the entire bottom edge. Emma was going to attempt to paint the shells along the bottom using rough textured paint to make them pop off the piece, in realistic shades of color, with shading for a realistic look. Then for the upper portion, the scooped out part where soap would one day rest, she planned to use a simple color and a gloss. Shiny and smooth meets rough, she speculated as she began painting a shell.

"Hey, Emma!" Cassy called from the head of the basement stairs. "Jacob's here!"

Jacob, Emma thought. He was supposed to be at work. Before going upstairs to see him, Emma put her paintbrush in water to soak, and made sure her masterpiece was in a safe dry place.

"Coming!" she called out.

Climbing the steep stairs, Emma was a little nervous. She didn't think Mrs. Rhodes would appreciate a boy dropping by when she wasn't at home. Her hand on the rail, she glanced down at her watch. Mrs. Rhodes had driven to town several hours ago to do her weekly grocery shopping. She shouldn't be much longer, Emma thought.

"Hey," Emma said with a smile, looking down at her boyfriend sitting at the kitchen table sipping on a can of pop. "I thought you had to work today."

"Got off early," he said on a belch.

"Gross!" Emma Katherine laughed.

"Thought I'd come by and see if you wanted to go for a ride!" he said with energy she wasn't feeling.

Emma looked down at him skeptically and said, "I don't think I can go. Mrs. Rhodes isn't home, so I can't ask if it's okay."

"Go ahead, Emma Claire!" Emma Katherine exclaimed. "I'll go for a ride if you don't want to go!"

Emma pursed her lips thinking, well, if Emma Katherine thinks it's okay then it must be okay.

"C'mon!" Jacob said excitedly, as he scrambled to his feet. "I've got a helmet you can wear."

Emma followed Emma Katherine and Jacob down the driveway where he had parked his blue motorcycle.

"I'll go first!" Emma Katherine said, as she jumped onto the back of the bike and wrapped her hands around Jacob's waist.

Jacob kicked the motorcycle into life, and laughing, they sped down the gravel drive and then down the country road.

Her hands on her hips, Emma watched the motorcycle become smaller and smaller and then watched Mrs. Rhodes station wagon become larger and larger as it came closer. Stepping onto the grass, Emma waved at her foster mother.

"How long's Jacob been here?" Mrs. Rhodes asked.

"About five minutes," Emma responded, as she grabbed a bag of groceries out of the car and followed her foster mother into the house.

"He came by to see if I could go for a ride," Emma said. "Can I?"

"Well, it looks like Emma Katherine is already on a ride," Mrs. Rhodes said, with her typical cheerful voice and grin.

Emma placed most of her weight on one leg and flung her hand to rest on her hip, and said with a grin, "Yeah! Can I go?"

"Yeah. You can go. Where you going?" Mrs. Rhodes asked, as Emma saw Jacob and Emma Katherine pull up in front of the house.

"I don't know. I'll go find out!" Emma said excitedly, and ran out the door.

"Where do you want to go?" Emma asked Jacob excitedly.

He slouched on the seat of the bike and ran a hand through his thick hair. "I don't know," he said with a grin. "Anywhere."

"How about the mall?" Emma asked with a brilliant grin. "I need a swim suit to walk beans in."

"A swim suit!" Jacob said, throwing his head back and belting out a laugh. Looking at her, he grinned. "You're going to walk beans in a bikini?" he asked hopefully.

"Yes!" she grinned. "Just who's going to see me out here?" she asked, sweeping her hand in the air.

"Uh—me...if I drive out here to see you," he laughed, as he looked into her eyes.

"Well I don't care if *you* see me in a bikini," she said, as she placed her hands lightly on his blue jean covered leg and batted her eyes to make him laugh.

"The mall it is!" he said, with another laugh.

"Let me run in and tell Mrs. Rhodes where we're going. Be right back!" she called over her shoulder, as she ran toward the house.

"Ready!" she shouted with a grin, as she ran toward Jacob. When she got to the bike, she swung her leg over, as if she were mounting a horse, then sat down and wrapped her arms tightly around Jacob's waist. "Woo Hoo!" she whooped.

The sun was warm on her face, and the warm wind blew her hair crazily around her head. She closed her eyes...feeling exhilarated! The stretch of country road the teens were on rarely experienced traffic, so the drive to the next large town where the mall was located was a serene, traffic-free one, just Jacob, Emma, with an occasional bug splattering their bodies.

A few mornings later, Emma, dressed in her new rust colored bikini with ties on the hips, walked through the field across the road chopping weeds down. It was eleven O'clock in the morning and the sun was already blazing hot. Pausing for a minute, she squinted up at the sun. Then, sweat trickling down between her shoulders blades, she walked to the end of the row, picked up her bottle of water with her grimy hand, and tried to drink away some of the heat. At this rate, she thought, the fields should be weed free by next summer. Placing the cap back on the bottle, she shook her head as she looked back down the row she had just walked, and swore the weeds had grown already, replacing the ones she had just cut out.

Walking beans was hot ass work—literally—Emma thought, as she left the field behind and walked across the road back toward the house ready to wash the dirt off. She was relieved the field was finally cleared of weeds. Caitlyn had been her occasional weeding partner for the last few weeks—welcomed company during the long hot days. Although she was right across the road from the house, it had still been kind of creepy to be in the middle of a bean field by herself. And joking around with someone made the day pass faster, and if she saw a snake, which she hadn't so far, she'd have someone to hear her when she screamed and bolted out of the field.

After dinner that evening, Emma was collapsed at one end of the couch watching TV in the family room. Caitlyn was lying at the other end of the couch; Carmen cozy on Mr. Rhodes' recliner, and Emma Katherine was propped on a pillow by the fireplace, when Mrs. Rhodes walked into the room.

"Mr. Porter called a little while ago. He's got one more field he needs to get done, but he needs it done fast. So...who wants to do it?" Mrs. Rhodes asked, as she looked around at the lazy group of girls.

Groaning met Mrs. Rhodes' ears, and then Emma said, "I'll do it!"

"Well, actually, he kind of needs you all to do it because he needs it done in two days. It's getting to the point he needs those weeds out or it's going to hurt his crop. The weeds are bigger in some areas of the field than the beans, and at this time of the season that shouldn't be happening," Mrs. Rhodes shared.

That could be cool, Emma thought, having them all walk a field.

"I'll do it!" Carmen said, "and so will Emma Katherine and Caitlyn!"

"Awe!" Caitlyn grumbled.

"Stop your whining," Carmen laughed. "What else you got going on!?"

189

"I don't want to walk beans this summer," Emma Katherine insisted, as Carmen and Mrs. Rhodes left the room.

Well, Emma thought, they were all walking beans!

As Emma walked through the kitchen later that night, Carmen called after her, "We're going to be in the field by six tomorrow morning."

She stopped in her tracks and spun around, and with a grimace of disbelief on her face she asked, "Did you just say…*six*…in the morning? You want to walk beans at *six* in the morning? I'm not even out of bed at that time of the day!"

Emma Katherine and Caitlyn began grumbling too.

"Hey!" Carmen shouted. "If you're riding with me tomorrow, be in the car at six tomorrow morning. It's going to be over ninety degrees tomorrow afternoon so I want to be out of the field before noon!"

Sighing, Emma continued on to her bedroom, silently swearing at Carmen as she did so. Six in the morning, who the hell got out of bed at that time of the day…during the summer?! She did…that's who, she thought in annoyance as she climbed the stairs.

The next morning, Emma drug herself out of bed at five thirty feeling as if she hadn't slept a wink. The loud booms of thunder and cracks of lightening from the thunderstorm had woken her after two O'clock. Finally, at three thirty, she had fallen back asleep. She hated storms…she had since her tornado experience. When she was in eighth grade, Emma and her sister Katie had lived in a foster home together, and one evening their foster parents had left them home alone during a bad thunderstorm. It had been a shock when what seemed to be at the height of the storm their foster parents had announced that they were leaving…and they weren't taking them with them. A half hour later, Emma realized that the height of the storm hadn't arrived, and it wasn't just a thunderstorm…a tornado was on the way. As trees fell down around the two-story house with the elaborate staircase and large windows, and roofs blew off the houses next door, and across the street, Katie tried to find a safe place for them to hide. The noise had been deafening, terrifying

Emma. Since that storm, Emma had been made aware of just how dangerous thunderstorms could be.

Emma, dressed in jeans and a long sleeve shirt with her swimsuit beneath, stood at the edge of the large weed infested bean field with the left over water standing in the rows from last night's storm. Gross, she thought with distaste.

"Spread out!" Carmen shouted. "Let's get going. I want this field done before it gets too hot out!"

Examining what seemed to be an endless bean field, Emma noticed a beautiful purple clover patch that extended—she counted—eight rows wide, in the center. There are no beans in that mess, she thought, as she began ripping tall weeds out of the ground, her shoes already soaked and heavy with clumps of mud. She stopped at the clover patch and looked at all the bumblebees swarming, and then looked up at her foster sisters now half way into the patch, bees all around them. Leaning against her pole, Emma thought, as she shook her head and swatted away a bee, they're nuts, and walked back down the row. Let *them* get stung she thought. *I can't walk through that shit!*

"Where're you going?" Carmen shouted.

"I'm not walking through those bees, and it's just all weeds anyway. There are no beans in there!" Emma shouted back, as she entered a row several rows beyond the clover-infested rows.

As she clomped through the muddy mess, the air thick with humidity and biting flies, Emma kept telling herself, *just think of the paycheck you'll be putting in the bank...and thank God, this is the last field!*

27

Emma stood swaying and clapping her hands to the beat of the gospel music. She looked around the large room that had two seating sections with an aisle down the center and a stage, the focal point, where the worship leaders were playing guitars, tambourines, and a piano, and were belting out the best Christian music she had ever heard in a church. Singing her spiritual heart out, Emma watched the woman with short blonde hair on the stage lead the congregation in celebration of God. Light filtered behind her from the almost wall-to-wall window covered by white curtains and adorned at either end by lush green ferns. A glow surrounded the woman, created possibly by the light of the window, or Emma suspected, by God's light shining inside of her.

The church of several hundred members had begun six months ago with just a handful of families, one of which had been the Rhodes family—as a Bible study group in a home in the country. Emma peeked behind her and smiled back at a woman that smiled at her, and then continued to scan the room and the people in it. It was so cool, she thought as a warm feeling enveloped her, to be part of a baby church—a part of its growth. She knew she wasn't one of the adults or a leader or anything like that, but still, she was part of something, something that had included her in its very beginning. That was something she couldn't say about most things in her life, having so few roots. But this, she thought as she turned her attention to the pastor that was telling everyone to be seated, was a beginning…a foundation.

Seated on the folding chair, knees crossed and skirt smoothed over her knees, Emma hunched over in prayer, and then listened to the weekly announcements, one in particular catching her attention. Church Camp. Emma's thoughts travelled to a time years ago when her stepmother had allowed her to attend a weeklong church camp. At the time, when Emma had still been living with her dad—her stepmother had still lived with them—she had been maybe eleven or twelve years old. She had been so excited to go away for an entire week, and fantasized that her family would forget her, and she could live with the nice people at the camp forever, never to feel beatings or any of the other bad things ever again. Sighing, Emma thought, but they *had* come for her, and over the next few years the abuse had gotten much worse for her.

The church camp she had attended as a young girl had been within an hour from her dad's house. Now as she listened to the pastor give the details, she realized this camp was different. This camp would be for an entire week, but the real exciting part was that it would be on a college campus in Michigan. Oh how she would love to go, she thought, but doubted it would be possible. Who would pay for it, she considered. The Rhodes had done so much for her already, but with five kids of their own, there would be no way they could afford to send her, and besides, she'd kind of be afraid to go with people she didn't know that well. She knew all the adults and kids at church, but for some reason, no matter where she went she felt like an outsider. God, she prayed as she looked up at the ceiling, *if only I could get rid of that feeling or whatever is wrong with me…and feel like I belong somewhere…to someone.*

It looks great, Emma thought, pleased with her handiwork. She had completed a couple of ceramic pieces she would be entering at the county fair. Shaking her head, carefully she placed the shell adorned soap dish back on the table in front of her. I'll never win, she thought, but how cool that I get to enter something in the fair! Never in her wildest dreams had

Emma thought she'd be entering anything in a fair, and bonus…she had a family that was going to have a booth! In addition to teaching ceramic classes, Mrs. Rhodes spent hours creating beautiful pieces to sell at the fair. Mr. Rhodes had stuff he was selling at their booth too, wood working stuff, not junk, but fancy things that he had created during the winter in his wood working shop. So basically, from what Emma had been told by Emma Katherine, they would get to spend a lot of time at the fair, hanging out at the booth, wandering around if they wanted, and then of course, they had to make sure they got their pieces they were entering in on time. The fair had a whole schedule of events; a demolition derby, horse show, beauty pageant, and what Emma was interested in, the craft and baked goods competitions. Mrs. Rhodes and Carmen were going to bake cakes, breads, and pies for the bakery competition. Of course, Emma thought, Mrs. Rhodes and Carmen would be winning lots of blue ribbons for their cakes! Pausing for a moment, a ghost of a smile playing around her lips, Emma looked across the room at nothing in particular and thought…it was like a Disney movie!

Standing in the Rhodes' living room, trying to peak behind Jacob to see what he had tucked in his hands behind his back, Emma asked curiously, "What do you have behind your back?"

"Now—now," he said with a goofy grin, as he looked down at Emma. "Give me a minute," then he turned away from her. Craning her neck, Emma tried to see what he was doing. Without warning, he jumped his six foot four frame around, and startled, she shrieked and then let loose a peal of laughter.

Smacking his arm she laughed, "You turd!"

He punched her arm lightly with something soft.

Emma looked down at his hands and saw maroon colored punching gloves, and grabbed them trying to yank them free from his hands.

"Hey!" she said in excitement. "I want to try them!"

He wiggled his hands free of the gloves, then stood behind her and helped her with them, lacing them for her. She gave him a quick jab to the stomach!

"Ouch!" he said, pretending it hurt, and then he scampered out of the room, returning just as quickly as he had left. He had brought another pair of gloves, Emma noticed with a grin, as he tucked one under his arm and shoved his hand in the other.

"Okay, now stand up straight," Jacob, instructed. "Then jab like this," he said, as he snapped his arm forward real quick, his face sheltered by his other gloved hand.

Snap! Emma's arm went. "How was that?" she asked seriously.

After about a half an hour of Jacob teaching Emma the art of defending herself, the lesson broke down into a giggly, half boxing, half wrestling match. Emma was giggling so hard, she could barely thrust her arm out to make contact with Jacob's gloves, and he was no better. She got one last jab in, then, exhausted, they collapsed on the couch in the room at the back of the house. She grabbed a handful of his thigh and pinched as he howled like a girl in a high-pitched scream causing Emma to laugh even harder. He wrestled her to the carpeted floor, and grabbed her leg, the soft part of her inner thigh and mercifully pinched lightly. Breathing hard, they climbed to their feet and collapsed onto the couch again.

"So you're going to a church camp?" Jacob asked, as he tried to catch his breath.

"Yeah," Emma said breathlessly, as she stared over at him slouched at the opposite end of the couch. She wondered what he thought of that, his girlfriend going off to Nerdville.

Mrs. Rhodes had talked to her the Sunday night after the announcement had been made about church camp, asking her if it was something she might like to do. Emma had responded that she knew it was awfully expensive and didn't think she'd be able to go, but thought it would be really cool. Mrs. Rhodes had managed to perform yet another miracle much to Emma's amazement. She had requested and received a voucher from her caseworker paying for her trip.

"I'm leaving next week," Emma said, as she tried to read his expression. Did he think she was a nerd for going to a church camp, she wondered. She hadn't really given it a lot of thought, but maybe kids her age didn't go to church camp. What if he broke up with her, she stressed.

Looking down at the floor, he shook his head and said, "Cool."

She wasn't sure if he really thought it was cool or was just saying the word, cool, but it didn't really matter, because she was going. Over a month ago, when her pastor had asked, as she did every Sunday, if there was anyone that wanted to come forward and accept God as their Lord and Savior, Emma had felt a warm presence wash over her, and knew that Sunday had been the day to walk forward. It was an experience she knew she would never forget. She had stood at the front of the room in front of the stage area—a glow from the window illuminating her—when the pastor had pressed the palm of her hand to Emma's forehead. Three other people had stood around her, one each side, and one at her back, laying their hands on her too. A warm wave had washed over Emma, taking her to a place where nothing hurt, and a brilliant light met her as she fell back. For a few moments, she had been gone from the small church in the town of Largo, Indiana. Too soon, Emma became aware of her surroundings, the light less brilliant now, and the wave that had engulfed her making her dizzy, receded, and she knew...her world would never be quite the same. *She* would never be the same. Carefully she had climbed to her feet making sure her heels did not catch on the hem of her dress. As she had walked back to her chair, Emma realized that nothing around her had changed, just some small something within herself. She knew she was still the same girl with all the same problems and insecurities, but somehow her heart felt more...open, and it scared her a little because she knew an open heart could be a hurt heart.

"It's going to be cool," Emma commented. "I'll be staying on a college campus somewhere in Michigan. Pretty laid back. I'm riding up in one of the parent's vans. Caitlyn's going too."

Jacob scooted over and rested his head on her lap. "What are you going to do while I'm gone," she asked, as she smiled down at him and ran her fingers through his hair.

"Oh," he said lazily, as he reached behind his head and placed his hand against her lower back, "hang out with Doug if he's around—work... sleep."

Leaning over, she kissed his lips gently, and then whispered, "Just try to stay out of trouble while I'm gone."

"Of course," he grinned.

28

Dropping her borrowed suitcase on the twin bed, Emma looked around the college dorm room with four beds. She sat down next to her bag, not sure what to do next. It had been a long drive, but not as miserable as she had anticipated. Her van mates had sung, and talked most of the way, with Emma happily joining in. Upon arrival, she had followed her group into a large lobby, just a big open space with couches, and chairs, similar to the kind at the children's home. The coordinators sorted out everyone's paperwork, assigning rooms, and roommates. And here she was…at church camp.

A few mornings later, way too early for Emma, she twisted, touched her toes, and stretched right along with about 50 other teens and adults. The first day Emma had arrived at camp, she had been given many forms to fill out, and one had been a list of her choice of daily activities—exercising had been one of the activities she had chosen. There was no pressure to attend the activities chosen. If the spirit moved her, they said, she could change her schedule for the day. It was just a way for them to have an idea how many people they could expect for various activities. So far, she had kept to her schedule, except for one afternoon she had opted out of hanging out at the pool for a few hours, choosing instead to just wander around. There were a few activities that were a must, the daily church service, which Emma wouldn't have missed, and meals, which she wouldn't have missed either.

The services were different from back home—the feel was different—which may have had something to do with the entire set up of being able to walk about an entire campus, walking past some activity or another that was going on a good part of the day. Emma loved being outdoors, and that could have something to do with her deep connect with her spirit that week, walking around campus—being outside in the sunshine. Just stopping and sitting on the grass or a bench, just watching, listening, thinking…praying soothed her soul. As she sat on the grass with the warm sun beaming down on her—knowing she was safe—she watched the other kids at camp walk by, play Frisbee, do some weird form of stretching or often she saw people praying with and for one another. All the while, nature mingled with it all, the white fluffy clouds in the sky, the breeze caressing her skin, and the birds singing her a lullaby. It was pure serenity—a time and place where Emma's thoughts were still. It was more a time of feeling than thinking, and she felt she wanted her life to be different somehow…have meaning, or…she wasn't sure. It was just a feeling that had begun to grow inside her.

One afternoon, Emma stood in the center of the church, her hands holding onto the wooden pew in front of her. She glanced over at a boy, seeming to be propped up by two of his friends. Emma had heard he'd had some things going on, that he was sick, and he looked sick, she thought as she turned her attention back to the church camp pastor. It was a good place for the boy to be, Emma considered as she glanced down at her hands. Looking out of the corner of her eye, she saw the teenage girl standing next to her, a girl that was staying on her floor in her dorm building.

Focus, Emma, she chided herself. The service was drawing to a close and she was becoming antsy, ready to grab some more of the beautiful day before it was time for dinner and prayer group. Distracted again, Emma looked around the beautiful large church facility, with polished light colored wooden pews, carpeted floors, and elaborate stained glass windows. Her eyes travelled to the front of the church and watched the pastor as he wrapped up the service. Let's say, Amen, Emma thought… *then we can all be dismissed…*

"There is someone, someone in this room that has difficulty hearing. They cannot hear out of one of their ears," Emma heard the pastor say. Now he had her full attention.

Emma's heart caught in her throat as she stared at the pastor.

She watched as he scanned the crowd in the large room, and continued, "Something happened to your ear when you were little. I'm supposed to pray for you."

Tears sprang to Emma's eyes as she looked down at the back of the bench in front of her, thinking, he *can't* be talking about me.

"Someone," he repeated. "There's someone in this room that I'm supposed to pray for…for your hearing."

Emma turned and looked around the room to see whom he was supposed to pray for, who would walk down the aisle, but no one walked down the aisle. It was so quiet in the church that Emma could hear her heart pounding. The pastor and Emma waited, but still no one walked down the aisle.

She watched as the pastor held his hand out, as if to grasp someone's hand, as he said, "The Lord wants me to pray for you, to bless you, to let you know you can be healed. Someone who suffered damage to one of their ears when they were a small child…"

Emma's heart was racing; she felt light headed, barely able to breath, and as hot tears sprang to her eyes, she knew the pastor—that God—was talking to her. She looked down at the back of the seat in front of her while trying to grasp that God would know her.

Her head still down, Emma slowly scooted past the blur of people that were sitting in her row, and then walked down the aisle toward the pastor.

She stopped within a few feet of the pastor, and he asked, "What's your name?"

Shyly, she answered, "Emma."

He took her hands in his, and leaned forward toward the left side of her face. She wanted to shift her face so that her right ear would be towards him, just in case he said something to her, so she would hear, but she couldn't. Something had rooted her to the spot—she was unable to move a muscle.

Her hands in his, he leaned toward the left side of her face, toward her ear.

Emma...Hear me," the pastor whispered into Emma's left ear, the ear she hadn't heard sound, not clearly and concisely, for as long as she could remember.

His voice echoed in her ear. She wanted to raise her hands and cover her ears the sound was so loud! A blast of heat blazed through her body, beginning at the crown of her head, and radiating slowly down her face, chin, neck, arms, fingertips, chest, torso, thighs, all the way to her toes. His voice had been so loud to Emma that she thought surely the entire congregation, even those in the very back row, had heard him. But as she pulled away and looked into the pastor's eyes, and whispered, "Yes," she knew no one but her had heard the whisper—God's whisper in her ear that hadn't heard sound in so very long. Seeing the shock on Emma's face, the pastor held onto Emma's hand for a moment more, until she released his hand, and slowly, thoughtfully, she walked back to her seat.

Later that night, as Emma lay on her side on her bed, her roommates already asleep, she thought about her afternoon, the whisper in her ear. She had heard him, she assured herself...had heard the pastor's voice—God's voice...someone's voice in her left ear, the ear she couldn't hear out of. But as she lay on her bed, snug under her covers, she thought... but I still can't hear. She dozed off to the thought, maybe it's a simple matter of faith...

Two weeks later, the Rhodes' house was a flurry of activity; baking for the fair was under full steam! Delicious looking and smelling baked goods were on every available surface in the kitchen, ready to be loaded into the station wagon. Mr. Rhodes already had his truck loaded with whatever it was he was going to use to create their booth, that and boxes of ceramics to sell, and of course, the creations he had made. It was an exciting day…fair day!

Emma had four pieces ready for the fair, and the entry form to go with them. She was ready, now if everyone else could get it together and get out the door, she thought impatiently.

"Emma Claire," Mrs. Rhodes called out, "could you grab that box and take it to the car?'"

Yes! Emma thought, anything she could do to get the show on the road, no feat too small or too large.

"Sure!" Emma answered, grabbing a box filled with various kitchen utensils.

And it looked like they were off, Emma thought, barely containing her excitement, and beaming as she opened the back passenger door and climbed onto the seat.

Thirty minutes later the station wagon, following behind Mr. Rhodes' blue truck, pulled up to unload everything they would need for their booth. After helping Mr. Rhodes unload the truck, Emma began unloading the car. She was anxious to see just how they planned to create a booth. As she looked around, she saw there were several booths nearby. Shrugging her shoulders, she expected a plain, wooden table… and after that, she had no idea.

"Emma," Mrs. Rhodes, said, "why don't you go wander around. Check out the fair."

Emma's eyes lit up at the idea. She didn't mind helping her foster parents with whatever they needed, but if they insisted, then she was out of there!

"Okay!" Emma said happily. It was still fairly early in the morning—ten–so it wasn't overwhelmingly hot just yet. If she wanted a look-see, now was the time, she thought as she strolled away down the paved path.

"Emma!" Mrs. Rhodes exclaimed. "Look," pointing at her soap dish safely held in a glass case. "You got a blue ribbon!"

"Where?!" Emma asked excitedly. Then seeing the blue ribbon lying next to her ceramic piece, she grinned, and said, "Sweet!"

It was the third day of the fair and the judging had ended for all craft and baked good entries. Mrs. Rhodes and Carmen had placed in just about everything they had entered, with many firsts, just as Emma had suspected they would. The surprise for Emma had been that her silly ceramics she entered had placed in several categories and had won a first place for her ceramic soap dish!! *Whoo Hoo!* she shouted in her head.

"I can't believe I got a first place!" she said with a big grin.

"Why not?" Mrs. Rhodes asked. "You worked really hard on it. It's beautiful."

"Thanks!" Emma said, standing before the case admiring the ribbon that would be in her hands in a few days. The fair had been an experience for Emma; the smell of food—hot dogs, pizza, and sweets—hung heavy in the blistering hot afternoon air. The days had been sweltering hot, with a fine dust kicked up when the crowd walked off the paved path in the game and rides area of the fair. She had experienced everything the fair had to offer, French fries drenched in vinegar, elephant ears dusted with powdered sugar, nauseating rides, and games where she threw change into colorful dishes. What she was going to do with the dish when she won it, she didn't know. It was the exhilaration of the challenge that kept her trying again and again. There was even a game of ring toss, which earned her a giant sized baby blue colored teddy bear that she had to lug back to the Rhodes' booth.

One evening, Emma walked over toward the stable area of the fair ground. She wandered around until she found the one where Andy used to work, *that summer,* the summer before he went away to military school. With her arms crossed over her chest, Emma stood outside and stared into the dark stable, remembering the stormy evening when she had watched Andy shoot some kind of horse medicine into his vein. She had been terrified, but she couldn't stop him. Emma shuffled out of the way, as a boy about her age came out of the stable leading a horse. Turning, she glanced back and imagined she heard Andy's voice, his laugh, and saw the ghost of the cute boy that had been her friend. With a heavy heart, Emma thought, but that had been a lifetime ago, and deep in thought she walked away.

It was the last night of the fair, and Emma sat snuggled into a chair under the shelter, smug that her family had such a luxurious booth set up. She should have known Mr. Rhodes would practically build a home away from home. It was more of a shelter than a booth, she considered as she nibbled on French fries, setting the book she was reading aside. Mr. Rhodes had planned the booth for all weather conditions, fashioning a roof out of something, she wasn't sure what, and even had walls erected on all sides except the entry. They were protected from the blistering sun during the day, and now the blowing rain. It was dark outside beyond the boundary of the covered booth, and thunder boomed, but as Emma glanced around her dry home away from home, she felt pleasantly cozy as lights from Mrs. Rhodes' masterpieces twinkled at her, and lamps placed strategically glowed warmly. It was the last night of the fair, which meant the end of summer.

29

Emma knew she was pushing it when she elected to wear not only shorts on the first day of school, but a pair of funny looking backless sandals. They looked like sandals Japanese girls wore with their traditional Kimonos. She figured it was the start to her senior year, and what were they really going to do…send her home? Placing her most charming expression of surprise on her face, Emma pretended she had no idea students were not allowed to wear shorts to school. The teachers had been cool about it, instructing her not to wear shorts again to school.

It was her last year of high school and Emma was going to make absolutely the most of it by joining every club she could get into, and intended to join the basketball team and the pom-pom squad again. Not only that, she was going to kick her shyness to the curb! She just had to stop being afraid of everyone, running away, and hiding away, feeling she wasn't good enough for friends or to fit in. This was it—her last chance—her senior year she was going to be all she could be, all she had dreamed of! At the start of the school year, Emma jumped at every opportunity to sign up for clubs, joining the yearbook staff, journalism staff, was elected to the student council, which wasn't difficult given the small size of her class, and she convinced her art teacher to allow the students to create an art club, and she was elected president. She felt as if she were finally making a space for herself at the school, and making friends.

Jacob had decided to take a year off before starting college. His dad had owned the bank and asked Jacob if he wanted to get into the business, to take it over, but Jacob had declined, so his dad sold it and was going back to college himself. Jacob insisted he just needed a little time to figure out what he wanted to do with his life, and a year off should do it. Until he decided, he was going to continue working at the gas station full-time. It seemed strange to Emma, almost an empty feeling not seeing Jacob every day at school. Since her early days at New Point High, he had been there, making sure he ran into her in the hall, making her laugh, and playing around. He just had that special kind of way of brightening the darkest, most gloomy of days, and now with him gone, she had the opportunity to figure out how to brighten her own day.

As Emma doodled on her lined notebook paper, she wished the classroom had the power to swallow her up, taking her out of her math class. Pressing her forehead onto the palm of her hand, slowly she scraped the sharp lead of her pencil back and forth, tearing a hole in the paper. You are so stupid, she thought. *Good God! How fucking hard was it to pass a stupid Algebra class...well for you apparently impossible! Shit!* Her head still in a downward, defeated position, Emma scanned the room, the room full of annoying freshman that comprised the class, she being the only senior. It wasn't as if she had tried to flunk her math class. She had agonized, some real snot nosed, tear streaming homework sessions, and even tutoring from her math teacher hadn't helped, but then her math teacher, last year, had been just a kid himself. So here she sat, in a pre-Algebra class with children, she thought as she ripped a hole the length of the page. Looking up toward the teacher she considered, at least she had a decent teacher this time, her Biology teacher, Mr. Perry. He was a great teacher—patient—he cared, and she babysat his son sometimes on the weekends. The semester had started out so great, Emma thought. She had managed to understand what the hell the man was saying in class, and what he wrote on the board, had been confident when she handed in her homework assignments. But at some point, she had begun to get lost in all the letters and numbers. It just wasn't natural to her to combine reading and numbers. Flopping her chin on her fist, tears sprang to her eyes as she thought about the times she had stood at the front of the class while everyone else was figuring out problems on their papers. Embarrassed, with tears in her eyes, she had told her teacher she just didn't get it. She hated math!!

Mr. Perry had told her she was trying too hard, thinking about it too deeply, and she didn't understand that either. Wasn't that what she was supposed to do, she worried...think deeply. Then there had been her history class—history, of all classes—that she had begun failing. What was happening, she wondered in confusion. She wasn't stupid. She was doing the work...but she just couldn't remember or grasp what the teacher wanted her to know for tests in history class *or* math. Sighing, she realized it was a foreign language to her. What if she couldn't pass? What if she proved to herself she was an idiot? What if she proved to everyone that foster kids really couldn't be anything...what if...?

The day Mrs. Rhodes had seen her first report for the semester— the D's—she hadn't gotten mad. She had sat Emma down, and they had talked about her grades, allowing Emma to explain why she thought she was failing and how Mrs. Rhodes could help her. Sitting at the kitchen table, the ceiling light glaring down on her, she had cried and explained she didn't know why she was failing. Math class had started out so well, she had explained, and then it just didn't make sense anymore. And failing history made no sense to Emma because she loved the class. Something just did not connect when it came time to take tests. One of the problems, Emma explained, was that she didn't know what the problem was. How could she fix something if she didn't even know why it was happening? Mrs. Rhodes had suggested finding a tutor to help Emma sort it all out, to help her learn how to study better, and help her understand her math. Surprised by the suggestion, but pleased that Mrs. Rhodes cared enough to help her pass her classes, Emma had agreed.

She hated feeling like one of the Special Ed kids that had been at one of her other schools. This wasn't her, she agonized. She was a smart kid, so why was she so stupid now? As she had over the past few years, Emma feared it was just too late to make up all she had missed, academically and in other ways. Maybe people were right, maybe she couldn't catch up and have her dream of being like everyone else.

The end of class bell rang, and not too soon to suit Emma. She was happy to be out of the miserably embarrassing class that was a testament to her academic failure.

"Emma!" Mr. Perry called after her.

Clutching her textbook, spiral notebook, and yellow pencil, Emma turned from the door and walked to her teacher's desk, knowing he was going to make sure she knew what the heck the lesson had meant today.

"Yeah," she smiled. He was such a nice teacher—she knew that— really trying to help her. It was a strange concept for her, teachers, and adults that wanted her to succeed, but it didn't minimize her humiliation.

"You okay? Do have any questions?" he asked with concern.

"I think I got it," she said, with little confidence that she truly did, *get it!*

"Well just ask me if you have any questions. Remember, I don't mind hanging out for awhile after class to answer your questions…okay?" he said persistently.

Smiling, she said, "Okay." She did have questions, but right now, her brain hurt, and she knew she'd just start crying so there was no point in asking anything.

"I have to get to my next class," she said, as she started to walk toward the door.

One more class, Emma thought with a heavy sigh, *then loser me gets to head on down the road to the tutor.* She had expected to see a tutor *after* school, not *during* school, but that was all Mrs. Rhodes could schedule. There was a woman a few blocks from the school that used to be a teacher and she had agreed, for a small fee, to tutor Emma during her afternoon study hall. So each afternoon, Emma was released from study hall, and as she held her breath, terrified a vicious dog would find her and gobble her up, she walked the two blocks to the tutor's home. She was a nice enough lady, patient, even as Emma cried as she struggled to understand her math. The tutor had some great ideas about study-ing for history, things Emma had never been taught before. The lady determined that Emma wasn't stupid. The problem was that no one had ever really taught her how to study. All these years, somehow Emma had managed to listen in class and do well on tests, but as the work became more difficult, she needed someone to teach her how to study.

When the tutor asked her how she studied, Emma wasn't sure she understood the question, responding that she read the material when assigned, and then of course wondered how the teacher expected her to remember everything she had read for tests. No one had ever taught Emma the concept of using flash cards to study, actually memorizing class material, so when it came to fill in the blank questions she'd have a shot at having an answer. She taught Emma to answer essay questions in a strategic manner. Until her tutor had introduced the idea, Emma hadn't realized there was a process for answering questions on tests. Emma began to realize it was a miracle she had done as well as she had all her academic life, starting in grade school when she had actually managed straight A's. Perhaps she was smarter than she thought...

Later that night, Emma ran through her familiar nightmare, fever-ishly hot, wisps of fabric catching at her arms as the sound of pounding feet drew nearer. Gasping for breath, Emma shot up out of her dream! Shakily she placed her hand to her chest feeling the racing of her heart. She licked her lips. It felt as if she had been running a marathon, her skin clammy with sweat, and her heart pounding crazy. What did it mean she wondered...her dream? It was always the same, so real, but it wasn't, she reassured herself, because where in the world was there some crazy room with giant sized bolts of fabric just blowing around in the wind, and who would chase her...*who was chasing her?* Emma, in a seated position curled her knees toward her chest and stared at the end of her bed.

Her heart stopped for a moment as she stared at two red glowing circles at the foot of her bed. What looked like glowing, demonic eyes, the shape and size a little larger than what eyes should be, was staring back at her. They were glowing from the foot of her bed, where just days ago, she had placed her oversized stuffed blue teddy bear. But her bear did *not* have red glowing eyes, she gasped in fear. She froze. Feeling sweat of terror bead up around her hairline, Emma choked out, "In the name of Jesus be gone. In the name of Jesus be gone!" thinking surely the Devil had followed her from her dream. But her prayer had no impact on the round red glowing eyes, with bright red centers now the size of golf balls! It was so close it could touch her if it wanted, she thought in horror, fearing at any second it would do just that! Holding her breath, Emma bolted out of her bed and almost fell down as she sprinted over to Emma Katherine's bed. Scrambling to get under the covers, Emma recalled that they had gotten into it earlier that evening about something, she couldn't even remember why now. She snuggled up next to Emma Katherine, and whispered, "Emma—Emma Katherine, can I sleep with you? I had a nightmare."

"I don't care," Emma Katherine mumbled, and rolled over on her side, falling back asleep.

For the rest of the night, Emma slept cuddled into the safety of her foster sister...where no nightmares could reach her.

30

Turning her head first to the right and then the left, Emma asked, "What do you think? I'm having my senior pictures done in a month so I want a new haircut, something more grown up. Any ideas..." Emma asked her hairdresser.

Mr. Curtis was Emma's hairdresser, and one of the members of the congregation at church. He had been cutting her hair since her arrival at the Rhodes' home and now with senior pictures looming, Emma wanted something new to represent the new, older her.

Standing behind her as she looked forward in the mirror, Mr. Curtis pulled her hair up and back, showing her what she would look like with much shorter hair. She liked the idea of a crisp, clean designed haircut, but if she went any shorter, her hair would be shorter than Jacob's hair, actually shorter than most boys she knew.

"I like it," Emma said. "Yeah. Cut it all off."

An hour later, Mr. Curtis swiveled the chair, with Emma seated on it, around so she could see her new creation.

"What do you think?" he asked.

She reached up, and smiling, touched her very short hair. "I love it!" she exclaimed. No one at school had this cut. She would be different, but this time, in a good way. Mr. Curtis swiveled her chair around and handed her a mirror to provide a view of the back of the cut. Holding the mirror in her right hand, Emma raised her left hand and grasped the very short strands of hair, too short even to skim the collar of her sweater. Running her hand over her neck, she felt where Mr. Curtis had shaved the wisps of hair away.

"Okay!" he said. "Let me show you how to take care of your new cut."

Emma listened attentively as he explained how to blow dry her hair to get the swept away, feathered look, and then he showed her various types of curling irons and the effect they would give her new look.

"Wow! Look at you," Mrs. Rhodes said with a smile, as she walked over and stood behind Emma looking at her in the mirror.

"Do you like it?" Emma asked with a smile, as she looked back at her foster mother through the mirror.

"I love it!" Mrs. Rhodes said, smoothing the side of Emma's very short hair. "It's sassy!"

Shaking her head, her fresh hair cut flying about as she did, Emma said happily, "I feel sassy!"

"Well, are you almost ready to go, sassy?" Mrs. Rhodes laughed.

Emma climbed off the chair, and with a smile, gave her hair one more shake. "Ready!" she laughed.

"You can show the girls at church your new DO," Mrs. Rhodes said, pleased Emma looked so happy, such a change from the girl that had arrived on her doorstep the summer before. They were off to the church for a spaghetti dinner. It was something new the church was trying out, Wednesday night spaghetti-dinner-get-togethers.

"What do you think?" Mrs. Rhodes asked, as she held up the crushed velvet chocolate brown skirt with a slit at the hem to provide easier walking, and a matching blazer.

"Oh my gosh!" Emma exclaimed in happy surprise. She reached out to touch the soft fabric, in awe of the outfit Mrs. Rhodes had created for her to wear for her senior pictures. "I can't believe you can sew something like this...make this, I mean," Emma said with sincere appreciation. "It's absolutely beautiful." Emma took the blazer from her foster mother and held it gently in her hands.

Emma could see the embarrassment on her foster mother's face, always so humble. Not for the first time, Emma considered how different Mrs. Rhodes was from most people she had ever met. Talented, giving, funny, warm, and generous—she could be the center of, well, everything if she wanted, but instead she was so humble, giving the glory for everything in her life to God. She felt a kindred spirit with her foster mother, at least in one way, with her soft, gentle heart, wishing she could be more like her in other ways too. One day she hoped to find the strength to be okay with who she was—little though that might be—and perhaps one day have the courage to just be, not needing to belong to any one person, content in knowing that where most people might fail her, God would not...*one day.*

Still holding the blazer, Emma stepped forward and hugged her foster mother.

"Well, it really wasn't anything," Mrs. Rhodes said. "Anyone could have done it. I just followed the pattern."

Emma beamed because she loved the outfit, and how endearing the woman that stood before her was. It was okay, she thought, to be who she was—to be soft, and she sighed...soft.

"I'm going to go try it on!" Emma squealed.

"Well wait a minute," Mrs. Rhodes laughed. "You need the skirt too."

Spinning around, Emma said, "Oh...Yeah!" and grinning, she practically danced to the bathroom to try on her new blazer and skirt. A few minutes later, she walked out of the bathroom and headed straight to the mirror hanging on the column by the table.

"What do you think?" Mrs. Rhodes asked.

Emma looked at her reflection in the mirror, noticing how the soft brown fabric caught the light making shadows in the creases and folds. She turned, and touched the toes of one foot to the floor, as if she were wearing a high-healed shoe, exposing the back of her leg between the slit in the skirt. Continuing to examine the blazer, layered over her white turtleneck and skirt, Emma smoothed the front of her skirt with her hands, and tugged at the hem of her jacket, pulling away any puckers.

Quickly she spun toward Mrs. Rhodes and gleefully said, "I love it! It's gorgeous!"

"Well I'm glad you like it," Mrs. Rhodes said with a grin.

Smiling, Emma thought, not for the first time, that Mrs. Rhodes had one of those happy kind of voices, as if she was just on the verge of laughing. She had never met such a consistently happy person. Emma sighed. It was really happening—she was having senior pictures taken. Someone was actually going to pay lots of money so she could experience a day just for her. Mrs. Rhodes knew a couple at church that owned a photography studio. The husband was the actual photographer, and the wife was his assistant. To top off the exciting news that Emma was going to have fancy pictures taken, Mrs. Rhodes had bought a pattern, selected the most luxurious fabric, and then made time to create the outfit Emma would wear to commemorate her senior year in high school, for all of time in New Point High's year book. It was like a dream.

Pivoting on her toe, Emma turned back to the mirror and examined her reflection once again, buttoning the one large brown button on the jacket. Staring into her eyes, eyes that matched the color of her suit, Emma thought about her senior picture that would one day be bound in the New Point High School's yearbook. She loved New Point High. It was different from any school she had ever attended. One of her many favorite things about the school, was the art class field trips. Occasionally during class, Ms. Blake, Emma's art teacher, and the other students, the ones that had cars, would drive a few minutes outside of town and park along the country road, their destination, a grass covered field. Lying in a field, they would stare up at the robin egg blue sky, as white fluffy scenes passed by. Nature's play—for Emma and her classmates—helped them see deeper than the surface of the world.

When Emma was in junior high, one of her English teachers and social studies teacher had realized she had an artistic gift, and had encouraged her to keep working at it. Her gift had been detected when special projects were assigned that required drawing, whether it was animals, or scenes related to characters in a story or historical project. Emma had the ability to capture whatever she studied and chose to draw.

During the past year, Ms. Blake had helped her further develop her gift to the point she had sold a few oil paintings, and had been asked to paint a mural on one of the walls of the teen Bible study room at the new church building. She'd already chosen a scene from the Bible and had begun sketching the outline on one of the walls in the classroom. Her goal was to create an almost ceiling to floor mural, something she had never tried before, and prayed she'd be able to create a painting with lifelike dimensions.

Her hand pressed to her stomach, feeling the soft fabric of the brown velvet jacket, Emma sighed once again and reflected, *I can't believe this is my life.*

"There's a bathroom in the back," Mr. Fisher, the photographer said, as he pointed behind Emma down a narrow, dark hallway.

Emma craned her neck and then turned, looking in the direction Mr. Fisher had pointed. It was dark back there, she thought, and a little creepy. Dark places weren't particularly her favorite places.

It was senior picture afternoon, and Mrs. Rhodes had dropped Emma off at the Fisher studio several minutes ago. Nervously, she looked around the studio and wished she wouldn't have left her alone, knowing it was silly to be afraid of one of the couples from church. Shaking her head, she tried to brush away her fear.

Her purple school bag, filled with everything she thought she might need for the next few hours, was slung over her shoulder. She had crammed curling irons, make up, hairbrush, and a simple pair of earrings into the bag. There was one little accessory she wished she could have left at home, the big, fat, juicy zit on her chin that she had woken up to that morning. Folded over her arm, hanging on hangers, Emma carried her brown velvet suit, cream-colored cowl neck sweater, and a second sweater for a wardrobe change.

Uneasily, Emma walked down the short hall, peaking about to find the bathroom, and then finding a small rough room with a toilet and small sink, she squeezed inside and shut the door behind her. Placing her bag on the floor, and hanging her outfits on a hook, she looked suspiciously around the cramped, cluttered, dimly lit room. She leaned toward the small oval mirror placed above the white sink and looked at her chin where she had squeezed and picked at the zit, now looking much worse than it had before she tried to make it disappear. Of all mornings for a zit to pop up, Emma thought in annoyance.

"Come on over here, Emma," Mr. Fisher said. With his free hand, he indicated the small round stool she was to sit on, holding a large black camera in his other hand.

Emma walked over to the stool and sat down primly on the edge, her knees tight together, and her skirt smoothed over her knees. She took in her surroundings, the rumpled cream-colored cloth on the floor, weird contraptions that looked like giant white umbrellas, and the lights that were blinding and hot.

Mrs. Fisher walked over and smoothed Emma's hair.

"Okay," Mr. Fisher said, "sit up straight, real tall, twist to the right just a little. Good! Stop! Now tilt your chin up, just a smidge, up a little more. Now look over at Mrs. Fisher. Don't move!"

Emma held her breath—trying not to move a muscle—feeling as if she might topple off the stool. This picture thing wasn't as easy as she thought it was going to be, Emma thought as her calf muscles screamed from holding her in position.

"Okay, you can breathe," he commented.

Good grief! It felt as if she were engaged in a rigorous workout in the blazing sun, she thought as she rolled the stiffness out of her shoulders and stretched her leg. Squinting, she peered at the lights, so bright and hot it felt as if she were being cooked!

A half an hour later, Mr. Fisher suggested, "How about if we get some shots outside? I've got the perfect spot in mind. Why don't you switch outfits and we'll get going."

Emma was curious as to just where the perfect spot might be as she walked back to the small bathroom to change into her luxurious suit Mrs. Rhodes had made for her.

Ten minutes later, Emma was seated on an ornate concrete bench surrounded by lush flowering bushes, green plants, rich colorful flowers, and the sun so bright it made her eyes water. It was the perfect spot, Emma agreed, as the sun warmed her back and the top of her head. The warmth inspired her to want to curl up on the bench and take a nap, like a content cat, but instead, she did as Mr. Fisher instructed, tucking, and twisting her body uncomfortably, and pretended the sun was not blinding her as she offered the camera a slight smile.

"Okay," Mr. Fisher said, after another half an hour of snapping shots from various angles. "On to the next location, the perfect spot!" he said with a smile.

I thought this *was* the perfect spot, Emma mouthed.

Looking back at the bench, Emma wrinkled her brow as she trailed behind Mr. and Mrs. Fisher through the garden area. The perfect spot, she reflected as she followed the two adults as they walked toward a small restaurant nearby. Emma stared at the building drawing closer with each step. The restaurant was a boxcar, actually, she thought, it was a caboose, the cute car that brought up the rear of a train. As Emma walked closer to the restaurant, she thought of another time she had been near a train, not so long ago, under very different circumstances. She had run away—had been lost, and scared—wondering what horrible nightmare God had planned for her next. Shaking her head, Emma scattered the remnants of her memories, realizing she wasn't that unwanted girl anymore.

She knew the story of the caboose, that it had been hauled into town and was now a quaint restaurant. Grabbing hold of the black bar, Emma pulled herself up the steps. As Emma walked down the narrow aisle, she looked with curiosity at the seats, bench style, with tables affixed between, and out the windows that lined the room. She walked to where Mr. Fisher was waiting, running her hand along the back of the plush seats. Beautiful, she admired with a small smile…the perfect spot for her senior pictures.

An hour later, Emma found Mrs. Rhodes waiting for her at the photography studio. "How'd it go?" she asked, when Emma walked into the studio.

"It was so much fun being a model for the afternoon," Emma beamed. "Mr. Fisher had some great photography shot ideas. He took pictures in the caboose!"

"He did?" Mrs. Rhodes asked.

"She's a great model," Mr. Fisher said. "Sometimes I need models for marketing purposes—maybe at some point Emma could sit for me. I'd pay her," he said.

"Wow!" Mrs. Rhodes said. "Well, we'll have to see. What do you think about that Emma Claire?" she asked.

Grinning, Emma said excitedly, "Yeah! I would love to."

"I'll get a hold of you, but it might not be until next year." Changing the subject, Mr. Fisher said, "Now, the proofs for her senior pictures will be ready right before Christmas. I'll call you, and you can come in and look at them."

"Okay," Mrs. Rhodes said.

31

Shuffling her clogs along the sidewalk through the colorful fall leaves, Emma thought about other leaves, piles of leaves along sidewalks that led to her elementary school when she was a little girl. There was something specific about every season that she loved, and during the fall, it was the brilliance of the leaves that created a glow outside, making her world seem brighter than usual. Then there were the leaves that had given up, let loose of their homes, slowly gliding to the ground that then made musical crunching sounds under her feet.

Halloween would be arriving in a week, not that she dressed up and trick or treated any more. But as the art club president, Emma had convinced Ms. Blake to allow club members to enlist the student body of New Point High to dress up in their favorite costume. To make the day even more fun, they would be awarding a prize for best costume. Who said high school students were too old for dress up, Emma had thought playfully Friday afternoon as she climbed the steps of the bus. She wondered what she and Jacob would be doing tomorrow night on their date. There were some good movies playing at the theatre she considered, as she walked back to her usual spot, the seat at the back of the bus.

At ten after seven, Emma walked down the stairs to call Jacob. He was over an hour late for their date and she was getting worried that something had happened to him. As she dialed his number, she tried to shoo the worrisome thoughts from her mind, visions of his broken body lying outside his car alongside the country road. What if he'd been in an accident, she worried. It didn't help her racing mind when moments later, she hung up the phone. *No answer.* Where was he, she wondered, now angry that he had stood her up. Then she chided herself, *what if he had been in an accident, you would feel terrible for thinking he stood you up!* Fifteen minutes, she decided, she'd call him again in fifteen minutes. She walked back upstairs and stood in front of her bedroom window that overlooked the field across the road, and the road that ran past the house. Maybe he just had to work late and he's on his way, she thought hopefully.

Fifteen agonizing minutes later, Emma walked back down the stairs and dialed Jacob's number again, and this time she was met by his husky voice, "Hello?"

"Jacob…are you okay?" Emma asked hesitantly, wondering why it sounded as if he'd just woken up.

"Yeah," he grumbled.

"Did I wake you up?" she asked in confusion.

"Yeah," he yawned.

"Do you have any idea what time it is?" she asked shortly.

"No," he mumbled. There was a pause, and then he said, "Oh, shit. I'm late for our date, aren't I?"

Relieved that he wasn't lying beside the road somewhere in a bloody heap, she sighed, "A little."

Still sounding half asleep, he mumbled, "I can be over in an hour. We can grab something to eat real quick, and just hang out for awhile."

"Okay," she agreed, wrinkling her forehead, as she wondered why he hadn't shown up for their date…why he was sleeping.

"K," he said so softly she could barely hear him. "See you in an hour."

An hour, Emma thought. That put the start to their date at what, like 8:30 or so, as she glanced up at the clock hanging on the kitchen wall. Four hours, basically, she sighed. She'd get to see Jacob for, four short hours.

At nine, Emma dialed Jacob's number again, "Hello," the groggy voice at the other end responded.

"Jacob!" she hissed in annoyance. "You haven't left your house! I talked to you over an hour ago. Did you fall asleep?"

"I'll be right there," he mumbled.

"Don't bother!" she said angrily. "I'm going to bed!"

What the hell, she wondered tearfully, and embarrassed, walked up stairs to her bedroom. She knew the entire family knew she'd been stood up, but they were all being nice and not saying a word about it. Just like most Saturdays, Emma had taken a bath, done her hair, and her nails...and for what, so Jacob could sleep at his house! Angrily, Emma yanked the baby blue sweater over her head, threw it on her bed, then thought better of the idea, and carefully folded it, knowing she'd regret the wrinkles the next time she chose to wear it. Sniffling, she pulled her nightgown over her head. Then she kicked off her blue jeans, and folded them too. Climbing under her covers, she pulled the stuffed Snoopy that Jacob had given her to her chest, hugging it as tears coursed down her cheeks.

Tomorrow was dress up day at school, Emma thought excitedly. It was going to be so much fun, anything to break up the monotony of a school day. They had chosen Friday as dress up day, in part because it was the last day of the school week, something to look forward to, and of course, because it was Halloween day. It had worked out perfectly that year, with Halloween falling on a Friday. She already had an outfit picked out, nothing over the top, just something simple; a little black eye liner to make freckles, red kerchief, plaid top, bib overalls, and you got yourself a cute little freckled country girl. Well, it was the best she could do. It would work.

"Well hello there!" Emma said into the telephone, still feeling the excitement from picking out her Halloween outfit for the next day.

"Hey, Emma," Jacob said quietly. "Whatcha doin?"

"Oh, I just got done picking out an outfit for tomorrow. You'd love it! The art club talked Ms. Blake into a Halloween dress up, so we talked to the principal and he agreed to it. So...I'm going to be all country tomorrow, with freckles and a bandana. It'll be a blast!" Emma bubbled. "Oh! And we're going to give a prize for the best costume!" Sighing happily, she asked, "How was your day? Oh...and what are we doing this weekend? We could go see a scary movie. Wouldn't that be fun...in honor of Halloween?!"

"Emma...Emma," Jacob interrupted. "I wanted to talk to you about something."

"Oh," she said, surprised into speechlessness. "Sure. What's up?"

"I don't know how to say this, so I'll just say it. I think we should break up," he said quickly.

Emma had been standing by the phone with excited energy, but now, the energy seemed to have sucked right out of her. She pulled out a kitchen chair and sank down on it. Break up...had he really said, *break up*, Emma wondered in a daze.

"Emma, are you there?" Jacob prodded.

"I—I'm here," she murmured.

"Did you hear me?" he asked softly.

"Yeah, I heard you," she said, still trying to register his words. "But—but why, Jacob?" she asked, as tears sprang to her eyes. My God, he was her best friend. Could they be friends now, and...why?

"I just...I just think," he sighed, "it would be best for both of us. You know we hardly ever see each other now..." his voice trailed away.

Emma didn't know what to say, so said very little. She was heartbroken, but she wasn't about to humiliate herself by begging him not be break up with her. It was best to fall back on what she had always done in the past, hide her feelings. That was the safest thing to do, she thought, as holding back her tears, she said softly, "Okay."

"We can still talk and be friends, Emma," Jacob assured her.

"Sure," she said unconvinced, wanting nothing more than to get off the phone. "Jacob, I've got to go."

"Okay," he said, his voice deeper than usual.

Standing up, Emma hung up the phone, and feeling as if she'd just been punched, pressed the palm of her hand to her stomach and walked to her bedroom. She felt lost, not sure what to do. Should she crawl into bed and try to go to sleep, even if it *was* super early. Maybe she should try to read a book to block it all out, or just go back downstairs and stare at the TV, yet another way to block out the reality that she had just lost, not just a boyfriend, but also her best friend. Jacob had been her best friend, her funny, encouraging, goofy, loveable, best friend. Emma climbed up onto her bed, scooted back against the wall, and wrapping her arms around her legs, pulled her legs toward her chin, and rested her chin on her knees. She couldn't remember the last time she'd had a best friend. No—no, that wasn't true. There had been a friend in junior high, a girl that had made life at her dad's house bearable.

Shifting her head, she leaned her right cheek on her knees and stared blankly at the white wall. A gaping hole, that's what she had…the space that Jacob had filled, had been a gaping hole before, and now, it was open and empty again. Turning her head once again, resting her chin on her knees as tears streamed down her cheeks, she thought, not totally empty—not the same—it's not quite the same. Jacob might be gone, her sisters gone…her entire past was gone, but this time she wasn't totally alone. She had the Rhodes family, and they were right downstairs.

Swiping her tears away, Emma climbed off her bed and walked down the two steps that led to the common area, then down the stairs toward the bathroom to wash her tears away. As she walked into the family room, she saw Mrs. Rhodes sitting on the couch, Mr. Rhodes on his recliner, and Caitlyn and Cassy lying on the floor in front of the fireplace. Grabbing a pillow, Emma scooted next to Caitlyn in front of the warm roaring fire, and smiled as she watched the goofy antics on TV.

At ten O'clock, Emma climbed to her feet and put the pillow she had been propping her head on away, as the other kids grumbled to their feet. Mrs. Rhodes asked Emma to hang on a minute.

"Are you okay?" Mrs. Rhodes asked. "I know you were talking to Jacob on the phone earlier. Did he say something to upset you?" She could tell Emma was upset and insisted, "Come here. Talk to me about what's goin on."

Emma curled up at the other end of the couch, grabbed a throw pillow and cuddled it in front of her. "He broke up with me," she said miserably.

"Awe," Mrs. Rhodes said with mixed feelings. She didn't want Emma sad, and she could see that she clearly was, but she thought it might be a good thing if Emma had the chance to date other boys. They were getting too serious. Jacob was the only boy she had dated since coming to her home. "It's going to be okay, you'll see. I know it hurts right now, but there will be another boy. I know he was your high school sweet heart... really your first love wasn't he?" Mrs. Rhodes asked.

Emma shook her head with a watery smile. The woman knew her, that was for sure, just as if she were her natural mother. Emma knew she was right about dating other boys, but Jacob was her best friend, and it hadn't even been her idea to date him, she thought angrily.

"You know, the funny thing is that I had never even thought about dating Jacob," Emma said sadly. "I never saw him that way. Just as a friend. He was so funny, making me laugh all the time." Hunching her shoulders she reflected, "I loved the way he made me laugh; I never thought he was, you know, dating material. But then he grew on me... just seemed so sweet. They say you should be friends and then date... some silly thing like that. But I think that is the dumbest thing ever because if it doesn't work out, well, not only do you lose your boyfriend but you lose your best friend!" Emma laughed painfully at how screwed up it all was.

"Well, dad was my best friend," Mrs. Rhodes said with a smile, "and it's worked out just fine for me."

Emma let a sigh be her response because she didn't know what to say to that. She was glad things had worked out for her foster parents, but knew she would never date a friend again. They were too few, to willingly throw away.

"You okay?" Mrs. Rhodes asked with concern.

"I'm okay," Emma said. "I'll *be* okay," she smiled.

"Okay, you better get onto bed," Mrs. Rhodes said tenderly.

Walking up the stairs, Emma smiled. Jacob had broken up with her, but it was okay. The gaping hole she had felt earlier didn't seem so big now.

32

"You should come out with us tonight," Deena insisted.

Somehow, news of Emma's break up with Jacob had travelled around the school, fast, and not by her lips. There were no secrets to be had at New Point High, Emma thought with a smile. It hadn't been a bad thing that everybody knew her business. It was like a big family, a big, nice family...what she had imagined families were supposed to be like, like at the Rhodes' home. Here she was, and no one was making fun of her because Jacob had broken up with her. No, instead they were offering to help her pick up her pieces and move on.

Hmm, Emma thought. Go out with a group of girls instead with Jacob. Wow! It could actually be a great opportunity to get to know girls in her class better, well, junior, *and* senior girls, since they all kind of hung out together. When she had been going with Jacob, she hadn't been able to hang out with the girls, not since she was only allowed one night out a week, and that was on the weekend.

What would she say to these girls she wondered, and then chided herself, stop being stupid, Emma! *You talk to them just fine at school, during basketball practices and games, during lunch, and during club meetings. Jeez, it's not as if you don't have a brain and can't think of something to say!* But, she wondered, what *did* girls do when they hung out together on weekends? Well, she was about to find out. Obviously, she didn't have a date that weekend—no boyfriend—no date—so she'd ask Mrs. Rhodes if she could go out tonight instead of tomorrow night. *Simple enough!*

"Deena, I'd like that. I'm going!" Emma committed.

"Cool! I'll pick up Tara, and then we'll be over at about seven. There's always a group of us that hang out on the weekends. Some of the girls will hang out for a while, and then leave early to hang out with their boyfriends. We'll just cram as many of us in the car as will fit!" Deena said happily.

Deena always amazed Emma. Besides Tara, she was the happiest girl she had ever met. They kind of reminded her of Jacob, just the girl versions of class clowns. The teachers loved them so much that any of their gags were just laughed off. Their Halloween costumes were a hoot, and they knew it…two sparkly, silver angels, with wings and all….kind of their little joke. They weren't bad, just mischievous. Actually, there wasn't a bad kid to be found at New Point High.

There was more clowning around time than actual schoolwork getting done during classes on Halloween dress up day. The Halloween costumes were a definite distraction, that and the kids were all talking about what kind of trouble they planned to get into that night. Toilet papering the principal's trees seemed to be high on everyone's list. Emma had never joined in on anything like that and wondered what all she had been missing out on…and just how much trouble she would be in after tonight. Toilet papering the principal's trees…that couldn't be good she speculated. Her first night out with the girls and possibly her very first grounding was coming. *How bad could it be…she'd be hanging out with New Point High kids…!*

"Emma, the girls are here!" Mrs. Rhodes called up the stairs.

Crazy as it was, Emma was actually more nervous to be going out with a group of girls than with a boy on a date. Dating could be nerve-racking, but boys were pretty simple really. They talked and goofed around about boy stuff, and if it was your boyfriend, you kissed and stuff. Emma and Jacob had finally moved beyond just the kissing stage over a month ago…so they had kind of gotten into a routine on date night. She had been comfortable…now, not so comfortable, she thought as she bounced with determination down the stairs. *Who needed a boyfriend!*

She walked into the kitchen and noticed the three girls were all dressed as she was, causal, in jeans, sweaters, jackets, and tennis shoes. One nice thing, she had to admit about not dating a boy, was you didn't have to waste time picking out the perfect outfit, or wearing perfume.

"Hey guys!" Emma said with a grin, feeling as if her nerves might snap like a bad guitar string.

It was ridiculous, and probably not healthy to be so nervous at the prospect of venturing into the unknown with girls she hung out with at school—knew she should have done this long ago. Hanging out just with a boy had not been a good idea, she realized as she stood in the kitchen, faking enthusiasm and confidence.

Not a single one of the girls standing in the Rhodes' kitchen had ever made her feel less than them, like at some schools where she had been made to feel like an outcast—a dirty foster girl. As she looked around the small room at the three girls, laughing and joking with her foster mother, she saw New Point Highs most popular girls, Tara, Deena, and Emma Katherine. Internally, Emma shook her head thinking, it just felt so strange, as if she were an imposter—because she *felt* like an imposter—but she didn't want to be. She wanted to be just like one of them.

"Hey, Emma!" the girls chorused. "Are you ready?"

"Ready!" Emma said, feigning enthusiasm to cover the fear and insecurity she felt.

The girls loaded into the car, Emma climbing into the back of the car as Emma Katherine held the front seat forward, and then Emma Katherine climbed in the front. Tara got in on the other side of the car next to Emma, and Deena got in on the driver's side and started the car.

"Hell yah!" Deena whooped, as they tore down the gravel drive, and then pulled onto the country road. "First stop, Megan! Next stop…the store to pick up toilet paper!" Deena shouted.

After picking up Megan, another girl on Emma's basketball team, and the toilet paper, Deena drove to New Point High's principal's house, and parked her car by the curb. Emma could see, even in the dark, a very nice, two-story, white house. Climbing out of the car, Emma wondered how in the world Deena knew where the principal lived. His home was in Largo, the same town as the church Emma attended, and as she walked toward a group of trees, she considered, what if it wasn't Mr. Parker's house at all, but instead they ended up toilet papering some stranger's house. Wouldn't that be something, she thought sarcastically.

"Emma!" Tara said, trying to muffle her voice. "Catch!" Emma caught a role of white toilet paper, and watched for a moment as the other girls threw rolls up high in the air...then streams of toilet paper, roll and all, fluttered back down to them. Okay, she thought, she'd just throw it up and over branches until the roll was all over the tree in a nice draping pattern. Kind of pretty actually, Emma considered, as the paper almost glowed in the dark, making a stark accent against the large dark trees.

"Hey girls!" Emma heard a familiar deep voice say pleasantly.

Oh, shit! Well, at least she knew they had the right house.

"Hey, Mr. Parker," Deena said just as pleasantly back.

Fearing shit was about to hit the fan, Emma stepped forward. She wasn't about to let the other girls take the fall for their prank alone.

"Hey, Emma!" Mr. Parker said. Glancing around in the dark, Mr. Parker asked, "So who all do we have here? Deena, Tara, Emma Katherine, Megan, and Emma? Why don't you girls come in for a minute for hot chocolate? Mrs. Parker already made some," he said with a grin, his white teeth glowing like the moon in the dark.

Hot chocolate, Emma thought, *hot chocolate.* He had known they were coming she realized with a grin. This must be something kids did every year to his house and he wasn't mad at all. Her hands crammed in her pockets to take the chill off, Emma grinned as she followed the girls leading the way into the house. *When good kids did bad things...they got hot chocolate!* Emma realized in amazement. She said a quick thank you to God, for letting her be accepted into the good kid's crowd.

After a few more hours of mischief, Deena dropped Megan off at her house so she could meet her boyfriend for their date, and Emma Katherine off at Jordan's house, and then they had just one more place to stop off. Emma didn't know where they were going next, didn't recognize the name of the person that Deena mentioned—the name meant nothing to her—but she had nowhere else to be and a little over an hour before curfew, so she was game for another stop. They pulled up in front of a small house in New Point. Deena knocked, and a couple of guys Emma didn't recognize let them in.

"Hey!" Deena beamed happily. "How's it going?"

"Hi!" Tara waved with a grin, as she walked into the cozy living room and plopped down on the couch.

Emma looked across the room when she heard a familiar voice, and was surprised, and not in a good way, to see Jacob walk into the room carrying a can of beer. He stopped and looked at her, a grin spreading across his face. She did not return his smile, but did say quietly, "Hi."

A few minutes later, Tara and Deena managed to get Emma alone in the dark hall and they both insisted, "We had *no* idea he was going to be here. Do you want to leave? We can leave *right now* if you want!"

Obviously, they wanted to be there, at whoever these people's house was. It had turned out to be such a fun evening, Emma didn't want to ruin it, and so she said quietly, "No. That's silly. It's no big deal. We were going to run into one another eventually…it's just a little sooner than I thought. We can stay."

"Okay," If you're sure," Tara said. Then in typical Tara fashion, she asked, "Do you want us to kick his ass? We can! Deena can hold him and I can kick his butt!"

Emma laughed as she pictured it, and said, "No! But thanks. I appreciate the offer!"

Not knowing anyone in the room, Emma stared at the glowing TV as Jacob walked over and sat down next to her.

"Hey," he said softly into her ear. "Can we talk?"

Continuing to stare straight ahead, she said, "Sure. Go ahead."

"I mean alone. In another room," he said.

Looking at him, she answered, "That's fine."

He got off the couch and held his hand out to her, and she took it in hers, allowing him to pull her to her feet. Clearly, this is not Jacob's house so where was he taking her, she wondered uncomfortably, as he led her down the dark hallway. Just how well did he know these people, she mused, as he walked into a dark room and flipped a light switch, bathing the bedroom in soft light. She stood in the center of the room, looking around as he closed the door. The bedroom was nicely decorated in deep browns and blues, with a bed she noticed, that was much taller than any bed she had ever seen before.

Sitting on the bed, his long legs stretched comfortably toward the floor, he pulled Emma close and said, "I'm so sorry. I don't know what I was thinking. I don't want to break up. God, I miss you."

Emma was still hurt and angry. He seemed okay to just throw her away the night before—seemed pretty sure of his decision, she thought. He couldn't miss her too much, she thought sarcastically. It'd only been 24 hours that they'd been broken up. *Just how much could he miss her… it wasn't even date night yet!* She stared into his brown puppy eyes thinking, it had been a pretty darned good night hanging out with the girls; she could get used to not having a boyfriend.

"Do you miss me…just a little?" he asked, as he wrapped his arms loosely around her waist, resting his hands at the small of her back.

"Sure," she said hesitantly, plucking at his shirt.

He pulled her tight to him, and she placed her hands on his shoulders, not allowing him all the way into her space. He kissed her gently, then with more intensity. Scooting back on the bed, Jacob encouraged her to follow. Lying down cuddled together, their kisses became more passionate. Slipping his hand between their bodies, Jacob unsnapped her jeans, and Emma's hand shot down between them.

"No!" she insisted.

"Come on," he smiled coaxingly. "It's a nice big bed…"

"I don't *know* these people," she hissed, surprised and not at all pleased with where his mind was going…and in some stranger's bedroom. "There are people right in the next room. What if someone walked in?"

Sitting up, Emma slid off the bed and stood up in the center of the room. As she stared at him, he now sitting up on the bed, she hoped his un-break up was not contingent on her having sex with him in this strange room. If so, well then they were off again!

He gave her one of his goofy grins, and said," Okay, fine. Wanna go hang out for awhile? I can take you home after."

Emma considered it…she'd been having fun with the girls, but as she walked back into the living room she realized the evening was breaking up. It seemed as if Tara and Deena were going to hang out at the house with the people she didn't know, so, she might as well let Jacob take her home.

"You don't have to be home for awhile," Jacob beamed. "Let's go see what kind of trouble we can get into!"

Okay, Emma thought as she walked with him down the porch steps, so she did miss his silliness and goofy cartoon character voices.

"Here," Jacob said, noticing when Emma shivered, "take my jacket."

Emma shrugged into his jacket, giggling as the sleeves flopped over her hands. "Perfect fit!" he grinned.

She followed him to the back of his car, wondering what the boy was up to and was even more curious when he pulled a carton of eggs from his trunk. *What the heck…?*

Clutching the carton of eggs under his arm, he led the way as they ran across the deserted street, the streetlight illuminating their way. Crouched behind a broken down car and some rubbish, Emma giggled and whispered, "What are we doing back here?"

"We're gonna have some egg fun, but if we get caught, be ready to run like hell!" he giggled down at her.

Egg fun, she wondered, as she wrinkled her brow trying to imagine what he was talking about.

She heard a car driving nearby, and then saw the headlights. Feeling his arm move next to her, Emma looked over at Jacob as he pulled back his arm and flung an egg. She watched as it sailed through the air, and then it dawned on her…egg fun, was throwing eggs at cars! Oh no, she thought as her heart skipped a beat. Eggs stripped the paint off cars, she realized, as in what seemed like slow motion, she heard the egg make a thunking sound as it hit the car passing by. Years ago, someone had egged one of her dad's cars; he had been mad…, and his mad was explosive! He woke up the next morning to a nasty mess, beneath which was a paint job issue.

She looked over at Jacob grinning and giggling, as he said, "We'd better get going."

Yeah, she thought, we'd better before we get caught and land in jail for a little Halloween egging fun.

Twirling a pom-pom, her skirt flaring up and out, Emma swiped her white and purple pom against the girl next to her waiting her turn to twirl. As she stood in place, her arms tired from the weight of the poms, Emma continued to shake them to the beat of the music blaring through the gym. The noise in the gym was deafening with music, hands clapping in time to the beat and hooping with excitement for the basketball team's halftime show. Senior year on the squad was much more fun than junior year, with all the routines memorized, and now used to being in front of a crowd. She grinned when she saw Jacob in the stands waving at her. Waving her pom in the air, she waved back.

The song over, Emma and the rest of the squad ran off the floor. "Hey!" she smiled breathlessly, happy to see Jacob. "What are you doing here? I thought you were working tonight."

"My boss let me leave early so I came over to see you," he grinned, as they walked out of the deafening gym.

In the hall, Emma stood on her tiptoes to give him a tight hug. He took her by the hand, and drew her down the hall to a more secluded spot and kissed her, she pulling away, afraid someone would see. It may be after school hours, Emma thought, but it was still the school…and no kissing was allowed! Besides that, she didn't feel comfortable making out with her boyfriend in front of a crowd, or for that matter, anyone. Her shy and timid nature had travelled with her from her abusive childhood, to the hallway in New Point High.

Letting her pull away, Jacob asked, "Can you go for a drive?"

"I doubt it," Emma said with a grimace. "Mrs. Rhodes is not going to let me go out on a school night. You know that."

Laughing, he responded, "They are so strict. What do they think's going to happen if you go out on a school night, turn into a pumpkin?"

Laughing, she joked, "Maybe!"

Emma knew there were parents that allowed their kids to hang out with friends on weeknights, to go to dinner, movies, or just drive around, but the Rhodes just were not that kind of family. Sometimes they allowed boyfriends over to the house just to hang out on a weeknight until an acceptable hour, but dates, leave the house to hang out… no.

Ever since Jacob had broken up with her, the day before Halloween, Emma worried Jacob would dump her and find a girlfriend that had more freedom, or someone older. Now that Jacob was an adult, he could come and go as he pleased, well, actually, his senior year he pretty much had just as much freedom as he did now, she reflected.

When he had broken up with her, even though it had been just for a day, he had said it was because they hardly ever saw each other. She knew he was right. As busy as she was, Emma considered, with basketball practice or games most nights a week, and when she wasn't playing basketball, she had pom-pom practice, or was at the boys' games performing the halftime show; she didn't have a lot of time to hang out with Jacob, even if she *were* allowed to hang out during the week. With all she had going on, she was scrambling to get her homework done after school on the bus and at night after games and practice. Her tutor had been a tremendous help, so at least when she squeezed in study time, it was effective time. Math was still stressful and as much effort as she put in, she'd expected a much higher grade than a C, but at least she was no longer failing…just herself she thought…failing her higher expectations. History class was going much better too, with a more acceptable grade, of a B. Tutoring sessions had ended over a month ago, and as embarrassed as she had been to need a tutor, she was glad she had agreed to go. Not one of her classmates had made fun of her for seeing a tutor, and bonus…no dogs had attacked as she walked to the tutor's house.

"Come on," he coaxed. "We can sneak out. No one will even know."

"Jacob," she laughed uncomfortably, as she glanced toward the gym doors, "Mrs. Rhodes is in the gym. She'd know if I left the building. I don't know how she does it…it's as if she has some super-radar or something. I'm telling you, she knows when one of her kids is up to something!"

"Hey, you two!" Mrs. Rhodes said, as she walked into the hall and looked there way.

"See! I told you!" Emma hissed with a smile.

"What are you two up to?" Mrs. Rhodes asked with a grin.

"Just hanging out," Emma said with smile, wondering once again how the woman did it…how she knew just the right moment to make an entrance, when one of her little chicks were about make a break for it and break a rule!

"Hey, Mrs. R," Jacob said with a grin and a giggle, feeling like he'd just gotten caught, although he hadn't done anything.

"You're gonna miss the game," Mrs. Rhodes said good naturedly, and knowing.

Emma tugged on Jacob's hand, pulling him with her to the gym door and all the noise. "Come on," she said with a grin. "Let's go watch the game!"

"I can't stay long," he shouted, as they walked along the floor trying to find a place to squeeze in on the packed bleachers.

Emma looked up at him in disappointment, offered a sad smile, and shook her head as if she understood. As she cuddled next to Jacob on the bleacher, Emma wondered, now that he wasn't in school, doing homework, or playing basketball, what he did with all his free time. They were worlds apart lately, Emma thought, tucking her hand in Jacob's strong grasp.

About fifteen minutes later, Jacob hugged her close, and said, "I've got to get going."

"I'll walk you out," she said, disappointed that he was leaving so soon. As little time as they spent together, she'd hoped he would stay for the entire game.

"No, that's okay," he said with an absent smile, waving his hand in dismissal when she began to rise to her feet.

"Oh…okay," she stammered.

Leaning down, he quickly pressed his lips against hers, and then with an occasional *excuse me,* squeezed his way through the bleachers, jamb packed with students, parents, and teachers. With her hands clasped under her chin, Emma watched until he disappeared from her sight around the corner by the gym doors. Sighing, she turned her attention back to the senior boys' basketball game, just in time to see New Point score three points as the team dressed in white and gold, with a purple stripe around the hem of their shorts, ran down the court. Absently, Emma watched as the tallest boy on the team, Adam, loped down the court. Such a nice kid she thought, but at six foot, more like seven foot something, she considered, the gym seemed much too small for him, barely able to max out his speed at full court. With a heavy sigh she thought, the fun had just officially been sucked out of her evening, and wished New Point would hurry up and win so she could go home.

33

As she rinsed a glass and placed it in the sink ready for drying, Emma was deep in thought about the upcoming Christmas break. She didn't realize she was smiling as she scrubbed at a plate, thinking she had a few more weekends to earn money for presents for everyone. Since the little incident in the gym, Jacob had seemed more himself, like the old funny Jacob she knew. He hadn't missed, or been late for any dates. Maybe it had been work stress and adjusting to life as a grownup—no longer in high school—she considered.

Jacob had mentioned a pocket watch he'd like to have for Christmas, and she'd already bought it. It was beautiful, with a hunting scene on the case. He loved hunting pheasant, so it seemed perfect for him. She was so proud of it, and knew he'd love it! It had taken weeks of babysitting to pay for it. For her foster sisters, she would buy the most beautiful sweaters she could find at the mall. She loved wearing pretty things and knew they did too.

Things sure were different for her now, her thoughts drifting, remembering a time when she'd had very few clothes, or food. She had been a scrawny, starving, scared little kid then. When she had lived with her dad, things were so bad she'd had to borrow clothes from her sister— clothes her sister had borrowed from her friends. Memories took her to a different kitchen in a two-story house. She remembered standing in the kitchen at the sink washing a pair of stretched out tube socks, using dish soap as laundry soap, hoping that if she put them over the heat vent on the floor overnight they'd be dry by morning. They never were. More times than she could count, she wore wet uncomfortable socks with her worn out, stinky tennis shoes to school. It hadn't always been that way, she reflected. Before her stepmother had left her dad, she'd had nice things to wear, things that fit and were clean, and even food to eat. But even still, the beatings had been just as bad.

"Emma, you're slowing down!" Caitlyn said impatiently.

"Oh! Sorry bout that," Emma said with a smile, as she came back to the present, to the clean bright kitchen, and her three foster sisters waiting for her to wash the dishes so they could dry and put them away so they could get on with their evening.

Later, as Emma brushed her teeth, her thoughts returned to the past, thinking, those certainly were some days. She plunked her toothbrush into the container on the bathroom sink and then straightened and turned toward the mirror hanging on the wall. She bared her teeth, flicking her tongue over her crooked tooth. Then she looked into her green eyes, masked by brown contact lenses, and thought about other Christmas', ones with her dad, stepmother, two little brothers, little sister, and her two older sisters, Amy and Katie. Christmas morning had been the best morning of the year, and not because of the presents that her stepmother had bought and were overflowing from the table to the floor, but because no one hit her. It was as if that one day of the year was her gift, her free pass of a morning free from physical pain, and bruises.

Slumping her shoulders, Emma drew closer to the mirror and examined her nose, so much like her older sisters' noses, and thought, their lives shouldn't have been so painful, the stuff of nightmares. Things just hadn't turned out as she had dreamed, Emma thought sadly, as she walked to her bedroom.

"Are you ready?" Mrs. Rhodes asked with a skeptical grin.

As Emma walked down the stairs, she could hear Jacob and her foster mother talking, and she smiled knowing what Mrs. Rhodes was talking about. It was a Saturday afternoon with Christmas on the way, and Emma had decided she needed a marathon-shopping day, and Jacob was going to join her. He has no idea what he is in for, Emma grinned.

"Sure! How bad can it be?" Jacob answered Mrs. Rhodes, with a giggle.

"Well, okay," Mrs. Rhodes laughed.

"Hi guys!" Emma grinned, wondering if Jacob was up for the Christmas shopping challenge. Typically, Emma's date night during the school year began after six, but today it was to be an extended day, and at two O'clock, Emma felt daylight was burning so they needed to get a move on!

"Whatcha talking about?" Emma grinned, as she placed her hands on the back of a kitchen chair and cocked her hip. "Our marathon shopping day?" she asked excitedly. "It's going to be so much fun!"

"Yeah, fun for you, but I'm not so sure how much fun it's going to be for, Jacob," Mrs. Rhodes grinned.

Emma threw her head back and laughed. "Oh come on, he'll have lots of fun," she grinned.

Jacob batted his eyes, put his hand over his mouth, and said coyly, in his best girl's voice, "Shucks, it's just gonna be us girls today. Perhaps I'll find a lovely, dainty little bracelet, and maybe we'll have time to have our nails done." Flinging his hand forward, wiggling his fingers he said, "I'm thinking a sassy shade of pink. What do you think?"

Emma doubled over as laughter burst from her. Wiping a laugh tear from her eye, she asked, "Are you ready, sassy?"

As they drove down the country road in the direction of the mall, Emma grinned, "You are such a goof ball!"

"Well shucks, Ms. Scarlet," he said, with a flutter of his lashes, "taint nothin'."

The half hour drive was spent laughing and joking around, and when they arrived at the mall, they found a spot to park his car in the packed lot. Then, hand in hand, they laughed and skipped like two small carefree children toward the entry of the mall.

Emma still had more shopping to do for Jacob, but it would have to wait, she realized, as he hugged her from behind. Not much chance of sneaking away, besides there'd be plenty of shopping days yet with the family. Today, she was focusing her shopping on her foster sisters, still not sure what to get her foster parents. Then there was Will; what to get a little boy, she wondered, knowing it was sure to be an adventure shopping for toys with Jacob. She was not disappointed when two hours later, Jacob, and she bounced on big rubber balls through crowded aisles in the toy store.

It had been a wonderful day of shopping, people watching, and snuggling Jacob's arm as she admired all the Christmas trees and sparkly decorations. She'd gotten a comfortable jump on her shopping—just one gift she hadn't found, something for Carmen. Emma sighed as she walked beside Jacob through the mall, ready to wrap it up for the day.

She gasped and tugged at his arm. "Look!" she said excitedly, and pointed at a rack of sweaters.

"What...more shopping?" he asked good-naturedly.

Darting over to the rack, hoping...hoping it was the perfect sweater for Carmen, Emma lifted a sweater off the rack. It was as if the heavens had opened and beamed down on her.

"This is it!" she said, turning toward Jacob. "It's perfect!"

She held in her hand, a long-sleeved, soft to the touch, salmon colored sweater. It was beautiful she thought, falling in love with the sweater, and for a second, entertained the idea that she should keep it for herself. *No, Emma,* thought as she shook her head. *Christmas is about giving, and giving a sweater I love, is what it is about.* Besides she considered with a small smile, she had already found some really cool stuff on sale that she hadn't been able to resist, kind of pre-Christmas gifts to herself!

"It's beautiful," Jacob said, humoring her. "Are you going to get it?"

Looking at the price tag, Emma loved it even more. Seventeen, ninety-five! Sweet! "Yes!" she said, whisking her way through the tight aisles crammed with clothes and shoppers.

Forty minutes later, the kids walked into Jacob's house. Next on their agenda, a movie.

"Oh, something smells good," Emma said, sniffing the air.

"Smells like mom's been baking her Christmas cookies," Jacob said, leading the way to the kitchen. Sure enough, there were tins lined up on the kitchen counter, just waiting for them to eat them.

"What kind does she bake?" Emma asked, as her mouth began to water.

"All kinds," he said, as he took lids off four tins exposing sugar cookies sprinkled green and red, iced sugar cookies in the shape of stars, chocolate chip cookies, and then also kind of cookie she didn't recognize.

"What's that?" she asked, pointing at the mystery cookies.

"My favorite!" he said, picking up one of the mystery cookies and taking a big bite out of it. "Snickerdoodle."

She looked at him quizzically, still not knowing what it was.

Seeing the look, he explained, "It's got cinnamon and something else in it. Here," handing her a cookie, "try one."

"Mmmm," Emma murmured, closing her eyes as the cinnamon flavor melted in her mouth. Opening her eyes, she looked up at him and gushed, "Oh that is good."

Grabbing a plate from the cabinet, Jacob grabbed a handful of cookies, two cans of pop from the fridge, and then he led the way back to the family room.

"Where are your parents?" Emma asked, surprised they weren't home.

"Probably out with friends to dinner and cards," he answered, as he clicked the TV into life.

Monday evening after dishes and homework were done, Mrs. Rhodes sought out Emma. "Whatcha doin?" Mrs. Rhodes asked, as she peaked her head into Emma's bedroom.

"Flipping around the hardboard canvas she had been working on for her to see, Emma said, "This."

In her free time, when not messing around in the basement creating her own design of ceramic sweater pins, Emma liked to draw and paint, and what she was showing Mrs. Rhodes, was a tiger she had been creating using Cray-pas, a type of oil color. She loved using the colors because of the vibrant colorful effect, and they blended easily.

"That's pretty," Mrs. Rhodes admired, looking at the picture. "Emma, I wanted to talk to you about something."

Looking down at her artwork, trying to decide how to emphasize the light effect, Emma said, "Sure, what's up?"

"Well, first, the proofs for your senior pictures are in. I'm going to pick them up tomorrow and bring them home so you can see them," Mrs. Rhodes said with a smile.

"Emma's head snapped up, as she said excitedly, "They're *in!* Have you seen them yet!?"

"No, I'm going to pick them up *tomorrow,* then we can *both* see them," Mrs. Rhodes said with a grin. "And, something else...I had a call from your caseworker today. Your stepmother called and wanted to know if you'd like to visit with your brothers and sisters over Christmas break."

Emma stared at her foster mother for a moment, sure she hadn't heard her correctly, "My stepmom, Debbie?" she asked.

Debbie wasn't Emma's stepmother anymore. She hadn't been since she was twelve years old. Her real mom had bailed on Emma and her two older sisters when Emma was just two years old. She couldn't even remember her real mom—her face, her voice, what she smelled like. For ten years, Debbie had been the only mother Emma had known, and she'd thought she might end up living with her after she had been taken away from her dad because of abuse, but it hadn't worked out…wasn't meant to be she supposed.

Since she'd been attending church, Emma realized that God really did have a plan for her, and living with Debbie had not been part of the plan. God's plans were a mystery to Emma; she so often wondering where she'd end up—what would happen to her after she graduated from high school. *Would she be alone, thrown out into the world with no family?* No matter how much she loved it at the Rhodes' home, she knew she was still just a foster kid and shouldn't expect too much after graduation. Eighteen was such an exciting age for kids her age—for the kids at New Point High—but for Emma it represented the unknown. She'd talked to Mrs. Rhodes and her guidance counselor about future college plans. They insisted they would help her find a way to attend; it was just a matter of funding. She'd taken the ACT test, a surreal experience for her, and had even visited the college campus she wanted to attend in Largo. After graduating from high school, it sounded like she would have somewhere to go, but what about a car, she worried, and the rest of her life…where would she belong, who would she belong too, who would be there when she needed someone?

Mrs. Rhodes shook her head, yes.

"At her place?" Emma asked, as memories of her family rushed through her head like a river rushing through an underground cavern. "Will—will Katie and Amy be there?" she asked, deep in thought.

"I suppose," Mrs. Rhodes said cautiously, as she watched the war of expressions battle across Emma's face.

With a sigh, Emma asked, "When?"

"A few days after Christmas. Spend the night, for a night or two," Mrs. Rhodes said slowly.

"Overnight?" Emma asked softly.

A storm of emotions, small at first, grew into tornado size within Emma. Finally…finally she had begun to accept her life, a life where she wasn't constantly thinking about her sisters, dreaming up ways to see them, to be with them…to live with them! Leaning back against Emma

Katherine's dresser, Emma drew a knee toward her chest, draping her arm over it, thinking about her battered, bloodied, and bruised, heart, as it began to ache again. She felt pieces of what was holding her together fall away. Could she handle seeing them, she agonized, and have pieces of the scabs on her heart rip away. How long would they be in her life… one visit, two, just to have her heart broken again when they left…*again?*

She still worried about them, wondered if they were okay, but lately, more and more, she felt they were fine. It seemed that anymore, as she thought about her family, it just hurt, a reminder of people she loved, and missed—of not belonging, never belonging. They had all left her—just left her alone—and now here they were, she thought, as tears escaped from her lashes.

"Emma," Mrs. Rhodes said softly, "do you want to pray about it?"

Emma's foster mother knew what tore at Emma's heart. Over the past several months, their church family, and officially accepting God into her life, had helped Emma begin to open up, and many evenings had found Emma sharing her inner most fears, hopes, and thoughts with her foster mother. Her childhood had left her lost, angry, abandoned, and scared…feeling so unloved. Often Emma didn't know who she was supposed to be, how to act, because she had never seemed to be enough for anyone, and it showed because her entire family had left her, even the bad ones. What did it say, Emma had asked, when even bad people didn't want you in their life? The adults that should have helped her, hadn't; instead, they had just turned away from her, choosing to stand by her dad…*the bad guy,* just like so many others that had preferred bad people over her. How was that supposed to make her feel, she wanted to know, and why had God allowed all the bad things in her life…all the bad people? Did He hate her? Was she cursed to live a life where only bad happened, where people were constantly hurting her, and then throwing her away? So many whys for such a young girl. Mrs. Rhodes had prayed over her, just as her church family had done, for healing, hope, and faith. She just had to believe, they said, believe in

God, and that there is a plan in all things…that purpose can be found in everything, even the sad things.

Emma closed her eyes as Mrs. Rhodes pressed one of her hands to her forehead, and in a clear voice, she prayed, "Lord, I pray a prayer of protection and peace over your daughter. I pray that you give her the shield of faith, Lord, to protect her from the enemy's arrows, and give her the belt of truth so she will be able to decipher the Devil's lies, and the breastplate of righteousness. Fit her with your armor, Lord, to keep her safe from all that is evil in this world. I pray that you will comfort her, and let her know your love for her. And Lord, give her a vision—a vision of the plans you have for her life. Amen."

"Amen," Emma said quietly.

The room was bathed in quiet for a moment, and then Mrs. Rhodes asked, "Do you want to talk about what's bothering you?"

With a big sigh, Emma said, "It's really hard, I *want* to see them," she said adamantly. I miss them so much it hurts, but it brings it all back, all of it. I spent a lot of time trying to figure out how we could all be together, over the last few years. Even as little girls when we lived with our dad, we were always trying to think of ways to get away from him… to run away, and those plans always included us all together. So when we began being separated, I didn't change the plan, but it seemed as if they did. They all forgot me. I still think about all of them, still miss them…a big piece of my heart is missing, where they should be, but aren't.

"I'm sure they love you, Emma Claire. I'm sure God has a plan for all this. I don't know what it was or is, but, I don't know, maybe God knew with everything you and your two older sisters had been through, you each needed a little different kind of healing, and that's why God allowed you to go to different homes. You said you and Amy had some issues, didn't you?"

"Yeah," Emma said, as she looked down at her fingernails. "It was never easy for us, at least not as we got older. And it all started with our dad. He used to make us fight; he wanted us to beat the crap out of each other. It was crazy! I know he had issues as a kid. Being picked on by other kids made him real mean, but why would that make him want Amy and me to fight? But that's a stupid question, isn't it?" Emma laughed painfully. "Why did he do any of the sick things he did?"

"You shouldn't even try to figure a sick mind out," Mrs. Rhodes insisted.

"Sometimes I thought Amy hated me, maybe because I should have been able to save her from all the bad stuff our dad did—or—I don't know. I couldn't save any of us, not even me," Emma said sadly. "But now," she sighed, "now I don't have a family. I don't know them. I haven't seen them in what feels like forever, but I want to know them, to belong...to be part of them."

Looking up at her foster mother, Emma said, "I'm the only one of us kids that doesn't belong—that isn't a part of the family. I *love* living with your family," Emma rushed to reassure her foster mother, "but it still hurts to be unwanted by my entire family, so unlovable. I still feel like that little girl, the one whose mother didn't love her enough to stick around, and—and—I missed everyone, *miss* everyone, but I don't think anyone misses me. If they did, where have they been?" She shook her head and looked down, repeating, "To not be worth caring about... When I go see my family, I will see a bunch of people that belong together... where I don't belong." With a resigned sigh, Emma said, "I just don't think God has a place for me."

"Emma Claire, you do belong. God loves you, and so does your family, and so do we. We will always be your family, you know," Mrs. Rhodes insisted.

Smiling a small haunted smile, Emma said softly, "Thanks."

"So do you want to set up a visit then?" Mrs. Rhodes asked.

"Sure," Emma replied, thoughtfully.

"I have an idea," Mrs. Rhodes said brightly. "Why don't you make them presents? You have plenty of time to make gifts out of ceramics. I've got some new stuff in, some cookie jars, and even Christmas stuff, some trees and nativity sets. I bet dad could make something special if you wanted, something to go with a nativity scene, or string lights in one of the ceramic trees."

Perking up, Emma said, "That's a great idea!" She thought about the various pieces in the basement and on the shelves in the room next to the kitchen. "Yeah, I have plenty of time." It flitted through her mind… *maybe if I bring something it could kind of break the ice…at least it would give them something to talk about…something.*

34

"Get your stuff off my bed!" Emma Katherine shouted.

"Fine!" Emma shouted back, as she whipped the poster sized white cardboard off her foster sister's bed. When Emma had gotten home from school twenty minutes ago, she had ran upstairs, dumped her school books by the bedroom door, and threw the self-portrait she had been working on in art class on the closest, safe place, Emma Katherine's bed. She had planned to be back up stairs and have the portrait moved before Emma Katherine saw it, but she had gotten side tracked by a phone call. She knew Emma Katherine was right; she shouldn't have her stuff on her bed, but...*whatever*...she was in no mood to argue with anyone. The upcoming visit with her family had her on edge. Her nerves were crackling worse than any PMS she had *ever* had!

"Fine!" Emma yelled, as she wadded the picture up as tight as the stiff paper would allow. "I'll just fucking throw it in the garbage!"

"You don't have to throw it away," Emma Katherine called after her. "Just keep it off my bed!"

Emma stormed into the kitchen and slammed the wadded up portrait into the garbage can.

"What's all that shouting about?" Mrs. Rhodes asked, as she walked from the family room into the kitchen. "And what are you throwing in the garbage?" grabbing the wadded up paper out of the garbage.

Without responding, tearfully, Emma ran down the basement stairs, with the intention of working on one of her ceramic pieces she was going to give as a Christmas present. A few minutes later, after asking Emma Katherine to explain what had happened, Mrs. Rhodes followed Emma to the basement.

Standing next to the table, Mrs. Rhodes stared down at Emma. "What's going on, Emma Claire?" she asked with concern.

"Nothing," Emma said, not looking up. "I just didn't want that stupid picture anymore."

"But I thought you were entering that into the art competition, you know the regional one. It's a big *deal*. All the counties in the area within one hundred miles are participating. You did a really *good* job," Mrs. Rhodes said, placing her hands on her hips as she continued to look at the very distraught teen.

She sat down next to Emma and watched her dip a paintbrush in water. "Emma Claire, are you sure your fighting with Emma Katherine has anything to do with the picture you just threw away?" Mrs. Rhodes asked softly.

With a heavy sigh, Emma slumped on her chair, the keyed up feeling suddenly gone. Shaking her head, she said, "I don't know," and sighed again.

"Do you think maybe this has something to do with the visit?" Mrs. Rhodes asked, suspecting that was exactly what had her foster daughter in such a mood lately.

Tapping the wooden part of the paintbrush on the table, Emma rested her chin on the fist of her other hand. "Maybe. I'm sorry. I didn't mean to blow up. Maybe it *is* eating at me and I just didn't realize it," she confessed.

"Well, *we* all knew it!" Mrs. Rhodes laughed. "You have been one very cranky girl the last few days."

Emma looked at her foster mother, and wrinkling her nose, asked, "Have I been that bad?"

"What, you mean besides biting everyone's heads off, and stomping around the house...nah," Mrs. Rhodes said with a smile.

Emma laughed. "Why didn't you say something to me?"

"Oh, I figured it would blow over eventually," Mrs. Rhodes responded easily.

Climbing to her feet, Mrs. Rhodes said with a smile, "I pulled your portrait out of the garbage."

With a sigh, Emma said, "It's ruined now, so you might as well put it back in the garbage." She had worked so hard on the piece, and she knew it was good...but she knew she couldn't enter it now, not all crumpled.

"Enter it anyway," Mrs. Rhodes insisted. "The crumple gives it an interesting look...kind of like life."

Emma laughed, "Only you would find something positive to say about the picture I just ruined."

"Well, I still think you should enter it," Mrs. Rhodes said, as she walked up the steps.

As Emma began painting a ceramic picture frame, she thought... she wouldn't have much choice. It was either turn in the crumpled mess, or receive an F for the self-portrait project.

The next few weeks were a blur, with the ending of school until after the new year, and all the homework that came with it, finishing up Christmas shopping, and intense gift making. Emma had picked out greenware, giving careful consideration as to what would be the perfect gift for whom. She had selected a cookie jar, a soup dish, picture frames—she thought she'd give copies of her senior picture to everyone so they wouldn't forget her—and some other odds and ends ceramic stuff. It had been a lot to cram in and still enjoy her Christmas season... one of her favorite times of the year. Of course, she also spent as much time as was allowed with Jacob too. It was just such a warm time of year, and time spent in church with her foster family emphasized what it was all about for Emma.

Christmas morning, Emma rolled onto her side and blinked her eyes, trying to coax herself into full awake mode. How did these people get up so early on non-school days, she groaned. Flopping her arms above her head, she glanced over at Emma Katherine's bed knowing even before she looked that her bed would be empty...Yup. Everyone was awake and downstairs she knew by the sounds of the awakening house...the sounds of voices and laughter. Mmmm, and she could smell rolls. That's enough for me, she thought as she pushed up into a seated position. Homemade cinnamon rolls on Christmas morning...could anything be more perfect, she wondered with a hungry smile. Sliding to her feet, she bent over, grabbed her brush, and ran it through her short hair, and then she walked down the steps to the common area and grabbed her red robe off the hook.

With a happy smile, Emma walked down the red-carpeted stairs thinking about her Christmas Eve the night before. Mrs. and Mr. Rhodes had allowed Emma to spend the evening with Jacob and his family. His family celebrated Christmas on the eve of Christmas, something Emma had never heard of before. His entire family was there, his two sisters, one with her little girl, and the other with her husband. Of course, there had been a lot of laughing during their formal dinner, and then lots of presents to open after, even presents for Emma.

Jacob's mom and dad had given her several gifts, but her favorite had been a red clutch purse. It was really cool! Jacob had given her a purse as a gift also, one she would use on a more casual basis, similar in design—a clutch—with colorful stripes wrapped around the leather, and the clothes he bought her for Christmas had to have cost him an entire months pay. She had received three sweaters from Jacob, one a beautiful gray angora—just beautiful, she had gushed—one with soft pastel designs at the wrist, and the other was brilliant blue in color. The stack of gifts had been overwhelming for Emma, not what she had been expecting.

What had pleased Emma the most was seeing Jacob's face when he opened the blue box that held his pocket watch. After he had opened the clothing boxes filled with shirts and sweaters from her, she had presented her special gift to him. As she watched him crack open the box, she could see by the grin on his face that he really loved it. He held it, dangling from the gold chain high in the air, and examined it, then passed it around for his family to see.

Synching the belt of her robe tighter, Emma stood in the kitchen for a moment and watched the Rhodes family—the kids picking through their stockings in front of the fireplace while the parents watched. Hallmark card moment, Emma thought with a content smile. As she walked toward the noise, she wondered if there would be a repeat this Christmas of the grand horse adventure—Emma Katherine's horse escaping from the barn. As she stood in the entry of the family room, Emma was greeted with a chorus of, "Merry Christmas!" from the entire family.

A few days later, nervously, Emma walked into her stepmother's house, forty-five minutes from the Rhodes' home. She walked slowly toward the sounds of her brothers' and sisters' voices, her heart racing as she wondered...would her little sister and brothers remember her, or had they forgotten her. Had too much time passed? Was it too late to be part of their lives, for them to want to know her, to love her back? Did her little sister, Laura, still remember when they were little girls of just four and nine, when Emma cradled her on her lap as they sat on the worn, old, cold linoleum floor, when they watched TV? Would Laura remember when she used to brush her beautiful long curly hair, or that as the youngest sisters, they had shared the same bed, and Emma had tried to keep her warm and safe at night? Would she know how badly she had missed her, and loved her? And her two little brothers, Robby, with dark chocolate brown eyes and hair almost as dark—a beautiful soulful little boy, so soft and sensitive—and Timmy, so fair with blonde hair, so young when he had left, would they even recognize her, their long absent sister, she wondered. She had cherished her younger siblings when they had lived together, and now she agonized, would they know the jagged hole that had ripped into her heart when they had left. And what of her older sisters, Katie and Amy, had they missed her, and were they okay? And Debbie, her stepmother, did she know, or did she even care that to Emma, she had been just as much her mother as she was to Laura, Robby, and Timmy—how much she had missed her when she went away?

Trembling with fear and longing to be part of their world, Emma stepped into the kitchen and made a memory…just in case it was a long time before she got to see them again. Sniffing, she pasted a grin on her face, pretending to be confident, and happy, instead of how she really felt, like crying, running, and hugging them, not wanting to let them go ever again.

Her two little brothers, sitting at the glass kitchen table, not so little now, turned toward her and grinned. Then Laura walked into the room with Amy following close behind, her face lighting up when their eyes met. Amy rushed across the room and hugged Emma, and with tears burning her eyes, Emma clutched her older sister tight. She heard Katie's voice as she entered the room say, "What's all the fuss about?" her way of breaking the tension, and Emma's body shook as she both laughed and cried. Emma felt a huddle of arms encircle her from all sides as her brothers, sisters and stepmother hugged her…a hug that was long overdue and needed by them all.

Sitting curled up in the corner of the couch, Emma sipped a cup of hot chocolate with marshmallows floating on the top. Emma stuck her tongue into her chocolate drink, trying to grab a passing marshmallow, but missed again. It had been a Christmas to remember, Emma reflected as she looked over at the Christmas tree, the colorful lights twinkling brightly at her. Propping her elbow on the headrest of the couch, she pressed her jaw onto the palm of her hand and looked out the window at the falling snow. There was something comforting about nature's white blanket, she mused, as a piece of wood in the fireplace made a crackling sound.

Mrs. Rhodes sat at the other end of the couch sipping a cup of black coffee, and with a grin, asked, "Now aren't you glad you turned in your self-portrait project for art class, even if it did have a few wrinkles?"

Smiling, Emma said, "Yes." And then laughing, "I still can't believe I won a first place with that piece of garbage!"

"It isn't garbage," Mrs. Rhodes insisted. "It's beautiful. It's Emma Claire with a few wrinkles," she laughed.

Laughing, Emma said, "You are so funny! But, apparently, at least one of the judges had your way of thinking when they looked at it. Good grief!" she exclaimed. "Mine was the only portrait that was wrinkled. It stood out, that's for sure."

"It didn't stand out because it was wrinkled," Mrs. Rhodes assured her foster daughter. The *girl* in the picture stood out."

Emma tilted her head and smiled.

Changing the subject, Mrs. Rhodes asked, "So how'd it go with your family?"

Looking at her foster mother, Emma smiled and pensively asked, "Do you think it's okay to love two families?" meaning the Rhodes family as well as her biological family; her two older sisters, little brothers, little sister, and stepmother. It was a question that had been weighing heavily on her mind ever since she had gotten home from her visit at her stepmother's home. She loved her biological family, but she loved her other family too, her foster family. But, she wondered, if she loved the Rhodes wasn't she betraying her other family? It was all so confusing, she worried.

"Emma," Mrs. Rhodes said with a warm grin, "Before you arrived at our home over a year ago, dad and I prayed. We prayed that God would send us a very special child. Our prayer was, *Lord, please send us a child that we can see you working through.* Oh, Emma," she said with pride shining in her eyes, "it was you. When I look at you, I know God is good, and works miracles, because, bless your heart, He gave you a bigger than usual heart—a heart big enough to love everyone—to love the world."

With a reflective sigh, Emma smiled as she watched her foster mother take a sip of coffee. If there were more people, Emma thought as tears pricked her eyes, like her foster mother—kind, strong, and filled with love and purpose—what a different world it would be. Reaching up to tug at the small post earring in her ear, Emma reflected, maybe it *was* possible to belong, and love two different worlds. Emma took a sip of her now warm chocolate, and considered...*a heart big enough to love the world.* She glanced at Mrs. Rhodes—the woman that had loved her enough to keep her safe, taught her how to hope, and had a heart that loved the world—and smiled tenderly.

The past year had found Emma letting go of dreams and beginning to dream new dreams, gingerly embracing what might be, opening her heart to trust and hope, and allow God to reach her...knowing He was there, even for the lost children like her.

As the snow fell heavier outside the bay window, and the fire crackled in the fireplace, Emma snuggled deeper into the couch. She stared into the fire, brilliant colors of orange, red, and blues dancing dizzily about, and considered, for some kids there were many easy roads home, travelled by bike, car, or even a short walk. But for Emma, it had taken almost her entire childhood to travel to the Rhodes' home.

About The Author

With over twenty years experience in management, human resources, and project management, it was during the recession that Carol Knuth changed direction and began her pursuit of writing and publishing. Her first book *The Garbage Bag Girl* was the first in the series, her break out novel. The book details the heart-wrenching unique challenges at-risk children face, their strong will to survive, and as with her own life, spirits of endurance.

Carol Knuth currently resides in Kentucky with her family. She is the president of Dream Swept Publishing and she advises various organizations and boards that support the improvement of at-risk children and women's lives. Her interest in at-risk children stems from her own childhood spent in the foster care system.

Author photograph by Nikita Gross
www.carolknuth.com

ALSO BY CAROL KNUTH

The Garbage Bag Girl

21421382R00146

Made in the USA
Charleston, SC
16 August 2013